A Crimson Wolf

Slaves of the New World :3

Ashley Capes

For Brooke

Chapter 1.

The *chromata* rose around Mia in a petrified forest where tree trunks of blue loomed from sluggish fog. From somewhere beyond came the muted squawking of gulls, suggesting an ocean, but the scent of damp air carried no trace of salt.

Instead, she could smell only a general dampness as her boots crunched across the frozen, thin branches and leaves that littered the hard earth. It was as though shards had fallen from the trees to lie untouched for years, as though she was the only one to ever walk the path between the silent trees.

"Hmmm." Such a thing seemed unlikely, judging by the sturdy, clean signposts that she passed. Most bore freshly turned earth at the base, as though newly installed. Each signpost bore the same sign – a grey and blue kingfisher, its beak like a spearhead. Yet there was no sense of anything surrounding them, no wagon marks or spaces cleared for temporary camps.

Just the echo of her footfalls over untouched ground.

And despite the uncertainty to the place, the almost drab nature of its colours and the chill to the air, she could not fight the urge to leave quickly. A tiny fear lingered. What if Nyath had not truly been defeated? But above that concern was a bittersweet feeling she could not turn from.

As ever, in the *chromata*, her sight was restored.

She slowed, to raise her voice. "Guide?"

Her words did not make much of an impact in the forest of stone.

Lightning flickered in the distance.

She waited, but no thunder followed and so she raised her voice once more. "Am I here to see something else?"

Was she in the forest to learn about the pilot?

Or Thomas? Or Ethan? Without encountering something new, she wasn't sure what the petrified wood and kingfisher represented. And by now, days out from Brightnest, Mia had already chosen Nicholas' successor – a vision came and went; in it, both Francis and Selena, older now, were guiding a young woman.

It was that girl, who stood feeding a sparrow from her palm, that would lead Brightnest in the future.

When Mia woke, she and Ethan would continue to trek the coastline, heading for Viterra and hopefully, clues about locations on the steel map they had uncovered. She still could not quite see David's plan, but it was clear that she and Thomas had been protected and chosen as important tools by others.

And it was a just cause, a cause she believed in... but it was hard to fully reconcile David's kindness and conviction to protect them, with David as a manipulator or even something of a puppet master...

"Mia!"

The *chromata* vanished.

She opened her eyes to darkness, and a shape bent over her, no more than a shadow before the full moon. Ethan, and his voice had carried a note of concern.

She rose, reaching for her blindfold in the hush. "Is something wrong?"

"There are lights approaching."

Mia tensed. "Where?"

"From the coast," he said. "I'm going to get a better look, wait here."

"Right."

Mia tensed where she waited. So far, their trek east had been slow, along broken roads and through barren hills, and sometimes venturing down to the coast to detour craters or noxious swamps, the stench burning her nose and throat.

Last night, with darkness falling swiftly, they found a concealed depression ringed by trees. It had become the perfect campsite, with a gap in the canopy lighting Ethan's work as he started a fire and cooked their meal, using the supplies provided by the people of Brightnest.

And until now, they had encountered no travellers and none of Williams' soldiers on their path either.

Fear built now – her senses offering a clear warning, even as clouds seemed to cover the moon. *Things are about to change – those lights are trouble.*

Mia threw her blanket aside and reached for her pack, and the rifle that rested nearby. She checked on the bolt and shells, then waited. Would Ethan return before the lights reached them? *We're lucky something woke him, since I'm obviously no use.*

The rustle of leaves drew near, along with the sound of heavy breathing.

"Mia, we have to leave."

"What is it?"

The sound of their possessions being snatched up followed, though he kept his voice low. "Soldiers, heading for our camp. They've come from a ship anchored off the coast – I couldn't see any markings but it's big."

She bundled her blanket, stuffing it into her pack as she stood. "Who even knows we're here?"

"Exactly." Ethan took her hand, the grip firm, welcome. "If I thought this was just a random occurrence, I'd risk hiding here... but I doubt that's the case. What do you feel?"

No doubts. "They're seeking us."

"Then we have two paths. There's a trail that runs parallel with theirs, heading down to the water. It might surprise them, since they'll probably expect us to take our back trail and head for the hills."

"Lead us to the water, maybe we can hide further along the coast. The sand will be easier for me too."

"We'll have to be quieter, this way – I might have to carry you."

"Are you sure?"

"Not much in the way of even terrain."

"I don't want to be a–"

"You are no burden," he said, giving her hand a squeeze.

"Thank you." Mia let her pack drop to the ground, taking only the water flask, then wrapped her arms around Ethan's chest as he lifted her onto his back.

Then, he climbed from the camp with a grunt and began their descent. Mia held tight, the rush of night air on her cheeks, but could not get a clear idea of their path. Ethan moved at a fair pace but did not seem to be rushing, pausing often, perhaps to judge how or where to step.

Once, he leapt over a small brook, then fell into a crouch where he stopped, even holding his breath. She nearly toppled free, but muffled her own grunt at the impact.

Some ways off into the trees, the sound of footfalls, creaking branches and whispers reached her, light blooming. Mia kept still, drawing in a breath and holding it until the light faded.

"Tuck your head into my back for this part," Ethan said a short while after.

Mia did so and he was moving once more, and though it seemed he still took care, the occasional branch still scraped an arm or her back, though not enough to draw blood at least.

And it's better than being captured.

Ethan exhaled as he slowed, moving across ground now, steps sinking a little. The soft roar of the ocean was near, waves crashing gently. "Here," he said as he knelt.

Mia slid down, keeping a hand on his shoulder. "Should we rest a moment?"

"Maybe," he replied. "Moving at a half-crouch like that... was hard work. And that's not a comment on the effort of carrying you, either, My Lady."

She chuckled. "Quick thinking, as always, Ethan."

Something splashed, not too far behind them. Mia fell to the ground but Ethan was pulling her back up and into a run.

Mia scrambled to keep up, gripping his hand tight as she charged into the darkness. "Ethan?"

"It's a bloody longboat," he replied.

A shot echoed in the night.

"Give up!" Someone shouted, a clear tenor, rich enough to be a singer. "We only need Mia, remember?"

Ethan swore.

Chapter 2.

Thomas stretched across the divan, a cold glass of lemon water in hand where he frowned up at the ceiling with its wooden beams, hints of new spider webs visible. Light spiralled across the walls in jagged shapes as Elisabeth sat upon the windowsill, twirling an empty wine glass.

He sighed.

"Are you still sulking, even now?" she asked.

Thomas rose. "Sulking?"

She stood, and the bright Federation sun from outside obscured her expression. "I've already told you I'm offering Mia exactly what you are fighting for, Thomas. True freedom."

"I know that," he replied. *And that's hardly the problem – I don't* want *to find her.* Because if that happened, he'd have to confront the hurt he'd created. And it was there, lurking, waiting, even if Mia herself didn't know of the betrayal yet. *And you're safer with Ethan too.* "I'm just tired of waiting. This town is obviously another dead end."

"I see."

"Well, isn't it?" He tossed one of the cushions onto the

bed. "This is the fourth place already. If your network of informants is as good as you claim, then I think we should accept that my guess was wrong. Mia didn't travel west after all."

"I am not so sure about that, Thomas." Elisabeth left the window to join him, pushing him back against the seat so she could sit across his lap. "It is the logical choice to keep her distance from Williams. Her Gift will nudge her toward Alita's Shell."

"So you are *hoping*."

"Fine. But I maintain that any clues she has uncovered regarding Gatehouse will take her in the same direction. And if, once again, no-one has seen your sister when we reach Oriulla, then we will try one more place."

"The supposed Gatehouse Cemetery?"

She sighed as she trailed a finger along his jawline. "You doubt me on its existence? I have seen it."

"No, its value."

"That I believe we could confirm easily enough."

"If there's something useful there, then why delay?" Better to drive Elisabeth toward another task. And unless Mia and Ethan had found some clue or key to suggest a Gatehouse graveyard would help with the search for a pilot, it was *highly* unlikely they'd be anywhere near such a place; a place where 'the mountains met a golden stream'.

Not very specific.

"I'd hate to travel all that way just to have to back track to your sister."

"Rule it out – or in – anyway."

Elisabeth chuckled. "You're being awfully transparent, fool. Just leave the thinking to me, will you?"

Thomas shoved her to one side as he stood. "That your clever way of telling me you don't want to share what you know?"

She did not seem perturbed at him casting her off, where she still waited on the divan. "Perhaps."

"What's really inside Alita's Shell?"

"I don't know... for certain."

"You've said as much before, Elisabeth."

"True."

Thomas shook his head as he started for the door and the stairs beyond. "Fine. I'll be at the bar. Let me know when Wilkins comes back with absolutely no news once again."

"I will."

Thomas left their room and started down the creaking staircase. Murmuring and muted percussion sounds rose as he descended, passing three colour paintings, often landscapes, all with plenty of blue sky above.

Elisabeth's soldiers half-filled the taproom, shirts unbuttoned as they spoke and laughed, happy but not rowdy, if the calm faces of the waitresses were any indication. At the bar, two men worked before a long wall lined with glasses, jars and bottles of alcohol, most of it a typical amber but there were a few black and also green liqueurs too.

A large mirror rested behind much of the bottles but Thomas avoided it, taking a seat a little further down. *Who wants to watch themselves drink?* Thomas nodded to one of Elisabeth's men as waited, then ordered an ale when the owner approached.

The big man had a wide smile and a grey beard but no hair, instead he bore the spider web tattoos of a Bruiser. Former Bruiser at that. Like more than a few people in the

Federation, he bore old slave tattoos – in this case, both the black and the white.

Yet there were just as many folks with no tattoos upon their brown skin, people who had *not* been enslaved by the Williams dynasty. People who had been free, since the Uprising nearly a century ago now. And like Carlos from Ethan's crew, they sometimes bore dreadlocks, other times they wore white or orange headbands and wristbands.

"Someone was looking for you earlier," the barkeeper said as he handed over the drink.

"Oh?" *Surely no-one from the Federation knows me here? Leaving who else to come calling? One of Williams' lackeys?* "Someone from the Hog?"

"Don't think so," he replied. "Said his name was Jonas."

Thomas straightened. "Jonas?"

"Right. Mentioned not having seen you since the palace. Said he's staying at the Luna Hotel."

"Was he a tall fellow, little older than me? Almost unnaturally blue eyes?"

"Right."

"Okay, thanks." Thomas took a drink – a long drink – then set the glass down with a clink, pausing to tap his fingers upon the counter. Was the visitor part of an elaborate scheme from Williams... or was Leah's brother truly alive and waiting in a hotel by the name of Luna?

Chapter 3.

Thomas started from the bar at a stride. He barely paused to collect one of Elisabeth's men, gesturing to Jiro. The thin man handed his drink to one of his fellows. "Thomas?"

"I'm visiting the Luna Hotel and I could use some company – just in case."

"What do you mean?" the soldier asked as he caught up to Thomas in the doorway. His face was a little flushed. He'd probably had plenty to drink, but his balance or vision didn't seem impaired as the man counted bullets in his revolver's chamber. Newly promoted, to replace Oliver, Jiro now bore an insignia of crossed rifles on the shoulder of his jacket.

Not a traditional Kingdom marking, something Elisabeth had come up with to set her men apart.

"Just that I'm not sure what I'll find, yet." Thomas called back over his shoulder. "That's where I'll be if Elisabeth needs me."

Someone called back an affirmative, and then Thomas was leading Jiro into the sunny streets, detouring bright stalls and pink-blooming spiral cactus, these placed in huge terracotta pots. Their plate-like leaves provided plenty of shade, and folks gathered beneath them to talk and laugh.

"Sure is different here," Jiro said as they moved into an alleyway. Instead of refuse, it was mostly filled with crates and boxes. "I'm not used to a place that doesn't smell damp and dark."

"Shame the whole nation can't be like this."

"Right," the man said with a nod.

Thomas glanced at Jiro while they waited for the crowd in the next street to thin. It'd been impossible to get a truly accurate sense where Elisabeth's men stood. Were most along for the ride simply to escape Williams, or did they also believe that the dirt kings were wrong?

They continued on and a light sweat formed on Thomas' face before they reached the Luna, which was flanked by more spiral cactus and canopies. Additional shade cloth had been spread between poles upon the rooftop, as if to protect an outdoor dining area perhaps. *Not so different from the abandoned town of Marwin.*

"So, what's inside?" Jiro asked, a hand on his gun.

"Someone I knew from the palace – or a trap."

The man raised an eyebrow. "Just the two of us to spring it, then?"

Thomas laughed. "Well, if you put it that way, maybe not. I was more thinking, if it looks like I'm not coming back, then you could at least get Elisabeth or Wilkins."

"I'll be watching then," he replied.

"Thanks." Thomas approached the hotel, pushing through the doors to a quiet reception area lined with indoor plants, the green brightening the brown, muddy-looking stone. An older woman in a woollen shawl behind a long desk, rose.

"Welcome to the Luna Hotel. We have several rooms still available, traveller."

"Thank you, but I was hoping to visit a guest – Jonas."

"You've come early enough; he should be sober."

Thomas hesitated. "Sober?"

The woman nodded as she parted flower stalks and poured some water into a nearby vase. "He's not coping too well since the accident."

"Oh?"

"Perhaps I'm worrying too much," she replied. "Or speaking out of turn, actually. Room twelve upstairs, if he's in."

"Thank you," Thomas said as he started up the stairs then along a quiet corridor lined with doors, it too bearing its share of greenery.

At number twelve, he knocked. His body tingled, as though near a great mass of steel. "Jonas? It's me, Thomas."

"Come on in!"

Thomas turned the handle and stepped into a room cluttered with mechanical bits and pieces, cogs, springs and winches and belts. Even the bed was covered in bulbs, though Jonas himself sat upon the floor in a space he'd carved out, surrounded by hand tools and metal shavings and empty jars.

Jonas was still wiry, his face a little longer than Thomas remembered, a touch of grey to his short brown hair and the stubble on his cheeks too. He wore dark grey pants and a blue vest, blinking from behind his brass-rimmed glasses when he looked up.

When he rose to move forward, he was unsteady but not stumbling. "Thomas? It really is you."

"It is."

Jonas reached out, gripping Thomas by the shoulders as he smiled – the gesture seemed half in welcome, half to steady himself. "I wasn't sure I even believed it was you, you know. After all, I thought I saw you walking the streets with *Elisabeth* of all people."

Thomas shook his head. "I didn't know you were alive... or where you were."

"I was here," he said, glancing to the bed. "But that's another story. Tell me, when did you escape? Is Mia well? Who were the soldiers I saw you with? Deserters? Was that actually her?"

"Ah... in a way," Thomas replied. "But it's also worse than that; I'm more or less a prisoner at the moment. And Jonas – that *was* Elisabeth, you saw. And I'm helping her, for now at least."

He scratched at his cheek. "Truly?"

"Yes."

"Well then... I think I'll need another drink," he said, motioning for Thomas to join him on the floor, where he found a bottle and yanked the cork free. "Tell me the whole story if you can."

"I'll do my best," Thomas said. He noticed a toy train, half-visible beneath the bed, but no other hints to suggest a child, yet he did not ask about it... figuring out how to explain to Leah's brother exactly what was going on was more pressing. *And if I'm hesitating now... well, it's going to be* far *worse when I see Mia again.*

"Don't worry, I'm sober enough."

"Well, I'll still try to keep this brief," he replied, before starting to sum up as much as he could. "Eventually, Mia and I were separated and that's when Elisabeth captured me. But I think Mia's safe; she and Ethan escaped."

"I see. That's a ray of hope." Jonas took a long drink, then handed the bottle to Thomas. "And good riddance to Julian; thank you for that, Thomas."

Thomas spread his hands. "It is but one thing, perhaps. I've more failures in my name lately."

"Elisabeth?"

"Among others... I know she was not the main instigator when it came to... what happened to Leah. But she was like the others; she never stepped in."

Jonas' jaw was clenched. "Right." Then he shook his head and his shoulders slumped a little. "But we all do what we have to survive, don't we? I doubt Leah would blame you for anything you've had to do, Thomas."

Was that true? Thomas could not answer at first. *There's always a cost to survival.* "We do."

"Now, I don't expect you must tell me everything, but answer me this, can you? Do you trust Elisabeth?"

"No."

Jonas smiled now, and it was gentle, even a little glazed. "Ah, that's my boy. Good to hear. So, what does she want from you?"

Relief loosened his muscles, and Thomas took a drink of his own. "Elisabeth wants to use me for access to Alita's Shell. Have you heard of it?"

"I have."

"There's something inside that she wants. Something to help her escape Williams."

Jonas nodded. "Maybe there would be. There are more than enough rumours about that place. At least it seems you have an impressive leash at present?"

"There is a soldier waiting for me outside... and she does have a hold over me," he said, but again, could not reveal the full truth about that hold.

Jonas waited.

"Or maybe it's me. Part of me thinks she might actually succeed – I'm hoping I can use her to restore an airship."

"True freedom, huh?"

"So I hope."

"Then, you've given up on revenge?"

"Revenge?"

He found a new bottle, this wine with an unfamiliar label – local vintage. "You don't remember your promise?"

"No..."

"As I remember it, Warrick had twisted your shoulder right out of its socket." He chuckled. "Once we fixed you up, you made your promise. Fierce words, but still cute because you were still quite young."

Thomas opened his mouth to respond... but maybe he *had* made such a promise? A long time ago, Jonas, Leah and Mia were there too, everyone in one of the rose gardens, thorns and petals shining with dew...

And there'd been another boy back then too, a blond kid with freckles. *I* do *remember.* The boy had disappeared, and Warrick and Julian were laughing about it.

"I said I would kill them all. With my pruning scissors."

"Right. Though I don't blame you if you've got other priorities now; it's not like I made good on any of my bitter oaths. But I thought it was a gutsy thing to promise, even if it was just to yourself."

"Well... stopping Williams is one way to protect Mia."

"Think you can do that, even with Elisabeth's help?"

Thomas took another drink of his own bottle. "I don't know."

Chapter 4.

The Queen's voice held an illusory softness but was clearly the kind of voice that had long grown accustomed to commanding attention. And expecting answers. Even so, her tone was not curt.

A welcome contrast with Aiden's barking from where he, too, sat across from Mia and Ethan – two silhouettes before a generous row of portholes. Mia rubbed at her wrists and shifted upon the stool she'd been given.

Being free of their bounds was welcome but escape seemed improbable at best. They'd climbed down ladders and walked along clanking halls past the engine room presumably, where she heard many voices along the way, all with only the faintest sense of being upon water too, ending up eventually in the Captain's quarters, where the scent of old parchment joined lemon tea.

"Welcome to the *Albion*, please consider yourselves guests at present," Queen Marianne continued, after directing servants, sailors—or soldiers perhaps—to prepare food. "And while 'guest' may in fact be something of a euphemism,

I trust I will not need to change that, and that you will be willing to assist us?"

It was hard to tell from her voice alone, but while she did not sound like a young woman, she was significantly younger than Williams, just as the rumours at the Fortress had claimed.

"How would that be, Your Majesty?" Ethan asked, some wariness in his tone.

"A continuation, on a much larger scale, of your own goals, Ethan formerly of Woodend," she replied.

"The Queen is going to bring down Williams," Aiden added. "And Mia is an important part of that."

Is? That's presumptuous. "How did you find us?" Mia asked.

"Silas helped out there," Aiden replied.

"How?"

"That is not vital for now," Queen Marianne replied. "What I must know is whether we can count upon you both."

"You want to use my Farsight to guide your actions?"

"And the key I lent you," Aiden replied.

An interesting choice of words there. "The *Clara* needs more than just the key to the Ruby Heart, as I'm sure you know."

"Aye, I do."

"Then what *is* your plan?" Ethan asked.

"The fine details we will keep to ourselves for now, but we believe we can convince at least one other nation to crush the Kingdom forces here in the east," the Queen said.

"Like Europa?"

"Or Zhongguo. Or the New States; we have yet to decide."

"And the *Clara* is your bargaining chip?" Mia asked. "It hardly seems enough."

"No, but the airship will transport us there far swifter,

to better convince them. Few airships remain, even in the northern hemisphere, Mia." The shadowy outline of the queen offered a small shrug. "Nor in our half of the world, truly. But we would ask, will you aid us in choosing the correct ally? Someone whose soldiers would be liberators without then becoming occupiers."

"And what after such liberation?"

"I restore the east, unify the nation. We trade again, travel, become respected once more – and more importantly, slavery ends and people can work toward their own futures."

"With you upon the throne?"

"I trust no-one else, Mia."

Mia nodded. *A fair answer but that doesn't mean I'll automatically trust you.* "I think Ethan and I would like to speak privately a moment," she said. "We will have conditions of our own if we choose to assist you."

Aiden snorted.

Mia turned her head. "And I haven't forgotten Captain Hawkins and the people of Silver Rock."

"They are all well enough, girl," he snapped.

Now Mia turned to where the Queen sat. "I assume you don't keep him around as a diplomat then, Your Majesty."

Aiden shot to his feet, but the vague movement of Marianne's arm rising stopped anything he might have said. From beside Mia, tension seemed to pour from Ethan. The Queen's voice bore just a trace of amusement. "Aiden is certainly useful... when he remembers his role here." The woman rose herself. "Your meals will arrive soon, but please use my quarters here to speak as long as you need."

"Thank you, Your Majesty," Ethan said.

The two figures left then, the heavy steel door clanging

after, leaving Mia breathing easily where she sat. Ethan didn't seem so relaxed. In fact, he stood and began to pace, his footfalls a little brisk. "Is this the best time to antagonise Aiden?"

"Absolutely. We have the most power now, before we agree."

"Well..." He chuckled. "That's true. But I didn't know how the Queen was going to react. She's hard to read."

"Leave that to me, I guess."

"No warnings, then?"

"Not yet, which is a good sign," Mia said, pausing to stretch her legs before her. "Even from Aiden, which was a surprise."

"Then we're going to agree to help them."

"Everyone in that meeting knows we don't have much choice."

"This could be a blessing after all – chasing down locations on the map could be a *lot* faster now, and we'll have access to far more in the way of resources."

Mia nodded along with him but she found herself frowning at a new concern.

"Mia?"

She waved a hand. "No, it's fine. I agree, but now that I take a minute, I really do want to know how they found us. How exactly did Silas help them?"

"I'm curious too, but does that matter right now, for us?"

"Maybe not this very moment."

"This might not be any more urgent, but I want to know what the Queen holds over Aiden, to have taken the *Albion* from him."

"Something significant, surely. If Silas could find us

though, can he find the pilot too?"

"That's an interesting question." Ethan stopped his pacing. "Sounds like you're doubting what you saw in the *chromata*."

"No, but it's still not enough, is it?"

He took his seat once more. "Let's get to work on those conditions for offering our assistance. I get the feeling we're going to need *quite* a few things."

She smiled, straightening as she did so. Was hope returning? And not the kind of hope that was nearly indistinguishable from stubbornness or even desperation, but something warmer and even exciting...

"I think you're right about that."

Chapter 5.

Thomas blinked up from his cup at a new sound.

How many have I had? Light from outside was already changing, deeper shadows filling the cluttered room now. Up until a moment ago, it seemed that Jonas' calm, regretful tone had been all he'd heard for hours, a welcome reminiscence about Leah... but a new voice *had* called.

Thomas turned to squint at the shape standing in Jonas' doorway, black flak jacket and boots, hand on the butt of a revolver.

Jiro.

"Thomas? You're safe?"

"Not to worry, I'm not drunk," he replied as he stood – and his balance was good enough, thankfully. "Jonas, this is Jiro. Is something wrong?"

"You said if you hadn't returned..."

"Oh."

Jiro shrugged. "Well, Sergeant Wilkins is back and Elisabeth wants everyone to hear what he has to say."

Signs of Mia? *Unlikely... I hope.* "Trouble?"

"I think so. No smiles when I was told."

"Right then." Thomas navigated his way around the table. His balance was not terrible truly, perhaps he hadn't had too many at all? *Good.* He glanced over his shoulder at the door, to where Jonas still sat. *How strange to have met him here.* "Thanks."

Jonas lifted his cup. "Visit again, will you?"

"I will."

In the hall, Thomas hurried after Jiro, the soldier already at the timber balustrade, taking the stairs two at a time. Thomas shook his head, not daring to replicate the feat. Not that he was drunk... but, just to be safe.

The setting sun sent orange beams to sear his eyes, but he blinked his way into the nearest alleyway. He kept pace with Jiro somehow, the cool air of evening helping a little. "So, no sign of my sister, then?"

"It felt more tense than that," the sergeant replied. "Like fresh bad news."

Evening had fallen to purple and black shadows by the time they reached the First Inn, where it seemed the regular patrons had vacated the bar, leaving only the bartender wiping at unaccompanied tables.

Not that many tables were empty, considering Elisabeth's men packed the place.

Wilkins was pacing before those gathered, clothes covered in dust but clear circles around his eyes where his goggles would have protected him. Elisabeth sat within the group, nursing a white wine. She raised an eyebrow at Thomas as he entered, but only gestured to Wilkins.

"Go on, Sergeant."

"As I said; they'll be here by dawn. No way to know exactly

who is among them, or whether they simply followed our trail or not, but there are enough to give us some trouble if we're not careful."

"It's Warrick, surely."

"Or at least one of his captains," the sergeant agreed. "Whoever leads the force, it outnumbers us two to one."

Some of the lingering warmth from Thomas' afternoon of drink faded. "That large? I didn't think the Federation would welcome so many Kingdom soldiers."

"They'll be bribing their way in," Elisabeth said with a shrug. "If we can do it..."

"But the Fourth Minster would have to be watching a force that big – he'll have men ready at least, surely."

"He certainly will." Wilkins nodded. "Long ago now, I faced Maximilian upon the battlefield; the Bloody Plains of Kimor. He'll know what's afoot here."

"Then isn't the Minister our cover to escape, if we need it?"

Elisabeth smiled. "Should have seen that myself, yes." She drained her glass and set it down. "Time to get a move on, then."

"My Lady?" Wilkins bore a slight frown, weariness clear upon his face.

"We'll head for the Gatehouse cemetery, right now. If this trip inland has been worthless, then we will at least see what can be found there before searching elsewhere."

"We haven't covered so much of Federation lands," he replied.

"True. But it looks like Williams is going to force our hand. I don't want to get caught up in something here; we need access to Alita's Shell and we'll lose it if we make too much noise."

He stroked his moustache. "That will be a close race, if we're slowed by the climb. We'll be exposed while within firing range."

"Split into two groups. I'll take Thomas and Jiro to the graveyard while you lead them away. Make it convincing, Sergeant."

Thomas caught a flash of worry in the man's eye, and the sergeant's old request to protect Elisabeth rang in his mind. *Pressure I don't need.* Yet if nothing else, at least Mia would remain undiscovered; she was likely still safe too, hardly being alone out there.

"Don't worry so much," she replied. "At the very least, Thomas will be watching over me."

"Even so, My Lady, if even one car takes up your trail, you will be outnumbered significantly."

"Then Thomas will simply overturn their little cart," she said with a grin. "I doubt any of us have forgotten what happened at the Shell."

"Aye." Wilkins turned to Thomas. "Think you could do something like that? Overturn a steam-car or two?"

"Yes." And it wasn't a form of bragging either – such a thing *did* seem very possible.

Elisabeth was still looking pleased. "That was fast, Thomas."

"I can feel every piece of steel in the room – and plenty outside, I even have a sense of the Sand-Hog out there, beyond the edge of town. To me, it all seems pretty light." The faint humming, one that he'd long since come to suppress now, grew as he focused upon the minor vibrations in his chest and arms, even his hands.

"There you have it, Sergeant." Elisabeth clapped her

gloved hands together. "Let's make sure we have enough provisions, and I want someone to obstruct the road somehow, no matter how petty. Make it difficult for them."

One of the other men nodded, a fellow whose face seemed mostly jaw and brow, lending him a brutish look. "I have a few ideas."

"Excellent, make a start, Lawrence. Everyone else, get a move on."

The men began to file from the room with shuffling of boots, some heading to their rooms, others outside to prepare their own vehicles, those they'd taken from the hog and which had been purchased within the Federation during their search. *They're all about to get a fair work out.*

Elisabeth slapped Thomas upon the shoulder as she passed, heading for their room. "We have something to discuss as well."

Chapter 6.

Warm lamplight and candles cast the clutter in their room in a more favourable light –clothes and weaponry, mostly – as Elisabeth pressed her body against his. She placed both gloved hands upon his cheeks, the leather smooth and cool. "Will this be a problem, Thomas?"

"What?"

"Warrick, of course."

He frowned as best he could. "What are you getting at?"

"You still want him dead."

"Making me one of many."

She sighed, but she was smiling. "Maybe you are at that." She let him go then and moved to sit on the bed where she began to stuff clothes into a bag, spare revolver and ammunition belt mixed in. "So long as you keep to the path we've agreed upon; I won't accept you growing distracted here. Your sister is first priority when it comes to your freedom. And mine."

Of late, Thomas had been wondering about that. "Is she?"

"Of course. She's the key to opening Alita's Shell, we both know that."

"You seem to think the Gatehouse cemetery is just as – or more – important."

She tossed a belt knife into the bag then looked up at him. "Do I?"

"It seems that way. We haven't had a lot of success here, even with your extensive network of informants."

"As I recall, you had no better ways to find her, and so I maintain that it is a logical choice for her and Ethan to flee west."

"Maybe so. But even without clear traces, you don't seem too disappointed – meaning the graves are important."

"We've already talked about that: there are supposedly plans or documents useful to the *Clara* buried there."

"Is that all?"

"I won't know that until we open it up."

"Isn't it past time for playing coy, Elisabeth?" he said, folding his arms. "I've tied my cart to your horse – I need you to succeed so Mia and I can have our freedom. What do you gain by hiding things from me still?"

"Fine." She leant forward with a sigh. "When the basin first dried up, old man Williams searched and vandalised, but found nothing. This was in the early days of the Federation forming, you see. So he had time – supposedly he and his men spent a month digging."

"Looking for what?"

"As I said, plans, instructions for the *Clara*, or back then, maybe the Ruby Heart. He eventually found a steel coffin, emblazoned with a crimson-coloured wolf."

Tension had snuck into his limbs. "And?"

"Supposedly, it is the coffin of Jean, Gatehouse's leader. Williams' grandfather believed that important things were buried with him, but as you can imagine, something stopped him – the coffin was sealed; it could not be opened," she said. "And that's where you come in, Thomas."

"Ah." It always came back to his 'gift' – that was why she valued him. But maybe there truly *was* something important buried with Jean. *Something that could help the pilot? Or just anything we can use to stop Williams.*

"You don't need to look like that, you know."

"Thank you."

"I'm serious, Thomas. Some people are in no way useful; they accomplish nothing, their entire lives. You are different."

A little more distance opened up between them. "That's not the compliment you seem to think it is."

"Just remember that you need me and I need you and your sister, and we all want to see Williams finished."

"Do we?" *First time she's phrased it that way.*

"Of course."

"I thought you were planning to fly away, escape to a better life beyond the sea?"

"And on my way out, I plan to do as much damage as possible," she said with a nod. "The first strike is going to be today, and the next, once we have what's inside Alita's Shell."

He chuckled. "Something else you don't know, right?"

"Just pack your clothes."

***

The roads beyond town were lined with long, serpent-like shrubs of deep green undergrowth as they began to climb, the steam car labouring a little but holding up. While the countryside seemed a little less barren than most of the east, it was still no garden.

The plant life they passed *did* seem healthier somehow, even if it remained muted in colour. The shrubs were quite rounded in shape, and smooth at a glance, but according to Elisabeth, their leaves were sharp and poisonous.

"Then you have been here before."

"Of course," she said from where she leant forward from the back seat, red hair flowing in the breeze. "I wanted to see the coffin for myself."

"And?"

"And it's above an empty pool in what might have been a quarry once. No-one disturbs it, since most folks believe the area cursed."

"Cursed how?"

"Many escaped slaves are said to have died there. Wild animals do not visit the place, and stories about ghostly figures at night linger," she said with a shrug. "It hasn't stopped plenty of grave-robbers from seeking out the coffin, but no-one can move or break into it, so it's simply there, slowly being overtaken by dirt and weeds... or it was last time."

"What if it's gone now?"

"I'll be very disappointed." She tapped Jiro's shoulder. "Get ready, the fork is not far."

"Right."

"Besides," she said as she leant back, "We have to get there in one piece first, and we don't know how close those pricks really are." She flipped up both revolvers to check on their chambers and then snapped them closed again.

Thomas glanced once more into the side mirror. Mostly swirling dust, as it had been all day, but Elisabeth's caution was welcome. His matching worry wasn't precisely related to his own safety... that had changed. *Thanks to Silas, I suppose.* His fear was still more for Mia. What if she was somewhere in the Federation, facing similar threats? Was she truly safe? Ethan would be watching over her. *And she has own gifts.* Her Foresight would be just as useful as Ethan's skills. *You have to trust that's fine.*

Jiro slowed the car to a crawl, but did not stop the engine. From the back, lantern-jaw – or Lawrence – called from the boiler. "We've put a good distance between us and them."

"Perfect," Elisabeth called back.

The fork stood in a clear division. One trail climbed farther, stony walls rising and the undergrowth creeping across the uneven road. The other path was more well-maintained, with its road marker posts and smoother surface. It swung east, offering a gentler incline, and it was there that Wilkins and the others continued on, the rumbling of their flight soon beginning to fade.

Elisabeth hopped free then, rifle in hand, a pack slung across her shoulder. "Don't let them leave you behind then."

Thomas and Jiro joined her but Lawrence hesitated a moment as he took the driver's seat, brows drawn in worry. "You sure about this, My Lady?"

"I am. Just lead those to Talinmor and let the Federation troops deal with them."

"We will." He nodded, then he was steering the steam-car back after the others, puffs of steam whipped away by a growing wind. If the plan worked, Warrick would be fooled into following. Federation troops would stop them, at the least, leaving Wilkins and the others free to resupply and prepare for their next step.

Whatever that would be... probably rejoining the Hog, which was admittedly a little understaffed but even with a skeleton crew, there were none who could challenge the monster.

"Come on," Elisabeth said as she started jogging up the path.

Jiro hoisted his supplies as he followed, and Thomas tightened the straps on his own pack before starting after them.

It did not take long for sweat to start pouring from his temples and down his back. It was no mountain peak with thin air, but the trail offered little cover from the afternoon sun. The tallest row of trees were still some distance away, and only the snake-weed shrubs were available for cover if needed, barely enough to conceal him if he had to lay within.

He glanced back down the trail. No sign of the Williams' force yet.

"How far?" Thomas eventually called up to Elisabeth.

"We'll reach the cemetery before dark," she replied. "There's a depression off the trail a little ways further, I think."

"You think?"

"It *has* been a few years since I've been here, you know."

Thomas suppressed a sigh but it was not too much longer when they reached the depression, which included shelter in the form of a hollowed-out part of the rock face that would mostly conceal them. At least, it would offer enough time to *hear* someone coming before they were within sight.

The shade is nice too. Thomas let his pack slump to the stony earth with a clink, then reached for his flask. The sweat was already cooling and he exhaled; how wonderful water could taste.

When he lowered his flask, he caught Elisabeth glaring at him. "Yes?"

"Be careful with the lamps, will you?"

"They're fine."

Before she could retort, Jiro raised a hand. "I hear something."

A growl crossed the road beyond the shrubs.

Jiro lifted his rifle, and Elisabeth drew her revolvers. Thomas followed suit with the twin-shot he'd been given, and waited. Was it a wild dog or something bigger?

Dark fur appeared as long ears rose above the snake weed, revealing a long snout and bright yellow eyes. Long fangs protruded from the beast's mouth as it glared at them. It was probably the size of a pony – an especially large wildcat.

The claws were probably more like talons.

But it did not attack; only sniffing at the air, then moving on after giving them another glare.

Thomas lowered his weapon. *False alarm or ominous portent?*

Chapter 7.

"What's it like?" Mia asked from where she gripped the rail, cool breeze just a little cooler upon her closed eyes. She still held the silken blindfold, but it seemed a little grimy beneath her fingers, which made sense, considering how long it'd been since she'd washed her hair.

Something that would have to be rectified as soon as possible.

If I can find the energy; I'd sleep right here if there was a bed.

"The sea is pretty still and the sky is blue. There's a flock of gulls not too far away; they're near an outcropping of the reef. I can even see some stone snappers – they're bickering about something, by the looks of things." He paused. "Ever eaten one?"

"No, I don't really like crab all that much, I guess."

"Well, they're almost worth the risk." Ethan rested a hand on her shoulder. "Think they'll accept our demands?"

She smiled. "Who? The stone crabs?"

"I can see Aiden as one of them, actually," he replied, and she could hear his grin as he spoke. "But it's probably going to come down to the Queen. She seemed receptive enough."

"Maybe we should have asked for more, then – not just help finding Thomas and the pilot, but some guarantee that the *Albion* would reach out to but not seek to dominate places like Brightnest, or the mangroves and Silver Rock."

"True. But I don't think Queen Marianne wants to make a new empire."

"I hope that is so."

Now he leant against the rail beside her. "If that's the case, would you get a sense of it?"

"I'd like to think so. I'm hoping to dream, or visit the *chromata* again soon. We could use another clue to the pilot. Or Thomas."

"Maybe tonight, then," he said, then lowered his voice. "I notice you didn't mention the map before."

"No. Not yet," she said. "I want to be sure we can trust them."

"We may need it, if they're not convinced."

"But not until then."

"Agreed."

Mia sighed, a little more deeply than she'd meant to, perhaps.

"Mia?"

"I'm just tired, I think. It's all catching up."

"Let's get some rest then. Our room even has a bath, you know – as befitting honoured guests that we are."

She chuckled. "Maybe you're the one who can read minds now."

"It's not big enough for two, if that's what you're thinking," he replied.

"Take it easy," she said with a smile.

He took her hand. "Let's get some rest then, I'll work on the water while you take a nap if you want – thinking chaste thoughts the whole time, of course."

"That might make for some... strange things in the *chromata*, so maybe I shouldn't."

"I hadn't thought of that."

"Let's just get below decks first," she said.

"Right." Ethan said as he began to lead her across the *Albion*, toward the rumbling of the boilers.

When they had climbed down and reached their room – forty steps left from the ladder, portholes offering streaks of faint light, Mia stretched out upon the bed while Ethan worked on the bath.

Her body sunk into the mattress, the pillow too was surprisingly comfortable, though the bed was truly large enough for two people. She dozed, but did not fully sleep – giving Ethan only a mumbled answer when he asked about the bath, urging him to bathe first.

Yet it was not long before she woke a little, the sound of water trickling down Ethan's naked body to the steel floor seemed awfully loud... Had his idea been so bad after all? *Stupid time to think about that.*

She rolled onto her side. *Not yet.* Getting rest was more important – her limbs were not getting any lighter, as weariness born from days of uncertainty, of flight across uneven terrain, continued to pressure her.

Sleep would come easily enough; but the lingering concern was her Farsight. There was still no way to activate her Gift purposefully, and just as troublesome, she could not enter the *chromata* at a time of her choosing.

A large part of her value – in the eyes of the Queen, at

least – was that ability to foresee things. All useless if it couldn't be used for specifics...

Something warm but light settled over her and she exhaled faintly.

The *chromata* appeared.

It was the same limitless place, shadowy at first, and she could not move through it this time. Instead, Mia found herself seated upon a velvet-embroidered chair as the shadows bloomed into yellows, purples and reds – dancers in a glittering ballroom.

Exactly like the palace.

And yet, the room was not all candelabras and musicians in finely-tailored suits.

The dancers were soldiers. They spun and twirled in dark flak jackets and helmets, goggles concealing their eyes. Scores of them, all circling a pair who seemed caught within a halo of light... Thomas and Elisabeth.

Her red hair was almost blazing in the light and her face was bright with excitement – or passion. Thomas' own gaze remained locked onto hers, and there was an equal passion therein. But as they twirled, something more was revealed, one hand each held a gleaming blade.

Mia strained against the invisible bonds, fighting her way upright to lean over her rail. She opened her mouth to call his name but could not speak.

And then the *chromata* was gone.

Chapter 8.

Unease from her visit to the *chromata* lingered through the next day, like fresh claws perched on her shoulders. All through a breakfast of toasted bread and butter that should have been delicious, and a meeting with the Queen and Aiden, and now to the prow where she stood, gripping the rail once more.

The sound of the sailors calling to one another and the rumble of the stacks had long-since receded, so too the cry of sea birds nearby.

Thomas was still in danger – but he was at least on equal footing with Elisabeth… yet the passionate gazes… What did they mean? Was Thomas actually *sleeping* with Elisabeth? Or was the vision meant to represent some ploy to kill her, a plot Elisabeth seemed equally likely to undertake?

It's impossible to know.

But as much as that troubled her, didn't being frozen and mute within the *chromata* offer the chilling possibility that Nyath had returned? *Surely not.* Tension tightened all the muscles in her body, those claws digging deeper. *No, I dealt with him. He's gone.*

Which left some other explanation. "Something else happened there."

If only she could speak to the Guide.

"Mia?" A gruff voice neared, sounding as though it had called to her more than once.

She turned to a bulky shape, possibly with arms folded. The sun was bright enough that she squinted a little, even behind the blindfold. "Aiden."

"We've come up with a town to visit, based on what you've told us. Oriulla, it's near to the tip of the western side of the nation, beyond the White Abyss."

"Where Gods supposedly salted the very earth, four hundred years ago?"

"Right."

"And Oriulla has petrified trees also?"

"So the Queen tells us."

"How long?"

He grunted. "Three days – if we find whoever you're looking for right away, that is."

"I will know them."

"Good," he replied, and it seemed he did not doubt her. "In any event, while Ethan and Her Majesty plot out our course, she wants you to meet Jemima."

"Jemima?"

"She is a little like you – it's how Williams was able to find you at different times over the years."

Mia hesitated. *Someone else like me? They could know something!* "And Jemima is how you found us recently."

"Right."

Mia nodded. "Before we go, tell me something, Aiden.

Why did you give me that key? Was it some sort of gamble to keep it from Williams in case he called your bluff?"

"Only it wasn't a bluff now, was it?" he said, and his voice changed, as though grinning.

"But you thought Thomas and I would be able use it?"

"Maybe."

She waited a moment but Aiden didn't seem to be offering anything more. "Then you'll show me to Jemima?"

"I will," he replied. "And it's below, two ladders, so you have to be careful."

"Of course," Mia replied, but her thoughts turned to Jemima as she walked, eventually accepting Aiden's help when needed. Who was Jemima? How similar was her gift? And if she'd been liberated from the palace, did she know the Alchemist? Or at least, the source of her gift? *Maybe she'll know something about the chromata.*

"Here we are," Aiden said, the sound of old hinges squeaking open.

Their boots echoed a little inside, suggesting a large room – but the sound was not quite right, as though the walls had been lined with rows of something that absorbed... she inhaled. Lavender? "Where are we?" Mia asked.

"Jemima's room, obviously." Aiden quickened his step a little, and his dark shape paused before a lamp, which he opened up enough to reveal more shadowy shapes – one of them something far larger... The sound of tapping upon glass followed. "Are you awake, Jemima?"

A heavy sloshing of water came from where he stood.

Then, a few drops hit the stone floor. By the sound, almost a splat, it seemed thicker than water. Was Jemima in a large bath or some manner of *tank*?

"Is this the girl?" Her voice was difficult to age, but her accent suggested a woman from the islands east of Birnhale.

"It is, Jemima."

"I do sense her gift; we are similar after all."

"In some ways," Aiden replied. Mia frowned in his direction. *Is that a hint of shame?* "Mia, this is Jemima. I won't bother with descriptions, since you're both blind."

"Thank you," Mia said, unclenching her jaw as best she could.

But he was already speaking from the door. "Talk as long as you wish, I'll send someone to escort you back."

"You are very kind to worry over her," Jemima said. "But I'm sure she will be fine."

Mia drew closer, moving a little swiftly. What could she learn? "Hello, Jemima. I am Mia... the Queen said that you have Farsight too?"

"Well, my gift is not so strong as yours."

"You can tell?" she asked. "I've never met anyone else like me."

"Not your mother?"

"I do not know." *And I may never find out.*

"Well, it comes from family, so Williams must have taken your parents for his experiments. Him and that other fellow, David."

Mia blinked, mouth falling open.

"Who?"

"David. He was one of the nobles working for the king."

Chapter 9.

Thomas lifted the lantern, though it did not light much in the purple dusk.

The Gatehouse cemetery rose up around a basin where it was nestled within the hills. Tiny streams trickled down from the tree line above, splintering and fragmenting around uneven rock formations and small plateaus scattered with dark shapes, probably headstones.

Darker shadows flitted from branch to branch, but since they were quite small, he did not pay them much heed. Instead, Thomas started up the basin's slope, Elisabeth and Jiro in tow. His boots stirred no dust, the cracked earth and wind-worn stone seemed to hold the memory of water; a dampness lingered upon the air. *Like it's beading on my arms and face.*

"People say this place is haunted by what exactly?" he asked as they drew near the first row of headstones. All were shaped like peaked leaves, standing upright, the names and dates too faded to read. Based on where the waterline must have stood, he doubted the basin had always been filled –

since it was unlikely Jean and the others would have created graves *beneath* the water.

"Some manner of curse, I believe," Elisabeth said as she pointed. "Jean's grave is up there."

"Curse?" Jiro asked. His voice was a little tight.

"Supposedly the digging of the graves disturbed something."

"And that's what the grave robbers encounter when they come?"

Elisabeth shrugged. "I saw nothing like that."

Thomas paused on one of the uneven landings, the ground underneath more stone than earth now. *How did they manage to make graves here? And why?* There was always a chance the pieces were mostly markers only, representative of other final resting places. *But Jean's coffin is here.*

"What is it?" Elisabeth asked him.

"Just thought I'd light these now. Light's beginning to fall."

She bent to help him unpack, and then light two more lamps – one of which she handed to Jiro. "It's the next ridge."

"Right." Thomas lifted the pack, somewhat lighter now, and climbed up the last few irregular 'steps', placing his booted feet carefully. Here, more water trickled down, stones glistening in the warm light.

Now that they stood closer to the tree line, the basin's edge was darker, but something caught the lamplight nearby. It was half-visible, gleaming between gaps in a stony mound; the open gravesite littered with broken tools and faint traces of old campsites. There was even an old pot bearing a long crack.

Beside the mound stood a simple wooden sign with

painted lettering – quite clear strokes, in fact, the paint was newer than the wood itself.

Only a few steps closer and the coffin itself became clear where it lay, half-covered in dirt and rubble.

The gleaming surface was a coppery colour, faintly orange... unlike any material he'd ever seen... unlike steel or iron, since his body was not responding to it. *Or is it? Something this large should be setting off my senses but I only feel... I don't know.*

He knelt at the edge, setting the lamp down.

"Here it is then," Elisabeth said. "Notice the marking?"

Thomas nodded. A crimson wolf lay curled around an hourglass. There were no other markings, no headstone nearby either. Just the wolf and glass... which did not seem to be paint, and nor had it faded either. It was a vivid red that might have respond to the lamplight.

An image of the man from the photo album, with his mass of dark hair and big grin, flashed through Thomas's mind. Was this truly Jean's final resting place? How had it come to an end, how had they fallen apart?

"Recognise anything?" Elisabeth asked.

"The Gatehouse symbol, of course."

"I mean the coffin itself – that is Orichalcum."

He reached out to touch it. "Truly? I didn't realise–" A shiver ran through his very bones, almost sizzling across the surface somehow. It made no sense, but the sensation banished a creeping fatigue. His eye widened; it *was* a form of steel, or at least, a mineral, and it contained such strength, a latent power.

And if it really could be used as a fuel source, or any of the other things Elisabeth had mentioned, the coffin was also a thing of immense value.

"I believe so," Elisabeth was saying. "Based on the piece we found in the worm, it matches my notes from our last visit here. Back then, we could not move or even scratch the surface in any way."

"Hmmm." If even Williams' forces and their machines could not move the coffin, it made sense that it was still lying untouched. "But you think I can?"

"I *hope* you can."

"And inside?"

"As I said, I'm hoping Jean is buried with something that can help us unlock the *Clara*, perhaps some clue as to Alita's Shell. Maybe nothing. We won't know until you give it a try, will we?"

Thomas folded his arms, staring down. The longer he spent near the coffin, the more *alive* it seemed. The Orichalcum was... restless. Very different in look and feel to what they discovered in the worm, but then, all the acid and steel of his suit probably interfered.

And did I ever touch that piece without gloves?

"This isn't like the door to the Shell, if that's what you're thinking," Elisabeth said. "I believe that to be a different metal again, and we both know that your sister's song is the key there."

"Fine."

Thomas placed both hands upon the coffin, sliding them across the surface and applying a little pressure. *Forgive me, Jean.* Yet there was no seam. Even when he climbed down into the shallow grave, there was nothing he could use. Nor could he, as Elisabeth suggested, come close to moving it to check beneath.

Elisabeth was muttering. "Even with your gift... this has been a waste of time, then."

"Then should we make camp back in that hollow?" Jiro asked.

"Perhaps. It seems we haven't been followed at least. Very well, let's–"

"Wait," Thomas said.

The Orichalcum was not so cold as he'd have imagined. Would it just need heat, like in the beginning? He rubbed his hands together, building heat, then gripped the surface once more.

Nothing.

"We will find another way, Thomas," she said as she rose.

"No, wait." He *was* close; the sensation that was overtaking his body had grown to a humming now, the Orichalcum responding. "I think I can do this."

"All right."

What did it want? The hum was building, anticipatory... "What if..."

Thomas swung his fist.

A deep, bell-like tone rang out across the cemetery. He blinked. *Not what I expected.* But was it progress? Thomas struck again, and this time his fist left a dent, and a second tone echoed. It was a soothing sound too, somehow ancient, full of music.

"Keep going," Elisabeth said, crouching beside him once more.

He punched the coffin again and a split ran along across the surface. Thomas gripped the edge of the Orichalcum and wrenched it open. No screeching followed, just another, thinner note, elongated.

Elisabeth slapped him upon the back as she leant over. "Well done after all. Let's see what we've got."

The dark hollows of a skull lay within, all the more shadowy due to the bleak white of the bone. As if it had hardly faced the ravage of time. *Or been cleaned.* Thomas pulled more of the coffin open, wrenching at it from where he stood in dirt at the bottom.

Then he leant back to catch his breath.

Jean's bones lay within.

And nothing else. No map, no journal, no hidden photograph or anything of use.

Elisabeth broke into laughter. "I half-believed, you know."

"What now, My Lady?" Jiro asked.

"We meet up with Wilkins and then plan our next move, though I think we're running out of options."

"Meaning?" Thomas asked. His own disappointment lingered. *Maybe I'd believed too.*

"That we continue to search the Federation, or we take a risk. I wanted to avoid this but I didn't think we'd fail to find your sister, to be honest. This is the safest place for them."

"What risk?"

"Williams has someone that might be able to find Mia."

"How?"

"Jemima is another prisoner, one of the Red. She has a gift that is similar to your sister's, though it is not so powerful."

"Truly?"

"Yes. There have been a few, over the years."

"I see." If Mia could speak to such a person, maybe she'd get some answers about her own gift, but returning to the capital was not just a risk. It was madness. "Isn't it too dangerous?"

"Perhaps. But we're already risking everything."

Thomas glanced back down at the coffin, where Jean's skeleton lay. *Was it really worth desecrating his grave?* "I suppose we are."

Chapter 10.

"David worked with Williams?" Mia's question echoed in the room, as though leaping from the water to the steel roof before being swallowed up by the lavender-lined walls. Mia struggled to control her voice. "But that doesn't make any sense!"

"No need to shout, dear," Jemima said. "It is as I said. He was there from the beginning."

Mia had no words at first. *How? How could this be? She's wrong, she has to be.* "He wouldn't do that..."

"It was David's idea, to search for people like us."

Mia shuddered as she gripped the edge of the tank, the chill of the steel rim somehow welcome. "But he saved us. And he *hated* Williams. Called him false king, the whole time we travelled together, he had nothing on his mind but freedom for the people."

"That I do not doubt; he had principles."

"But..." *Doesn't this mean he knew our parents and never said a word? That* David *was involved in taking us away from them?*

"Perhaps I should tell you what I can remember about that time, it may help." Jemima's tone had softened.

"Yes. Please."

The water sloshed and Jemima's voice receded a little, as though she was floating across the tank. "The more I sense or see about the future, the more I lose of my past. It may be that way for you one day, I do not know. But there were dozens of women they brought to the city over the years, and a handful of men too."

"But no children?"

"Not at first. But the people David and Williams found were... encouraged to conceive children. For a time, it was assumed boys did not share the gift. Still, the king required us to continue *bearing* children, though he clearly thought *caring* for them was a waste." Bitterness entered her voice. "But enough of that. Your parents may well have been strangers at first, or they may have come to the fortress together. I am sorry that I do not recall."

"I see." Mia could barely hear her own words.

"There was an entire wing of the palace for us. It was comfortable, but more than that I seem to remember fits of rage from Williams, demands for progress. David and another man, I cannot picture his face or name, but over time they came to doubt their methods, if not the goal."

Was the other man Nicholas? "Did that goal differ from their king?"

"In time, yes. I believe that is why they turned their backs on the palace. Once they left, everything changed." The water rippled again. "We were scattered, enslaved or sent away, and some of us remained in the palace. We who were deemed most useful."

"Williams wanted to use your power to extend his rule."

"Of course, he is a man entirely lacking in vision," Jemima replied. "David once told me that he imagined a future where war and plague could be avoided, where the nation could be healed and reunited with the rest of the world," she said, though her voice trailed off. "I was proud to be a part of that ideal, you know. Even if the way they went about it was wrong."

"What happened?"

"Over time, my memories weren't the only things I lost. There was a toll upon my body too, first my eyes and then... well, it has been decades since I was able to walk unaided."

"Williams used that against you."

"He did. I have had to seek out his enemies or those he desires, with varying successes, for years now."

"Silver Rock."

"Yes. But I saw something else that day, something I did not share."

"About me?"

"And Thomas. I saw you and he in a magnificent airship, the name 'Clara' painted on its side. You stood at the rails, surrounded by others but... I could not see their faces clearly, yet I felt the hope you all represented."

"Hope?"

"For the future. But I did not imagine I would meet you myself, dear."

Mia closed her eyes. "I did not think I would meet anyone like me. Ever."

"There are others, I am sure," Jemima said. "But now that we have spoken, I want to ask a favour – an old woman's favour, perhaps."

"What can I do?"

"I so rarely see or sense anything about myself – you have probably found your gift to be similar. But I simply want to know, what is in store for me… I want to know, is there an end to my suffering?"

"I…" Mia frowned. "Are you in pain now?"

"Less than usual, thankfully."

"Oh."

"But knowing that nothing will change, well, that is its own burden. So, Mia, will you try?"

"I will. I cannot control my gift very well. And the chromata is impossible to predict, but I will."

"Chromata?"

"You don't know it?"

"Not at all, dear."

"Sometimes when I sleep, I go there. It's like a world of dreams but I can control things, sometimes." *Not too often, recently.*

"I see. It does not sound familiar, but as I said, much is lost to me, especially of my youth. I no longer know where or when I was born, where I was raised. Or by whom."

"I'm sorry, Jemima."

"No need. I will look to the future instead. It will be a brighter one too, if you can help, if you can bring the light to these lands."

Light? Mia straightened. "Jemima, can I ask you another question?"

"Of course."

"What about a great bird of light, have you ever seen that?"

"Ah, now that I have. Twice in my life, I have dreamt of such a bird – as did the others. One woman claimed that her grandmother knew who it was, called the bird *Sephina* Goddess of the Day."

"Sephina?"

"Yes. But no-one else had heard of it. You saw it too?"

"Sometimes." Mia nearly said more, but there would be time later. David's role at the palace... it changed everything, didn't it? Long-buried questions, doubts and fears were still returning. Old pain.

She had more to ask. *There's a chance our parents didn't abandon us.* "You said David came to regret what he did."

"That I know. He and the king came to blows over it."

"But, noble goal or not, why did he *begin* using those methods?"

Jemima sighed. "I wish I knew, dear."

"Can you tell me anything more? You knew him then."

"And you knew him after, by the sounds. What do you feel? If he protected you, he must have been more than his mistakes."

Mia turned to lean against the glass, sliding down to settle upon the cold steel floor – her legs were suddenly weary. *Just like the rest of me.* "I don't want to think that he acted that way because of guilt. The concern felt real."

"Surely it was."

"But I don't know anymore." *Not after what he did to who knows how many people?*

"Well, I do know that at first, many of the people tested were slaves... perhaps I was too."

"Meaning?"

"That I think David believed he was giving them a better life."

Mia clenched her jaw. "But he was also taking them from

their families."

"Some, I have no doubt," Jemima replied. "I can only offer my own guesses if you want them, no justifications."

"I do," Mia said. She released her fist, almost as though the flash of anger had been too much. A dullness was falling over her. *How, David? How could you have done those things to children? To me and Thomas?*

"You'll have to decide how you feel about him but you don't have to figure anything out this moment, either."

"I suppose not." Mia hesitated. There was one more question. And yet, to ask it was a risk. *If she says no, the door closes forever, doesn't it?* "Jemima, what about my parents – do you think the palace would have kept any records about who they took?"

"I'm sure they did. After all, they wanted to know exactly from where the gift came."

Mia straightened now. "Then there's actually a chance I could learn something."

"If the King is defeated."

"Maybe it will be 'when' he is defeated."

"A vision of your own, then?"

"No," Mia said. "More like a promise."

Chapter 11.

According to Ethan, the deep blue and grey of the sea was ever-changing beneath the winds as the *Albion* sailed, days and nights passing alike. During their voyage, Mia found little time to visit Jemima. Mostly, she was working herself hard – either refining the plans for their search as they neared the town of Oriulla, or washing and repairing clothes, any menial task so that she might fall into a deep enough sleep to reach the *chromata*.

Yet each night was a failure, so far.

No visions of the future, no sense that danger or victory lay near. Just rest. A deep, satisfying sleep wasn't too bad. *And having Ethan with me makes a difference too.*

But now they sat in what was once Captain Hawkins' cabin, a large room filled with the scent of coffee and, based on the rustling of paper on the table before her, a room likely dominated by charts.

"I was hoping we'd reach Oriulla first, but it looks like we'll need to resupply in Talinmor," Aiden was explaining. "Not just water, but food as well, meats especially."

"And fruit," Felicity – the queen's maid – added.

He grunted. "If possible, I suppose."

"We will do our best of course," the Queen said. "I have not heard of particular shortages this far west, at least."

"Will we ourselves be a problem?" Ethan asked. "A kingdom ship, I mean."

"People tend to expect Hawkins, and so we're welcome anywhere," Aiden said.

"At first," Queen Marianne replied.

"They've all come around, Your Majesty."

"Thus far."

"And how does Captain Hawkins fare today?" Mia asked.

"Well enough, I imagine," Aiden replied. "And I don't want to have the same argument."

"I want to be sure. After all, that was one of our conditions."

The shadowy shape of the Queen leant forward. "And so we have all agreed," she replied. "Once we have landed and resupplied in Talinmor, you can certainly speak to him again, and you will see that once more, Captain Hawkins is not being mistreated."

Aside from what has already been done to him and his crew. Technically the Queen was correct, and Hawkins had been in fair spirits when she'd visited. But aloud, Mia only said, "Thank you, Your Majesty."

"Of course. Now, as also previously agreed upon, we would love to hear from you about our path ahead."

"Nothing has come to give me any pause," she replied, though it was growing wearisome to only be able to report the same thing – essentially nothing, since she was receiving no warnings at all. *Which* should *mean we're going to be fine.* "We are safe and will reach port in the same condition."

"Anything specific we need to consider?"

"No. Should a threat arise, I will know of it."

Aiden tapped a finger upon the table. "I'm surprised you and your brother managed to avoid Elisabeth for so long, considering how vague your gift can be."

"But we did," Mia said with a smile. He'd offered several griping comments before. "Be patient. I will know – as with the pilot, remember?"

"Well, we must reach Oriulla first in any event," the Queen said, speaking over Aiden. "That much remains clear. And now, I suggest we all take some rest."

Mia rose and started from the room, keeping close to Ethan though by now she was far more accustomed to the space. It was, as ever, the ladders heading below that gave her more pause but these, too, she was getting better at navigating.

Once she reached their room and readied to sleep, Mia sought Ethan's arms with a slight frown. "Why does she limit our time with Hawkins?"

"Hmmm. A control measure? To remind us that she's still in charge?"

"Maybe." Mia rested her head against his chest, the steady thump of his heart soothing enough to close her eyes, but she did not fall asleep, despite the comfort. Her failure to dream anything useful or return to the *chromata* competed with the same confusion that had lingered during the voyage. She sighed. *How could David have done that?*

"You're thinking about David again, aren't you?" Ethan said softly.

"I am. I'm sorry."

"Why?"

"Because it's interfering with my Gift."

Ethan gave her a squeeze. "I think you're being a little hard on yourself, you know. Learning something like that, about someone you trusted, it's not a light burden."

Was he right? *Maybe he is.* The pressure... did it mostly come from within? It seemed stronger than any expectations from the Queen and Aiden. "You sound like you know what it's like."

"I suppose I do," he replied. "But I won't bother you with it."

She lifted her head, reaching up to find his face. Her fingers caught his stubbled-cheek. "I can listen too, you know."

He chuckled. "If you put it that way – but it's not much of a story."

"I want to know."

Ethan kissed her fingertips. "Well, it was my father. He was about as close to the nobles as you could be for a common-born man, because he was a very rich merchant. My family owned the distilleries in Birnhale."

"Woodend? I thought Williams controlled that."

"Now, yes. But then, my father, like his before him, was responsible for nearly all the liquors in the city. Yet, he was also a gambling man." Ethan paused. "You can probably guess most of what followed."

"How did it happen?"

"I'm not sure the whole of it, whether Father was cheated or whether Williams was a better player, but his debts soon outstripped what we could produce and so, eventually, that's how I was blessed with my first tattoo."

Mia straightened. "He sold you?"

"And my mother and two sisters."

"Ethan..."

"To a vassal to the west, actually. But once I was old enough to do something about it... well, I'm still doing something about it, it seems." Now a smile had entered his voice.

"You mean Williams? Or your father?"

"Williams," he replied. "But I did eventually figure out what I feel about my father, but it took time. So, I guess I'm trying to say that there's no need to rush things when it comes to David."

Mia lowered her head to his chest, the burden a little easier to bear. And she nearly asked him more about his father, but had there been hints of reluctance to his words? "Thank you."

"Of course," he replied. "Want to get some rest?"

"Yeah."

Mia closed her eyes, and this time, she let his heartbeat accompany her to sleep.

When she woke, it was to the mattress shifting as Ethan rose. *Morning already?* But she was offered darkness only; he had not lit the lamp yet and their room bore no portholes. "Anything?" he asked.

"No. No warnings or dreams, no visit to the *chromata* either."

"That's good."

"Because a lack of bad news is a good thing?"

"Exactly."

She slid the blankets aside then, cool air finding a way to pierce her undergarments before joining Ethan at the basin, three steps only. She reached for where she left her cup, only to meet Ethan's hand. "Sorry," he murmured. "Thought I'd pass it to you."

"It's fine," she replied. She dunked the cup deep into the water barrel, to find the surface far lower than she'd remembered.

"Have you ever been this far west? When you and Thomas were hiding?"

"Not so far as Talinmor, no."

"Me either. But Carlos lived in a village nearby," he replied with a sigh. "I hope he's still alive. I hope they all are."

"Me too," she said.

"Well, let's keep our ears open in Talinmor for anything that could be related to the map too," he said.

"Wasn't the Thunder Forest supposedly in the south west?"

"It was. It doesn't have the sound of a Federation name – nor Kingdom, really, but maybe there's an old timer who might help."

"We're only visiting two towns in this part of the nation; it's probably a long shot, Ethan."

"Yeah, but I don't want you to have to do all the work," he said. "And I have my reputation to maintain."

"Reputation?"

"Precisely. I wouldn't be much of a rebel leader if I couldn't at least ferret out a few secrets, would I?"

"This might be harder than the dirt you usually have to dig through."

"You volunteering to be my shovel?"

She laughed. "The moment I have a useful dream, you'll be the first to know."

Chapter 12.

Thomas flinched awake where he lay upon his bedroll in the hollow.

A cool wind rustled leaves upon the trees, and the snake-weed too, causing blood-red embers in the fire to spurt up to a flickering flame. Just as quickly, they would die away before flaring again.

He glanced around their tiny camp; Elisabeth slept soundly, and somewhere Jiro was on watch... but those details were becoming unimportant as he rose. *What's happening?*

The threat of pursuit from Warrick too, that didn't matter.

Even a need to relieve his bladder was just a thought skidding across his awareness – he was being called.

Back to the cemetery.

Why? But Thomas couldn't stop himself as he rose and slipped from the camp, starting back up the trail. The darkness was his cloak, but surely he made enough noise that Elisabeth or Jiro would have noticed? Yet again, his concerns were pushed aside by an insistent desire.

Return.

And so Thomas strode into the night.

His thoughts were hard to marshal and his sense of time remained hazy, things only clearing a little when he found himself climbing the basin once more. The moon was high enough to light the gravesite, to reveal the barely adequate job he'd managed in terms of putting the Orichalcum coffin back to rights.

Elisabeth had expressed some interest in taking it with them, but just as Thomas had suspected, he'd not been able to lift it, nor tear a piece free. As though Jean's coffin *wanted* to remain a single piece, even after being broken open. Giving Jean a proper, second burial would have been the right thing... but they'd carried no tools.

Yet now, he was peeling back the Orichalcum once more.

It was easier the second time; quickly he revealed the pale bones once more. And then Thomas waited, haze fading a little since he'd returned as urged. "I am here." *Who am I even speaking to?* He squinted at the tree line, but found only shadows... and even as he did, it was clearly a gesture only.

It was Jean, *Jean* had called him back.

Take me.

"What?"

But no voice answered, and he spoke only to a *need* that lurked within the grave, a need that urged him to take the skull. He reached forth, once more not fully in command of his own limbs it seemed, and gave the skull a firm twist.

It snapped free of the spine and Thomas shuddered.

But he still lifted Jean's skull to rest beneath one arm, then pushed the Orichalcum back into place. The dent and split remained, but it was the best he could do.

Return.

And then it was time to head back to camp.

Thomas climbed down into the chill of the basin, careful not to drop Jean's skull, then began his descent at a jog. Despite a chill that clung to him after what had happened, he at least had full control over his body again. *And my thoughts, for whatever that's worth. I've got Jean's skull now... just not sure why.*

If he could return before dawn at least, he'd still be able to get a little rest – assuming rest was possible. He gripped the skull beneath his arm a little harder, as it seemed to grow heavier.

Touching the Orichalcum again had given him another burst of strength but he still frowned as he travelled. *Jean, what do you want from me?*

This time, he received no answer.

***

By noon the next day, at the crossroads to Oriulla, with Talinmor due to appear first, Elisabeth managed to flag down a farmer's wagon while they ate their meal of dried fruit and oat biscuits. Thomas arranged the pack carefully where they sat in the back, making room between stacks of timber and bolts of cloth.

So far, Jean's skull had not issued any more undeniable orders. *Thankfully.*

"Hmmm. Are you mocking me now, Thomas?" Elisabeth asked from where she lounged beneath the sun. Jiro was nearby, eyes upon their back trail, rifle in hand.

"Not that I'm aware of," he said as he slumped against the

side of the cart. "Why?"

"Well, you're taking extremely good care of those lanterns now."

He sighed. "Why don't we talk about Warrick, instead? Like, what if he's got Sergeant Wilkins pinned down, or worse?"

"I doubt that."

"A magnificent plan."

"If anyone is pinned down, it will be Warrick. The Federal forces around here are good soldiers, Thomas. Far more organised than the militia you saw in border towns, believe me."

"Shouldn't I have seen *more* of those troops near the border?"

"Maybe they were on manoeuvres. Or you missed them. Or maybe they've relaxed numbers there, since it's been so long since Williams made any threatening moves." She shrugged. "Everything will work out as planned, Thomas. Then we can circle around to the Hog once we re-supply. Warrick won't have any idea."

"That easy?"

"That's what I'm expecting, and I'm not wrong all that often."

Thomas leant back and closed his eyes. "Then wake me when we arrive."

Chapter 13.

Talinmor was not precisely a coastal town, but hints of the sea had still been visible beyond pale hills as the farmer's cart approached large steel gates, long walls of stone lined by sentries. Guards had also been posted before the less imposing fence lines that protected the town's crops; the green a welcome sight.

But while both barriers bore sentries, only the town walls featured steam-cannons. *By the look of those boilers, maybe near as powerful as the ones on the Hog.*

Which suggested Elisabeth's confidence might not have been misplaced.

As did the steam cars arranged in a camp upon the nearby plain – lined up opposite the crops. A Kingdom's banner of five spires flew above the camp, complete with the royal W, but the figures passing between tents did not seem as though they were preparing to launch an attack. Their numbers were in the scores, not the hundreds... Thomas leant back against the rail.

"It is as I promised," Elisabeth said with a small smile.

"So I see," he replied as the farmer slowed the cart to join the line of others.

Ahead, Federation soldiers in their dark red coats and leather helmets were questioning those who entered the town. The uniform, which was different to what they'd worn upon Thomas' previous visits to the west, did indeed suggest more organisation. Even the goggles had been painted red – no doubt to further differentiate their forces from the black of Kingdom troops.

"This won't take long, folks," the farmer called back. "At least, not if what you said about your sergeant is true; he'll have arranged things with the gate."

"How long has the town been doing this?" Elisabeth asked.

"Oh, since before that other Kingdom lot turned up."

"Bandits?"

"Right," he said. "They've even raided my little farm; didn't take much but they hurt the pajon crops."

Thomas glanced to one of the barrels. Inside would be a segmented plant of gold, bundled into thin strips; some people chewed on them raw, though they were mostly cooked with chicken or fish. Pajon was resilient enough to grow nearly anywhere, but its sale was outlawed in the east.

Another ridiculous Williams law.

"Take a handful if you like," the farmer continued. "Good yield."

"Thank you," Thomas replied, and opened the lid to pull a few straws free, handing them around. He bit into his, the faint spice welcome and vaguely familiar. *Eating them for the first time, with Mia and David... somewhere in the north west. Near a white fountain?*

He had not made much progress on the piece when the soldiers reached the farmer's cart. Two men approached the farmer, while another began a search of the contents, after gesturing for Thomas and the others to hop out.

"Hold it a moment," the soldier said, his expression not precisely unwelcoming.

"I believe you've granted entry to my sergeant – Wilkins, man with a moustache," Elisabeth said.

"Could be," the fellow replied, eyes still upon his task. "Ask Emilio, he'll know for certain."

Emilio turned at mention of his name, approaching with a slight frown upon his tanned face. "We did have some ex-Kingdom lads before. Said to expect you three, but we'll still need to search your belongings."

"Of course," Elisabeth said, handing over her pack.

Thomas hesitated before offering his own pack to the second fellow. Jean's skull was still in the bottom... "You're not squeamish, are you?" Thomas asked, when a hint of suspicion entered the soldier's gaze.

"What does that mean?"

"I have a skull in there," he replied.

Emilio paused in his own search of Jiro's pack. "Why?"

"A fallen comrade," Thomas replied.

"Find it," the leader told Thomas' soldier, who started removing items, blanket, food and water first, then the lanterns. Elisabeth glared across at Thomas, but he only shrugged. *These guys won't stop us – they'll think it's strange, but it's not a reason to detain us at all. I think.*

The soldier lifted the skull free with a wince, then unwrapped it upon the ground.

Jean's bone was bright beneath the sun. The hollows of

the eyes stared back, and the skull remained silent.

"…. You cleaned him?" the man asked.

Thomas nodded.

Emilio grunted, then gave a wave. "Let's keep the line moving."

Thomas repacked Jean's skull and his belongings, then joined Elisabeth and Jiro. Together, they passed through the gates and entered Talinmor, turning from the broad road and its carts and cars, closer to the buildings of pale stone.

"Thomas, you'll need to explain that once we get a moment," Elisabeth said, eyes scanning their surroundings.

"I will," he said without looking her way.

Instead, he glanced up at the covered walkways – they seemed to appear everywhere he looked, though he'd been suppressing the sense of the steel subconsciously. Most were constructed of metal frames and other pieces of salvaged scrap. Few of the coverings that stretched overhead seemed wholly watertight, but they provided more than enough shade.

Shopkeepers were smiling as they called for attention, and even the guards Thomas passed inside the large town appeared more at ease. *Are they more relaxed or does it just look that way, since I'm used to seeing dejected faces and tattoos?*

Though there were a few people, Kingdom and Federation alike, bearing tattoos. Most markings were faded, and one that lay on the wrist of a man who gave them directions to the hotel Wilkins had taken, seemed to have been clumsily burned away. *Not that I blame him – whatever it takes.* His own tattoo could wait until true freedom.

The *Brass Bell Hotel* was quite large, covering half a block, though once he saw the yard used to store steam-cars,

Thomas understood why. And sitting within the ranks were several he recognised from the Hog. "You haven't stayed here before?" Thomas asked Elisabeth as they paused at twin wooden doors to let someone exit, striding down the short flight of steps as if in quite a hurry.

"Only passed through last time," she replied. "But Wilkins remembered the name – I only hope he hasn't had to spend too much more."

"Bribes?"

"Of course. Whether we're Kingdom soldiers or ex-Kingdom soldiers, the Federation expects a price for travelling within its borders. Especially this far west."

"Are we so short on funds, My Lady?" Jiro asked.

"We will be soon..." She trailed off, hand upon the door where she glanced back to her subordinate. Her eyes had widened in shock.

Thomas turned.

Five figures stood within the street, and they, too, looked just as stunned where they stared back.

Ethan in his leathers and tan shirt, no cloak here, along with the hulking form of Aiden and his shaved head. They in turn stood beside three figures – a familiar young woman dressed in a pale-yellow skirt and dark pants, and a middle-aged lady with silver-streaked dark hair and regal bearing, a bearing that her nondescript cloak could not hide...

And Mia.

Chapter 14.

Raised voices, tense to the point of shouting, reached Thomas through the walls of the *Brass Bell Hotel* – not a full-blown argument, yet, but Elisabeth and Aiden did not seem any closer to an agreement.

But it was hard to focus on their words, not with Mia sitting beside him.

Her hair was a little longer, and the bright silk of her blindfold had faded but she was safe, alive. *And right here beside me!* Both more and less safe than before... he had to steady a trembling of relief anyway. Best of all, her expression revealed new confidence – even the way she'd entered the room and told him about everything that had happened gave him cause to smile. *Maybe I don't have to worry so much.*

"Are you still listening?" she asked, giving his arm a thump.

"Sorry. Just thinking that you've changed. For the better," he added. "It's nice to see you this way."

"I feel the same about you, Thomas," she replied. "I don't think we've ever spent so much time apart, you know; it's bound to have happened."

"Yeah." And now he hesitated. *Shit. How can I even* start *to talk about the other things that have changed?*

"Is something wrong?"

"There is, Mia." His smile had well and truly faded now. In its place, the doubt and shame he'd been able to set aside at first. "I don't know how to explain this, but I've let you down."

She put a hand on his shoulder. "I haven't told you everything yet either... about me and Ethan, you can probably tell."

"I can," he said. "And I'm happy for you – you certainly haven't let me down." And it was true, he had no doubts about Ethan.

"Thank you, Thomas," she said. "And if what you want to tell me has to do with Elisabeth, I think I can guess, you know."

He glanced down at her. "You can?"

"In my visions, I've seen you two facing off. It's like you're both poised to strike, but you're keeping each other *quite* close."

"Oh." Thomas exhaled. *Maybe she'll understand? She already seems to know...* But saying it aloud – wouldn't that just cause pain? Was the urge to confess simply the desire to unburden himself? *Selfish.* But to keep such a secret from his sister was wrong – worse, how could he betray Mia and her suffering, his own too, and then simply pretend it was not so? "I'm ashamed."

"I imagine you did what you had to do in order to come this far, right?"

Thomas nodded. *By God, I'm a wretch – just admit it and apologise! She's making it so easy.* "Yes, but I... I don't think..." He stood. "Mia... The way you say it, that makes me sound noble. But I slept with Elisabeth not just to try and manipulate her for my own survival, but I also... sought her bed."

Mia sighed. "I suspected as much."

"You saw?" He couldn't keep a note of horror from his voice – it rushed forth to overcome the shame.

"No!" Mia replied, giving him a little push. "Not like that, you fool."

"Oh."

In the quiet that followed, he moved the window and opened it. Air flowed into the room, but the fresh breeze did not ease his guilt. "I'm sorry, Mia. I know what she did to us but I convinced myself that–"

"Thomas, stop," she said as she rose. "It does hurt, of course it does. But there will be plenty of time for me to take out some anger on you later. Just tell me this, have you fallen in love with Elisabeth?"

"No, I have not." And it was no lie. He did, in some way, care for her. But it was not love; it had always been a relationship of convenience. *Honestly, I doubt she would let herself love someone else, to be that vulnerable anyway.* "She's both exactly who we always thought her to be, and a little more human than we thought, but I could never trust her fully and I do not love her."

Mia stepped closer, then gave him a good kick. "Good."

"You're letting me off easy for now," he said, rubbing his shin.

"I am, but I meant it, Thomas. We have bigger problems – mostly those two and the Queen, next door. But I found out something... it's about David." She laughed then, a bitter sound. "I'm far more upset about that, in some ways."

"What happened?"

Her jaw was clenched. "He was working *with* Williams, in the beginning. The Queen has someone like me on the *Albion* and Jemima told me some of the things she could remember from back then."

Thomas could not answer. *David...*

"They were looking for people like me. Taking slaves and others too, maybe our parents."

"Wait..." *But David fought so hard against Williams – it doesn't add up.* Mia's final words broke into the slight daze he'd found himself in. "Our parents?"

"And he never said anything, all those years."

Thomas shook his head, voice hardening. *How could he do that to us? Lie for all those years!* "Why?"

"Jemima said that it was to help people. He turned his back on it all, after clashing with Williams."

"What?"

"Supposedly, he thought people like us could make the kingdom a better place. I don't know what the final straw for him was."

"We have to know more." Thomas closed the window with a thud. It was a chance to learn the truth, to follow his hope. *That our parents didn't abandon us.* "And there's only two people left, who can tell us anything. Maybe three, with Aiden."

"Williams and Silas both seem like better bets."

"Right."

Mia tilted her head, listening to the voices in the other room. It seemed they'd died down. "Thomas, I know I've resisted this in the past, but I want to know too. I'm sorry

I used to discourage you... we probably still have to find a pilot first; and the *Clara* would make taking on Williams so much easier."

"Easier than the having both the Sand-Hog and the *Albion*?"

"Probably. And we don't exactly own either of those two," she said with a shrug. "Not the airship either."

"First step is still dealing with everyone in there and whatever they've decided without us."

"Ethan will have steered them in the right direction."

He chuckled. "I guess so. Well, should we go and see?"

"Before they start up again, yeah," she replied with her own smile.

Chapter 15.

The long table had been assembled somewhat hastily by the owner of the *Brass Bell*, who sent out food and drink soon after. As darkness fell across the yard, the man lit portable lamps too, assisted by a happy young server, and then bade them ask for anything more as he returned inside. The bearded fellow had obviously picked up on the heavy tension in his yard, where all were seated not too far from the steam cars, tents and supplies.

But the table had not broken into rival camps, precisely. It *did* seem that everyone had united under common goals – even if lingering agitation came from disagreement over where to travel *first*.

Logistically, it was clearly best to continue on to Oriulla first, and locate the pilot from Mia's vision.

And that was about as far as all could agree.

Elisabeth sat across from Thomas, Mia and Ethan, flanked by Jiro and Wilkins, where she urged a return to the border, to open Alita's Shell first. There, she was sure they would find something of great value, and something useful for the *Clara*.

The counter came from the head of the table, where Aiden and Felicity, the Queen's maid, flanked Maryanne. "I do not doubt the value of such a place; there are certainly documents within the palace that suggest as much, but we will be better served by securing the *Clara* first. I fear my pig of a former husband will have already moved to block us in that regard."

"Agreed," Aiden said as he folded his arms. "We can return from the New States or Europa with a larger force that way and wipe Williams from the face of the earth."

Wilkins stroked his moustache. "Convincing either nation would be impressive."

"You doubt Her Majesty, Sergeant?"

"Hardly. I doubt that which is unknown, the other nations. Can we really rely on them?"

Elisabeth slapped the table. "Which is why we should open the Shell first. We might need to bargain with what lies within."

"Isn't it time to tell us what you suspect?" Thomas asked.

She frowned at him, hesitating.

"A fine way to cement the slowly growing trust, dear," Queen Marianne noted.

"I suppose so." Elisabeth leant back in her chair with a sigh. "So be it. I believe that there is a store of Orichalcum within the shell, and more than enough to satisfy this poor nation."

"Orichalcum?" Felicity asked. "The mythical mineral?"

"Yes. Something that is not only of *incredible* rarity and

value itself, but is also a fuel source like no other. With a single load, we've estimated that the *Clara* could circle the world with no problems. It could change the way all transport is conducted here. Possibly across the world."

The Queen raised an eyebrow. "You know that the store is there?"

"Based on the books I stole from the Fortress, yes."

"But you haven't seen it?"

"No," Elisabeth admitted. "That's where Mia comes in."

Mia didn't respond, instead addressing the Queen. "You do not seem too surprised, Your Majesty."

"Not truly. I knew such a store existed, or was rumoured to exist, but I had expected to search much nearer the *Clara* – beneath its resting place, actually."

"The Shell is the safer bet, Lady Marianne," Elisabeth maintained.

"We should follow Gatehouse in this, shouldn't we?" Ethan asked.

"Both places bore the Hourglass," Thomas added.

Sergeant Wilkins stood to attend to a flickering lamp. Like the others, it had started to attract moths, their purple wings tinted with paler blue scales too. "Alita's Shell is closer, if we must search each place."

Queen Marianne was now nodding, though Aiden didn't seem too pleased. Was that because at one point, he'd have to travel with Elisabeth upon the Hog? Was he worried about the ship or something else? *And why does he travel with the former queen?*

"Then it's settled?" Ethan asked.

"So it seems," the Queen replied. "Let us return to the *Albion* at dawn, and head for Oriulla."

"Are you still certain you can find this pilot, Mia?" Aiden asked.

"I am."

"Then sweet dreams, I suppose," the former Bruiser said as he stood to assist the Queen with her chair.

The three left without ceremony, but Elisabeth waved Wilkins and Jiro away, leaning over the table, eyebrow raised. "Well, Thomas? Best you and I give these two their privacy, don't you think?"

Thomas glared at her, unable to face Mia.

"Very considerate of you, Elisabeth," Ethan said as he stood, slapping her on the back. "But if you could spare Thomas a few moments first, I'd appreciate that."

Elisabeth frowned. "Just so long as you don't keep him all night."

Once more, Thomas found himself unable to speak.

"Assuredly," Ethan said as she strolled off.

Silence filled the yard, until Mia sighed. "We have more important things to discuss, so let's skip–"

"Wait, Mia," Ethan said. He took her hand.

"Ethan?"

"Let's talk," he said. "We may want to say things aloud to one another now that the topic has come up. Thomas, you know that I care for Mia, and she cares for me, don't you?"

"I do."

"And you have no objections." The way Ethan phrased it was not precisely a question.

Thomas shook his head. "Not at all. I'm grateful, Ethan. You were there when I could not be. Mia is happy, I know."

Mia turned from Ethan, a trace of wariness in her voice. "So, you really aren't experiencing any well-meaning but misguided urges to interfere, like an older brother might?"

He chuckled. "No. I did almost feel that when I first suspected you two felt that way... but I could not wish for anyone better. And you chose him, Mia. That's good enough for me."

"Good."

"About Elisabeth," he said then, the lightness evaporating with his words. "I know not to trust her, and I share her bed while our alliance lasts, not because I have fallen for her."

"Glad to hear it, Thomas," Ethan said. "I won't come between you and Mia there, and I know you have spoken already, but don't underestimate Elisabeth simply because she purrs for you."

Thomas winced. "Fairly spoken." *And gentler than I deserve.*

"Let's move on, shall we?" Mia said, speaking a little quickly. "Or at least, change focus back to trust. I think we can all see, it's clear that neither Elisabeth nor the Queen are revealing all that they know about the Orichalcum."

"Agreed," Ethan said.

"Either way, I think it's obvious what her plan is for appealing to other nations for aid."

"So, we know she's looking for an ally, but how can she choose?" Thomas asked. "Has she already contacted them?"

"And offered what, exactly?" Ethan added.

"Right." Mia was nodding. "And Ethan and I never felt that the *Clara* was a suitable bargaining chip alone, so it looks like the Orichalcum is what she'll offer. If it *is* the fuel source it is claimed to be, I can see why."

"What still concerns me," Ethan started, "is that whoever she ends up bringing here, may well decide to turn on us and take all the Orichalcum. A whole new war could begin."

"Another reason why she wants Mia, right?" Thomas asked. "Her Foresight."

Mia nodded and lowered her voice. "We need to think about how to maintain enough power in this thing too."

"Think there could be a point where we become expendable?"

"Perhaps," Mia replied. "But believe me, I'll sense *that* coming, if it happens."

Thomas gave her hand a squeeze, unable to ignore a tiny sliver of doubt – was Mia trying to convince herself, after so long without a vision or dream?

Chapter 16.

Oriulla was not so different from Talinmor. Similar buildings of pale stone waited inside heavily fortified walls, joined by bright cacti too, but here, closer to the coast, muddy green eucalypts also towered. The bark was closer to silver than grey, trunks usually adorned by small pieces of painted wood in various colours, seemingly affixed by sap.

But he didn't get time examine them up close, since Elisabeth and Aiden were already striding into a large market, the space crowded by voices of the Federation folk. *Not so many kingdom citizens here either. We'll stand out.*

He edged closer to Mia, who walked with Ethan.

In the end, despite half the *Albion* wanting to accompany them on the search, it had been decided that five would be enough, and hopefully, enough to avoid the appearance of a threat.

Aiden still carried a heavy purse earmarked for bribes, and Elisabeth was hoping to meet one of her far-flung contacts.

But in the end, it was all up to Mia.

During their rocky trip upon the longboat, Mia had shared good news – even without a dream, she could feel the pilot now that they were close to the town. "He's definitely inside."

And while she'd urged them 'east' it didn't seem that the market was quite right... and the Federation soldiers stationed in their red and black seemed to agree, as a pair soon approached. One man called for them to halt before a nearby butcher, whose window displayed a mix of rabbit, chicken and lizard.

"Easterners are not always welcome here," the older man said in place of any greeting. "We trust you are passing through?"

Aiden narrowed his eyes, but thankfully, did not burst into a fit of anger. He'd had the same reaction at the gates. *But then, he's not a fool, just because he's short-tempered, I shouldn't be surprised.* Instead, Elisabeth answered with a nod. "We'd appreciate just a little more of your grace before leaving."

"Namely?"

"We're seeking someone to hire, actually."

The other guard scratched at his beard. "That so?"

"Yes. We need someone good with machines and we heard from the *Brass Bell Hotel* in Talinmor, that we might have luck here on Oriulla."

"The Bell, eh? Well, you can ask around – there's plenty of folks, but best if you clear out before nightfall."

"Many thanks," she said, as the two returned to their posts.

"Nicely done," Ethan said.

"I'm hoping we won't need so much time, but we have it now, at least."

"We're getting closer," Mia said. "Beyond the market.... near a glassblower."

"Right."

Once again, Elisabeth and Aiden quickened their step across the cobblestones. It seemed that they were both vying for the actual lead, as though competing, which was foolish for so many reasons – not in the least because neither knew where they were headed.

Still, by the time they reached the glassblower and its workshop, where apprentices were crowded around a glowing fire, Mia called ahead. "The three-storey building nearby."

Thomas paused.

A jail – the tallest building near the glassblower was a jail, its barred windows, lack of ornamentation and armed guards unmistakable.

"So, he's a criminal?" Aiden asked.

"Or a guard," Elisabeth replied. "In any event, let's see what it'll cost."

At the door, a pair of Federation troops stopped them, one man with a raised hand. The other tapped his revolver. "I don't think so, folks."

"Greetings." Elisabeth flipped a silver coin in her hand. "We are hoping to hire someone here, but we understand that as easterners, you might not be open to that possibility. We hoped you might be willing to negotiate."

The guard looked at the coin, then shook his head. "Who?"

"And for what?" the other asked.

"For mechanical work," she replied as she tucked the coin away. "I understand there's someone here who would be suited to that?"

The two exchanged a glance. "That'd be Marcus. I'll take you to him but you'll have to leave your weapons out here, understood?"

"Very reasonable."

Thomas glanced to Mia at movement – she'd straightened slightly; it seemed Marcus was the one they needed.

Perfect. Thomas lined up to hand over his rifle and belt knife next, before following the guard, who introduced himself as 'Damascus', into the cool building. The entryway held a long desk, but also steel barricades. Three men, each in Federation black and red and armed with revolvers and rifles, sat around a game of cards.

"You'll have to take care of his fines," Damascus said as led them through a bolted door into a well-lit hall lined with bars, but he stopped at the first cell to gesture. "This is Marcus," he said, then stood back with arms folded.

"My name's Copper," the prisoner snapped. He was a young Federation boy, maybe twelve or thirteen, and he leant against the wall upon his cot, swinging a polished stone through a piece of string; the game of cat's cradle seeming a little more complex than typical. He wore ragged pants but his shirt was of a fair cut, simply smudged with grease. His face was the same, dark eyes frowning at them.

Damascus shrugged. "Whatever you call yourself, this might be your lucky day."

"What do you mean?" He stopped to examine his 'visitors' as he approached the bars.

"He can definitely help us," Mia said with a nod.

Marcus frowned. "Help you?"

Aiden hefted the purse, letting the coins clink together. "We'll pay to get you out of here, if you'll work for us."

Hope and interest entered his eyes, though it was cautious. "Doing what?"

"Working with machines," Mia said. "But you'll have to leave Oriulla and travel with us, so it's not a small thing we're asking. What do you say?"

He grinned as he gripped the bars. "Nothing much for me here. You're on, lady."

Mia smiled. "Wonderful."

Aiden tossed the money to the guard, who caught it with a bit of flailing. "That enough?" the Bruiser asked.

"Take him," the man said. "This would probably cover his next fine too."

"We do need a key," Elisabeth said.

Damascus called for a subordinate, a stout fellow who scurried over and unlocked the door. Marcus – or Copper – grinned as he exited. "That's more like it. So, where are we headed? East?"

"Sooner or later, I imagine, yes," Elisabeth said. "But why don't we talk outside? You can tell us more about your skills."

"Well, there's plenty of people better than me but they don't all work as hard as I do."

"Lovely to hear," she said, gesturing for him to lead them from the prison.

Thomas hung back a moment, touching Mia's arm. "Isn't he a little young for all of this?"

Mia sighed. "Maybe, but it's dangerous for everyone, what we do... and it doesn't seem like he's that much better off here."

"You might be right, but let's agree to watch out for him; I don't want him thrown to the wolves."

Ethan nodded, though he rubbed at the stubble on his

cheek. "We've probably already done that, haven't we?"

"Only if we let it happen," Mia replied.

Chapter 17.

Thomas followed Marcus beneath the warm sun to the Albion's high rails, smiling as he did. The lad's wide eyes and even wider grin were infectious as he leant over to stare down at the ocean. "The waves are just bouncing off – this ship is amazing!"

"Wait until you see the engine room."

The kid pushed himself back. "Really?"

"As soon as we convince Aiden and the Queen, absolutely."

Marcus was already walking toward the base of the ship's stacks and their mighty bursts of steam, neck craned. "Think it'll be today?"

Thomas laughed. "I hope so. As soon as Mia returns, you'll get an answer."

"Sooner would be better, but I guess I'll have to wait."

"While you do, tell me, how long have you been working with machines?"

The boy scratched at his dark hair. "Since I can remember. When I was little, they said I would sit at dad's feet with a bolt and some nuts, just spinning them along the thread, over and over."

"From what you've told Mia, it sounds like that early start paid off."

He grinned. "Well, I was doing a lot better before they outlawed the racing. I nearly had an engine that could outrun the Michal Four-Part steam car."

Thomas whistled. *That* is *fast. The car and his progress — Mia was definitely not wrong about this kid.*

"There you are." Elisabeth approached from the prow, almost sliding across the decks to lean on the rail beside him. She wore a smile but it did not seem too genuine, as though it was for Marcus's benefit.

"Something wrong?" Thomas asked.

"No, but we should talk anyway." She looked to their pilot. "Copper, think you can manage not to fall in while you wait for this big lug's sister?"

Marcus nodded. "Sure thing." He slid down against the wall and pulled a small toolkit from his belt. Next, he produced a pocket-watch and flipped it open to begin his work, whistling as he did.

Thomas exhaled as he followed Elisabeth below to stride along the passage with its cloudy portholes. *Wonder if I could ever feel that kind of happiness — the kind where I'd want to whistle? Not that I blame him.*

They squeezed past one of Aiden's sailors on their way to a small room used for meetings, it seemed, where she closed and leant against the door. In the beam of light from the porthole, Thomas took one of the chairs and sat, stretching his legs to the small table as he waited.

"You seem comfortable," she muttered, but did not join

him, and did not add anything else.

Thomas straightened. "Elisabeth, what's going on?"

She tugged her gloves free and hooked them into her belt. "Nothing – yet, that's why I want to speak to you. I need you and your magical sister to keep an eye on Aiden; he's not telling us everything."

"Like you and I, then."

Elisabeth raised an eyebrow. "Are you telling me that you're keeping secrets from me?"

"Of course. And I'd be a fool to assume you aren't doing the same."

"Just so long as we still share a common goal, I suppose that won't hurt," she said with a smile, but while there was more warmth to it than then one she'd offered outside, this one did not last. "I can't have it taken from me, not this close. Years of struggle, of fighting, of suffering, *years*, to get here, Thomas."

He regarded her a moment. Once again, a touch of vulnerability had snuck to the surface. Was it genuine? *Is she really more than her ambitions?* Trusting her fully was not on the cards... *But it was certainly easier when she was just an enemy.* "This isn't just about you and Aiden competing, then?"

"You think we're competing?"

"Maybe you don't realise it, but it feels like you're both trying to... impress the Queen?"

Finally she did cross the room to settle into the chair across from him, a faint look of surprise upon her features. "You might be right."

"Nice to hear."

"She was a single bright light in the palace, Thomas.

Once, she took the time to ask if I was all right. The Queen herself. She stopped to ask a girl who had wandered into her garden to weep – and she asked if she could help, instead of immediately beating or chasing me away... that was like a rebirth."

"Then you trust her?"

"I do... yet I cannot fathom the connection between her and Aiden," Elisabeth admitted. "I know that he was once part of the plans David and Silas had, but Aiden turned his back on everything long before I came to my own realisation about the future. He *must* have a hidden agenda."

David. Again, doubt and confusion swept over him but he had to put it to one side. *Focus on Elisabeth and what she's saying, fool.* "You think Aiden has some leverage over the Queen? Because it seems the other way around to me."

Elisabeth nodded. "Which is why we need to watch them."

"Mia will know if there's something we're missing."

"I hope so."

"I'm more worried about Warrick. They might be able to cut us off once we head inland. That seems like something no-one has discussed yet."

"A lot of factors to consider," she said. "The weather, or how often he's stopped, and then the same for us, when we head for the Hog. Not much we can do until we know what's ahead."

"What about troop numbers at least?"

"I suspect we outnumber them still, especially with Aiden's men." She rubbed at her temples. "Why don't you get Mia to check on the skull you brought back, instead. That should be enough to occupy you."

Thomas blinked. Not a bad idea at all... maybe Mia could shed some light on why it happened. *That whole episode certainly slipped your bloody mind.* "I will, but I want to ask you something myself."

"I know what you're going to ask, and I've told you, there's something in there that we can use. More than the Orichalcum, but I don't know what exactly."

"Then what about the books you mentioned, the ones you stole from the palace."

"Safely locked away in the Hog. You want to read them?"

"Yes."

"So be it," she said.

A knock echoed down the corridor, followed by a muffled query. It came closer, and the voice clearer – someone asking for Elisabeth. She stood raised her own voice. "In here."

"Isn't the door locked?" Thomas asked.

She groaned as she stood, reaching the door just as the handle rattled. "Ah, My Lady?" It sounded like Jiro.

"A moment." She slid the bolt free and opened the door.

He glanced within, and seeing Thomas, his expression eased. "I have news."

"Inside, then." The closed the door behind him. "The pigeon?"

"Yes."

Thomas rose to join them. "It found us at sea?"

"Of course," she replied. "They're well-trained. In any event, what did it say, Jiro?"

"Williams has launched a second force from the border. Depending on exactly when the left Last Castle, they'll likely be close when we reach Alita's Shell."

She frowned. "That old bastard. But it might not matter

if we find what we need in the Shell."

"Don't we still need to reach the *Clara* itself?" Jiro asked.

"We can sail around anything he manages now."

"What if other ships are put into play?" Thomas asked. "The *Iron Whale* has enough firepower to challenge the *Albion*, doesn't it? And that's not counting Williams' own ship."

"It might well be a moot point, whatever our path."

"Why is that?"

"Because there's something in Alita's Shell, remember? Something we can use, the books just don't describe it properly."

"Tell me anything."

"It describes something called the 'Thorn of Souls'. What does that sound like to you?"

Dramatic name for a weapon... if that's what it is. But finally, she'd given in and shared some information! "It sounds like bad news."

She shrugged. "We'll find out in a matter of days now, won't we?"

Chapter 18.

Mia stopped when the sailor spoke, the woman's voice echoing below decks and forward where the dark of the brig waited. The sailor was one of Aiden's crew but again, like plenty of those upon the ship, did not seem as ill-tempered as her leader. "His room is here, Lady Mia."

"No need to worry about that sort of formality," she said. "Mia is fine."

"Oh, of course." With so little light below, the sailor was not even an outline behind Mia's blindfold. "Just let me get the door."

Steel clicked in steel and then a hinge creaked.

The faint scent of sweat within a closed-up room met Mia as she stepped within, dim shapes in lamplight. Copper and their guard followed.

"Mia?" Captain Hawkins's deep voice filled the space.

"Hello, Captain. I want to ask if you're well, but I suspect nothing has changed."

"Well, I want for little when it comes to food and wine, or

reading materials – that hasn't changed."

She nodded. He was also let free to deal with the occasional problem concerning the *Albion*, but hadn't spoken too warmly of semi-regular visits for fresh air. "Well, I hope to bring some good news today."

"Grand to hear," he replied. "About your young comrade here?"

"Yes. We've hired Copper to help with the airship. Can you show him how your ship works in the meantime, perhaps?"

Hawkins shifted closer, probably reaching out to take the boy's hand. "I'd be happy to do that, though I'm not sure the *Albion* and the *Clara* will have all that much in common."

"Anything you can show me would be amazing, Captain," Copper said. "I'm interested in pretty much everything!"

"I'll do my best, then," he said with a chuckle. A slight pause followed. "Assuming it's permitted by my masters?"

The guard shuffled his feet, but did not answer, seemingly more willing to let Mia do so. "They agreed," Mia said. "You'll have supervision, but it sounds like it'll get you out of here more often."

"I welcome that."

Mia reached out, and after only a slight delay, found the Captain's hand. "It is only the beginning. We'll convince them."

"If anyone can, I imagine it's you and Thomas."

The sailor cleared her throat, perhaps after exchanging a glance with their guard. "Ah... Mia. I think I should take you topside now. Her Majesty is probably waiting."

"I assume that means Copper will receive his first lesson from Captain Hawkins immediately?"

Silence. It seemed the two were once again exchanging glances, and then the guard spoke. "Just a moment and I'll take them both."

"My Lady, if you'd follow me?" the sailor offered once more.

"Thank you. Well, have fun you two," Mia said, directing her words mostly toward Copper, though she suspected Hawkins would be just as happy.

"We will!" the boy replied.

She followed the footsteps of her escort below decks, one hand trailing the wall with its regularly-spaced columns and their mighty rivets, every five steps or so. When they reached the ladder, Mia climbed up to find a cool breeze and warm sun, the shouts of sailors almost lost beneath the hammer of steel on steel. *Minor repairs?*

Two familiar voices were far nearer – Ethan and Queen Marianne, and when Mia squinted against the brightness, it seemed Aiden stood with the two.

"In a few days we will pass the ruins of Aderlen and locate a place to dock so that we can travel inland to meet the Sand-Hog, but there is no guarantee we can outrun Warrick. More, this news from the east concerns me. I'm growing increasingly worried about the king's ships and the *Iron Whale*," the Queen was saying.

"Is it faster than the *Albion*?" Ethan asked.

"Probably a match. So much depends on the weather we each face."

Mia joined them, her escort making apologies as she left. "Marcus is with the captain in the engine room."

"Thank you, Mia," the Queen said, and it seemed Aiden bristled at hearing Hawkins addressed as captain. "If I could also ask for your aid with a new threat."

"Williams' ships?"

"Yes. Admiral Fabian leads a squadron this way. Even if we send a landing party in time, the *Albion* may be vulnerable."

"I'll consult with Jemima before the evening."

"Excellent. We will, of course, make conventional preparations in addition."

"Has the *Albion* taken on additional weapons?"

"Some," Aiden said, explaining about several new cannons and their range, information she could not quite visualise. "But not enough to take on the *Iron Whale* and the other two at once. If it comes to it, I'll draw them away while the Queen continues to the Shell."

"Can you outrun them all?"

"Perhaps the smaller ships, but my men have been working on something to aid a retreat if the *Iron Whale* ends up able to keep pace."

"What do you have in mind?" Ethan asked.

"A smoke screen," Aiden replied. "But we've been trying to encourage the smoke to 'cling' to whoever enters it. That way, they won't be able to navigate."

"You can manage that?"

"Not yet, but Brandon is close. The problem is producing enough to make it effective on a large scale. But if we can take one or two ships out, then we'll have a chance," he said. "If possible, I'd rather sink them all."

Mia frowned. Who was Brandon? *Another prisoner like Jemima? Whoever he was, it sounds like he's an Alchemist... meaning he'd know Silas? Someone worth speaking to, maybe.*

"Unlikely, Aiden," the Queen said.

"For now," he replied.

Mia looked to his dark outline. "What do you mean by that?"

"No need to read into it," the Bruiser said before excusing himself.

The Queen did not address his comment either.

Chapter 19.

Thomas gripped the Gatling, legs braced against the edges of the steam car's platform as the car bumped along the barely adequate road. Heat radiated from the nearby boiler, but equally strong seemed to be the hum of the steel itself.

"Poor weather ahead," Jiro said from where he monitored the gauges.

Thomas nodded. Dark rain clouds approached, covering a large patch of the already overcast sky. The wilds of Aderlen were a mix of greying tree trunks and the faintly noxious scent of stagnant marshland — hills on one side and muddy plains on the other. If he glanced over his shoulder, he'd see Mia's car, and the Queen's too, where two of Aiden's soldiers, and Felicity rode.

Behind them, in turn, waited the coastal road that led eventually to a makeshift dock, where Aiden and the *Albion* had deposited them.

Will he really be able to lead Williams away?

Thomas squinted ahead, the goggles doing their job when

it came to keeping swirling dust from his eyes but impeding his view a little. *If nothing else, the rain will dampen all this.* Not being able to share his doubts with Mia, now that he'd finally found her again, was... unusual. Maybe she felt the same? At least she had Ethan and a couple of men from the Hog in her car. *Watching over her directly would feel better, though.*

The car slowed, and Thomas glanced down. Elisabeth had turned from the driver's seat, fiery curls flowing in the wind. "We're going to need more fuel soon," she called up. "Keep an eye out for something better than a single fallen tree, will you?"

"I will."

This close to the old border between Viterra and Aderlen, not so far from the marshes, the greenery wasn't so green, but nor was the place so arid as parts to the east. *And nowhere near as bleak as those craters of rust.* Debris from a mad general that slaughtered an entire city... so much of the past was lost.

But even if the surrounding hills were more alive, it didn't mean they travelled through a woodland either. *Maybe Aiden should have given us a little more coal.* The former Bruiser *had* amassed an impressive fortune, to have multiple steam cars aboard the *Albion*, and the wood and coal to spare in the first place.

What he'd offered got them at least halfway to Wilkins and the Hog, according to word received from the pigeons. So far, the sergeant also reported that Warrick was still nowhere to be seen.

Troubling. *Warrick had the advantage of numbers, so why didn't he attack Wilkins* before *the sergeant returned to the Hog?*

Once again, Elisabeth slowed the car, this time to detour a pile of trunks and stone, but there was more rubble beyond, and she was soon weaving her way through a wreckage of highway, avoiding cracks and holes that ran not only across the road, but into the plains. From the hills, a wind whipped down, bringing more dust and dead leaves.

Thunder boomed overhead. In the distance, lightning sliced through the clouds and the welcome scent of rain neared.

Elisabeth pulled the car from the road, coming to a halt before a large collection of old stumps, then climbed out, motioning for Jiro to do the same. "Let's set up some tents over there."

Thunder rumbled again.

Thomas looked back. Ethan was already pulling in nearby, but not right beside them, the Queen's car next, steam puffing as it rattled closer. She didn't line up too close either, but it was probably a token gesture. *If the storm hits, this could be the most steel around for miles...*

Before he could make the same observation aloud, another crack split the air. Rain burst from clouds, thundering across the plains, wind joining in. Thomas groaned, even as he leapt down to help Jiro with the tents. Together, they hauled canvas and poles to where Elisabeth was kicking away stones from an even space beyond the rows of stumps.

"Is this safe enough?" he shouted when they reached her.

"I'm hoping the old tree line will be at least something. Or better yet, that we're not in the direct path of the storm to begin."

"Think we'll be that lucky?" Jiro asked. Rain streamed from his helm, down his goggles and across his face.

"This close to Alita's Shell, we bloody better be," she said.

Thomas glanced to where Mia and Ethan were working on their own tents, and her thought echoed in his mind.

***

Rain pelted against the canvas of their tent, its green nearing black in the storm.

"Get out of those wet clothes." Elisabeth removed her jacket and started on her shirt buttons where she knelt upon the bedroll. The damp fabric clung to her body, revealing the curve of her breasts. "Warm me up, Thomas."

He hesitated, despite the chill of his own clothing.

She slid closer. "Stop worrying about your sister. She has Ethan."

That's not the whole problem. But Thomas removed his own flak jacket and shirt with a slight frown. "You still want to do this?"

"Of course." Elisabeth ran her hands across his chest and stomach. His muscles tensing at the clamminess but when she slid her tongue across his nipple, it was warm. "And so do you, obviously."

He lifted her chin, meeting her gaze. "That's not what I mean."

"Then tell me."

"Isn't there a new trust between us, now that we're all fighting for the same thing?"

Elisabeth grinned. "Thomas, you *like* that you don't fully trust me when it comes to the bedroom."

He didn't bother to deny it and couldn't prevent a blush either.

She kissed his neck. "Just stop thinking."

"Clearly, this isn't about us trying to manipulate each other anymore."

Her teeth grazed his shoulder. "No."

"Leaving what?"

Elisabeth bit harder. "Get these pants off me and find out."

Chapter 20.

When the storm eased, a new sound beyond the tent became apparent, and Elisabeth rose from beside Thomas with a soft curse. "That can't be good."

Something was rumbling closer – and not more weather, but vehicles.

Elisabeth leapt into her clothes and Thomas followed suit, the chill of damp fabric against his skin a far cry from pleasant.

"Weapons," she said as she finished with her boots and snatched both revolvers.

Thomas jammed his feet into his own boots and burst from the tent.

Puddles covered the hard earth but the sky overhead was clear and blue now. It could have been pleasant, but half a dozen steam cars, maybe more, approached from the north. "Who are they?" he called as he ran for his own car, where his rifle waited. *Maybe the Gatling is a better choice.*

"Don't know yet," Elisabeth replied from where she stood, hand shielding her eyes.

Ethan and Mia emerged from their tent, as did Jiro and the other soldiers from their own. The Queen and her men, who were already armed, approached first.

"Do we make a stand?" Ethan asked.

"Someone get me a spy glass," Elisabeth called.

Jiro leapt into the passenger seat of their car, then threw it across the camp. Elisabeth snatched the glass from the air and swung to face the vehicles.

"Who approaches?" the Queen soon asked.

"Federation troops, like I thought," Elisabeth replied as she held out the spyglass. "Take a look."

Thomas climbed back onto their car and lifted his own spy glass, the one affixed to the Gatling's shaft, and squinted.

A steady spray of mud flicked up from the cars as they grew nearer, and the windscreens were not always clear, but he eventually caught a glimpse of crimson on the uniform and a pair of goggles from one of the men. Another fellow stood behind a mounted weapon; something that seemed to lie somewhere between rifle and cannon.

And it did seem that the cars numbered six only, yet six cars and their men would be trouble if the soldiers had come to fight.

"Let's send up a white flag," the Queen said. "I want to see their response."

One of her soldiers, a stern-looking fellow, ducked into his tent. He emerged with an undershirt. Hands a blur, he pulled a belt knife and made two slits before affixing the makeshift flag to his rifle, then leapt onto his car to wave it back and forth.

Thomas turned back to the vehicles, now close enough to view individual soldiers. They were certainly armed with rifles and revolvers, but that didn't automatically mean hostility. The group did slow, but probably to navigate the uneven road.

Once the Federation soldiers came close enough to make out expressions, Thomas lowered the spyglass and took a hold of the Gatling, but did not fire. Both groups were already within range, and so far, no overt moves toward an assault had been made.

When the lead car stopped a short distance away, two figures were the only ones to step forth. One, a man, stood head and shoulders taller than the other figure – the fellow was easily seven feet tall, and his torso like a wall. At the least, his expression did not seem unwelcoming.

His second was well-armed, though she, too, did not seem to offer any threat when she lifted her red goggles, even smiling at them. "Your flag is noted," she said.

"Greetings on behalf of Highway Governor Bareo," the giant announced. "He has asked us to offer any assistance that Lady Elisabeth and companions may deem necessary."

Elisabeth chuckled. "This is welcome news... Captain? But I must ask at what cost?"

"Donovan. And admittedly, the Governor did express an interest in compensation."

"Then let us negotiate," she replied.

He nodded. "We will set up a pavilion, and refreshments. Your patience is appreciated."

***

Thomas joined Elisabeth, Mia and Ethan, *and* the Queen in the Federation pavilion, which was spacious, with folding chairs for everyone and space left over to walk to maps hanging on the walls. The Federation troops were well-provisioned, also, with plenty of fruit and wine to go with the water. *Not like back home.*

Captain Donovan and his sergeant, Jaya, were the only two at the large table, the rest of their men set to work preparing for an evening meal. "The Kingdom has been very active within our borders of late and this has made the governor curious," he said.

"And so he sent you south to investigate our precise location?" Elisabeth asked.

"That, and to offer sincere greetings to the former Queen of the East."

"That is kind of your master," the Queen said. "I am impressed he has been able to keep tabs upon me of late."

Captain Donovan nodded. "He is a tireless guardian of the Federation."

"And has he decided that I am now a threat?"

"Hardly, Queen Marianne," Sergeant Jaya replied. "But he senses turmoil and believes you and Lady Elisabeth are uniquely positioned to help the Federation circumvent it."

Quite the diplomat – both of them, really. Thomas waited for a reply from the queen, but she only nodded, letting Elisabeth take the lead once more.

"I imagine that Bareo knows we're heading for the Shimmering Ranges again."

"He does," Jaya said. "And in exchange for a reasonable share of what lies within Alita's Shell, Bareo has been granted certain authorities by the Fourth Minister, authorities which will allow him to not only aid you with our troops here, but also to repel any attempts by Warrick Williams to interfere.

In addition, a final boon can be granted. You are permitted to also remove generous portions of whatever you find from Federation territory."

Elisabeth's jaw worked but it was only a moment. "Please express our gratitude to both Bareo and Fourth Minister Maximilian."

"Of course."

"Should we discuss those shares?"

Captain Donovan nodded. "Certainly. The Highway Governor believes that a sixty-forty split of the Orichalcum is certainly fair."

Elisabeth straightened then, leaning forward as she did. "We would find sixty percent quite generous indeed."

"Wonderful news," he replied. "For such a share, the Fourth Minister hopes you can be relied upon in any possible future disputes between Federation and Kingdom."

"I would personally agree to that," Elisabeth said with a nod.

"Before I add my own agreement, I would ask: regarding your forty percent, does the Federation have an airship hidden away somewhere, Captain?" The Queen asked.

"Alas we do not. Yet I am sure it is clear that my superiors would wish to maintain a cordial relationship with any who might soon come into possession of one."

"Certainly."

Thomas almost smiled, hard to deny his own admiration. The Federation seemed to be doing a fine job on their part: doubtless well-aware that Orichalcum was useless to them without an airship, they were guaranteeing a functional relationship with Kingdom rebels by holding back a fair portion of a presumably limited fuel source. *Equally impressive is that they know or suspect what's in the Shell. Can we actually trust them?*

"It sounds like we've reached an agreement quite swiftly," Elisabeth said.

"So it has," the captain replied as he produced a document. "Let us sign and celebrate the accord with some of our finest wine."

Chapter 21.

Steam hissed as the sand-hog rumbled to a halt, dust swirling around two storeys of steel and iron; a monstrous wall of power. The main cannon hung above the engineer's dome, unmanned, and figures were not visible within the reinforced windows or the unshuttered portholes either.

Thomas had sensed it coming from a fair distance, standing beside their cars in the sun, and now the hum of the mass of steel pushed against him where the sand steamer rested. *It's familiar too. Like I'm recognising the specific pieces, like I know they belong to the Hog.*

A few soldiers soon appeared to wave from the rails but it took a short while before Sergeant Wilkins appeared from a hatch, starting down one of the ladders with some haste.

When he reached them, Thomas noted some wariness. The sergeant had brought the square-jawed Lawrence with him, both soldiers glancing at Captain Donovan and his Federation troops. Wilkins also seemed to recognise Queen Marianne, which probably shouldn't have been a surprise. But he spoke only to Elisabeth. "Welcome back, My Lady," he said. "I can report once aboard, if you like?"

"No need, Sergeant," she said. "We're all allies here, though introductions can wait – I want to know about Warrick."

"Certainly," he said with a nod. "Williams took the bait but did not follow the whole way. I sent scouts back and his troops had peeled off, eventually turning for the Shimmering Ranges."

"Hmmm."

Captain Donovan looked up to the Sand-Hog. "No matter his numbers, he could not compete with this beast, surely?"

Elisabeth nodded. "Agreed. And that means he'd be up to something."

"I hope to receive word of what, exactly, very soon," Sergeant Wilkins said. "Once we changed course to meet you, My Lady, we lost some time but Warrick will be at the Shell by now – possibly joined by reinforcements from Last Castle."

"We have spare pigeons, if you require them," Marianne offered.

"Thank you, My Queen," he replied, offering a short bow. Beside him, Lantern-Jaw blinked and hurried to follow. "That would be welcome."

"Of course. And none of that, gentlemen," she said with a small smile. "Here I require no formalities."

"How far to the Ranges?" Thomas asked.

"Three days." Wilkins replied. "And I expect to hear from our scouts tomorrow. We should be able to plan something at that point."

"Perfect," Elisabeth said as she led Wilkins back toward the Hog. "I could use some rest – and a bath. Let's load these cars up and get inside."

"Jiro, I'm leaving the car to you," Thomas said.

"No problem."

Thomas joined Mia and Ethan, climbing into the back of their vehicle as they started toward the ramp at the rear of the hog. He leant down from the gunner's platform toward the passenger seat. "Mia, what do you think?"

"About what Warrick's up to?"

"Right."

"I don't know. I *did* have a premonition earlier this morning, but it's about Alita's Shell."

"You see us there?"

"No, it was something like pale steel, with a coppery, faintly golden-tint. The colour is beautiful," she added after a moment, as though seeing it still. "It looks like a giant cannon, only shaped a little like a bulky spear. I can only guess, but it might be half the length of the Sand-Hog. Less, maybe. There's a line of carven thorns running the length, fanning out to circle the muzzle."

Hadn't Elisabeth mentioned something... "The Thorn of Souls."

"Is that what I see?"

"Maybe. Elisabeth told me that it's in Alita's Shell. I think she wants it as much as the Orichalcum for the *Clara*."

Ethan glanced away from the uneven earth, where they were filing toward the Sand-Hog's ramp. "Think she knows what it can do? What if it really is a cannon?"

"I'll watch her," Thomas promised as they passed into the shadow cast by the steamer.

Once they entered the hold and arranged the car – space for the extra vehicles was being created as soldiers moved supplies around and out into other rooms – Thomas led Mia and Ethan toward the dining hall. Their steps rang against the grilled floor as they passed steel-clad walls, large rivets and stacks of boxes.

It seemed some halls were narrower than his last visit... or maybe it was his senses adjusting to the blanket-like weight of the Hog.

The sound of the mighty boiler – of various boilers – lurked beyond the walls and the hum of the steel, the cold scent of the metal and faint traces of gunpowder; it was all another stab of familiarity. A troubling familiarity too. *This place... it's ridiculous. The Hog actually feels like home!*

Measured in the sheer number of days, or youthful memories, the palace could have fit the word 'home', but that had *never* been true. Anything before that dark time was a murky mess of impressions; dark hair, a scent of warm fabric and rain falling upon rocks by the water.

And the years of wandering with David? Those places were never solid enough to form attachment to.

David.

It was still so hard to understand. *What did he tell our parents? Did he lie? To the parents of other children too?*

"Thomas?" Ethan's voice bore a trace of concern where he stood. Mia had one hand upon Ethan's arm, no doubt due to the dim light.

"Huh?"

"You've really slowed down, is something wrong?"

"No, just thinking about this place." He shrugged. "Let's get something to eat and some rest. I'll push Elisabeth for more information about the Thorn of Souls too."

"Sounds good," Ethan replied.

But Mia moved closer, reaching up to catch his chin. "Don't hold things back, stupid. I can tell something else is on your mind."

Thomas chuckled. "Fine, but after we eat, all right?"

Chapter 22.

Thomas paced the decks to the fore, letting the afternoon sun warm him just as air from the Hog's passage cooled him – a pleasant mix but enough that his jacket became a little much, and so he slung it over his shoulder.

"I feel like I'm doing this a lot, lately," Mia said from where she leant against the rail.

Ethan sat beside her. "Doing what?"

Her face was tilted upward, hair fluttering in the wind. "Standing at the rails of huge machines and enjoying the breeze."

Ethan smiled from shade cast by the engineer's dome. "Maybe the next rail you stand at will be on the *Clara*."

"I hope so." She turned from the increasingly barren landscape as it rolled by. "What about you, Thomas? Ready to share? We've got full bellies and the nearest gunner can't hear us so all your conditions have been met, I'd say."

"They have."

"Is it about David?"

He could have smiled. *She almost always knows what I'm thinking – I've missed that.* "He's part of what I've been thinking about... I still don't understand," he said.

"Me either."

"But it's everything else too. I want to stop and line it all up, in case we've missed something."

She nodded. "Like what?"

"A bigger reason behind all of this?"

"But what is 'all of this'?" Ethan asked. "And do you mean with Williams? Or the Queen?"

"Maybe both, maybe neither," Thomas replied as he paused. "Help me if I leave something out, but I'm trying to put it together. I was thinking about David, and his purpose. *Why* did he take the steps he took? Both back then and before he died. When we were together, it always about our freedom, remember, Mia? He used to say 'you two must survive, for the future'. I used to think he meant *our* future, but maybe it was more. He knew we were different."

"True," she said. "He didn't share much else. And we didn't ask."

Thomas gave a shrug. "Probably too afraid."

"Right. We spent so much time just fleeing. Trying to survive while Williams hounded us – I definitely don't remember having a chance to sit and reflect on it all."

"So, when and *why* did the *Esmeralda* come into it? He wanted those birds to access Alita's Shell; he probably knew about it for a long time."

"I don't know, we were older," Mia said. "It seemed to take a long time before he started to head for it... I always thought he became desperate, as his mind began to fail."

"I thought so too but when you told me about... the

experiments, I couldn't figure out how that connected with us wandering and eventually fleeing for the north. What if he was waiting for us? For *us* to manifest whatever he'd set in motion when we were children, whatever he and Silas did."

"That makes sense," she replied.

Ethan straightened. "And you think the Queen might know too?"

"If she was recruited by David and Patrick at one point... maybe?"

"And we still don't know what hold she has over Aiden," Ethan added.

Mia adjusted her blindfold as she turned her back against the breeze. "So, what *do* we know?"

"All right," Thomas said. "Maybe we can't confirm this, but I think we can say that Williams – and David – expected us to be instrumental in whatever they had in mind. They both knew about the *Clara*, and probably would have had access to detailed records about Gatehouse, so they knew that Alita's Shell was important."

"And both Elisabeth and the Queen have read about the Shell, which is where they caught wind of the Orichalcum and this Thorn of Souls," Ethan added.

"But no-one's been inside yet," Thomas said. "And so they suspected or knew that something special would be needed to open the way."

Mia straightened. "The lullaby. *That's* why he taught it to me, and probably why it calmed him too. He was relieved I hadn't forgotten."

"Did he teach it to you?" Ethan asked. "It wasn't your mother?"

"I'm not so sure anymore," Mia said. "What if David taught it to *her* first?"

Thomas joined her at the rail. "Either way, he made sure you didn't forget it. He knew the Royal Mechanical Birds in *Esmeralda* weren't enough by themselves."

"Right, but how?" she asked.

"I don't know."

"Perhaps same goes for you, Thomas," Ethan said. "Silas obviously experimented on you and those who came before, with similar knowledge."

"Probably." Thomas winced at a particularly sharp bump, as the Sand-Hog's wedge smashed through something below, and it matched the equally sharp reminder that his life was as much a normal accident of birth as it was the machinations of a desperate group of rebels. *And for all we've uncovered so far, David and the others were well ahead of us.* "If only he'd just told us."

"He gambled on surviving long enough to tell us the truth when he thought we could handle it, I suppose," Mia said.

Thomas nodded.

"I think we have to accept that Williams knows as much or more than we do," Ethan said after a moment of silence between them. "Obviously, David and the others managed to hide some things from him but how much?"

"And we know Warrick will be waiting for us at the Shell," Mia added.

"That's part of why I want to go over this," Thomas said. "We're going in sure we have an advantage, with all this firepower, but what if we don't?"

"Or what if Elisabeth or Queen Marianne and Aiden are still holding back?" Ethan said. "They need you and Mia to gain access, but what for? What is so important about the Thorn of Souls? If it's so vital or powerful, wouldn't Williams have been wild with desperation to break in?"

"Elisabeth said that they'd tried in the past. But wherever they excavated, impenetrable steel walls were there, as if the mountain had grown up around them."

Ethan exhaled. "That's... troubling. But here's another question – why did Williams abandon the research once he lost you both, who were presumably his most promising candidates?"

"Has he done that?" Mia asked.

Ethan spread his hands. "We could assume that his switch to work on things like the Colossus suggests it... but that is an assumption, I'll admit."

"So, he was hoping to make something strong enough to break in?" she asked. "Or was the Colossus just another war machine?"

"Perhaps both."

Once again, the Sand-Hog crashed through debris below, hunks and fragments of tree trunks sent flying up from below.

"Maybe we still need to visit the locations on that map," Mia suggested after steadying herself.

"Hopefully Aiden did outrun the King's ships. We need Copper," Ethan said as he pulled a coin from a pocket. He flicked it into the air and caught it, repeating the gesture as he spoke. "Mind if I take a turn at summing up a few things?"

"Please," Thomas replied. The rebel seemed almost to be enjoying himself.

"We know or feel safe assuming the following: Williams

and all who worked with him, before and after the splinter, either know or at least *suspect* that one key to restoring the *Clara* is Orichalcum, and that the precious resource is in turn stored within Alita's Shell. Further, at a *minimum*, Elisabeth and the Queen are both aware of books taken from the palace that suggest a cannon-like object is stored there also, this 'Thorn of Souls'."

"Right," Thomas said.

"The journal we found mentioned Gatehouse hiding something – the Mist of Dawn, right?" Mia asked.

"That could be hidden inside too. I'm wondering if Williams doesn't know much about the Thorn of Souls? Or maybe he knew more than enough, and has kept it all secret, as have both the Queen and Elisabeth. And one obvious reason to do that would be because it is extremely powerful."

"Makes sense," Thomas said. "What about Gatehouse then? Did they know this too and so they sealed it away?"

"We might assume they did. After all, they mention hiding this Mist of Dawn to keep it from Williams."

"But David and the others thought it worth seeking out. Maybe to stop Williams," Mia suggested.

"That's where we need to focus, don't we?" Thomas asked. "*Why* does everyone seek this thing?"

"We'll, we know some of the motivations, or at least, the claims," Ethan said as he snatched the coin from the air and began ticking items off upon his fingers. "Gatehouse thought the Thorn was a dangerous weapon but we don't know for sure, why they didn't use it. Williams would want it simply for further dominance, to crush the Federation and maybe to expand beyond? He's said as much to you in the past."

Mia was nodding along with him.

"Next, David and Silas: either to destroy the Williams dynasty or keep the old man from attaining it. The Queen tells us she wishes to use the *Clara* and Orichalcum to bargain with other nations but had not mentioned the Thorn of Souls prior. And finally, Elisabeth wants it to escape, yet she too hasn't revealed the existence of the Thorn and so we have to wonder what they all know that we do not," he said with a grin. "That about it?"

"There's one more thing," Thomas added. "Elisabeth had us detour to seek out Jean's grave – she was hoping something helpful was buried with him, but whatever she wanted could be somewhere else? Marked on the map?"

Mia muttered a curse. "Thomas, I need to see Jean's skull. In private."

"Why?"

"Because it's important. I don't know why but there was a reason it called to you," she said. Then she shook her head. "I should have checked sooner, we had enough time on the ship."

"Then let's do that tonight. I'll bring him to you..." Thomas frowned. "If 'him' is even the right word."

"Spirit or not, I'm sure he doesn't think of himself as just a skull," she said with a slight smile.

Chapter 23.

In the darkness of their modest quarters, Ethan was not even an outline; he was a warmth, a sense of firmness where she rested her head against the smooth skin of his back, arm looped across his hip, the rise and fall of his breathing even.

"Are you asleep already?" she asked softly.

"No," he replied, though the word dragged a little, as though he was not fully alert.

"Thomas will be here soon," she said.

"I hope so; it's been a little too long, hasn't it?" Ethan turned to face her. "Maybe Elisabeth is trying to stop him?"

"No, he's not too far away – I can tell – and he's got Jean with him."

"Somehow that's a little unnerving when you put it that way."

She gave him a nudge. "Scared of ghosts, Ethan?"

"Not with you here," he replied. "Do we need to do anything to prepare?"

"It's fine. In fact, I think you can let Thomas in, now."

Ethan rose and the rustle of fabric followed, then his

footfalls crossed the room. Hinges groaned open and then the shuffle of a hurried stride approached.

"Sorry, it took me longer than I'd hoped," Thomas said.

Mia straightened.

Something faintly golden hovered in the room, resting level with what was Thomas' waist, at a guess – Jean's skull? The light grew taller, swiftly becoming man-shaped. The gold faded too, and in its place stood a man with wild dark hair, goggles around his neck. His shirt was open at the throat, smudges of grease and oil visible upon his pants too.

And, he was largely transparent.

Jean, legendary Gatehouse pilot.

"He's here," Mia said as she pulled her shirt closed and stood. "Jean, can you hear us?"

The spirit did not respond.

"You can see him?" Thomas asked.

"I can. It's a little like what I see in the *chromata*. Or when I dreamt of the bodies in Delilah's basement, only less solid." She paused. "Can I hold him?"

"Here you go."

She held out her hands and it seemed Jean himself approached, the weight of bone following.

The *chromata* sprung up around her.

Panelled walls in a large, lamp-lit room replaced the darkness. One wall was lined with glassware, a long bar beneath, and on another, the soft click echoed from a tall grandfather clock. Its numbers were unfamiliar, even if the arrangement was normal.

The rich scent of coffee filled the place, something that reminded her of the Fortress but it did not seem she was within Birnhale.

And Jean sat across from her, smiling from the leather-backed seat.

"Welcome, Mia." His voice was cheerful, his smile broad.

"You know me?" she asked. *Maybe it shouldn't be a surprise, considering what he is.*

He nodded. "Since your brother answered my call, I've been watching and learning as much as I can – and I gotta say, I'm relieved. I feel like I can depend on you two to finish what we started."

"You mean with the Soul of Thorns?"

"Exactly," he said, and his smile faded. He ran a hand through his hair. "You need to keep it away from the old demon's grandson – that's the current Williams."

She leant closer. "We will, but why, Jean? We haven't been able to piece together its purpose."

"I think I'll have to explain that if I can return," he said, even as he began to fade. "I didn't think it'd be this hard to be honest. Turns out I'm not strong enough to stay very long, sorry Mia."

"Wait." Mia reached out to catch his hand, and it *was* like holding flesh. Jean solidified a little. "I think I can hold you here."

Jean grinned. "Beauty and power, what a combination."

Heat rose in her cheeks. "Ah, well, I don't know for how long – this place is still pretty new to me."

"Me too."

"What do we need to do?"

"Use your Sand-Hog to carry the Soul of Thorns to the *Clara* – I'll help you install it, since it should be filled by now."

"Filled?"

"Right – that's why we sealed Alita's Shell, to give it time."

"Time for what?"

"To heal everyone," he said. "Or so we believe. When we found it, the Thorn was incomplete and the notes from the Forefathers weren't all that clear, I will admit."

Mia hesitated. Forefathers? Heal everyone?

"Sorry, I'm jumping around a bit," Jean said, and once again he started to fade. "You've probably been thinking of it as a weapon, right? It *can* be. It could probably shatter half a city, but that's not its true purpose."

Jean was a bare outline now.

"Wait." Mia gripped a little harder, though the sensation of holding an actual hand was gone – it was more like grasping for falling grains of sand. "The healing?"

"Right." His voice was a whisper now. "Go get it for us, Mia. Your song will open the Shell and Thomas' blood will handle the rest."

"Jean!"

The final grains slipped through her fist, leaving his chair empty.

So close.

Mia rose, but her legs buckled and she slumped across the tabletop with a groan, vision dimming as exhaustion swept in.

Chapter 24.

"Has Mia awoken then?" Elisabeth asked without turning from where she frowned through the narrow window of glass and steel mesh. To do so, she had to lean over the bank of controls, first giving the pilot a little nudge. "Give me some room here, Norman."

"The periscope *is* still functional, My Lady," he replied.

"I know that." She pointed down at the line of Williams' men where they blocked access to the pale stone of the Shimmering Ranges, which were bright beneath the sun. "It still doesn't make sense. We can roll the cars easily; do those fools want to die?"

"Mia's fine now," Thomas replied. And what she'd shared had been heartening and troubling in equal measure. *Not much time to figure it all out though.* Jiro had been sent to fetch Thomas, who hadn't had a chance to return to Elisabeth's bed last night.

So long had Mia simply sat still, holding Jean's skull, that Thomas and Ethan had began to discuss how to wake her, until finally Mia had toppled. Ethan caught her but she did not wake at first. Yet when she did regain consciousness, it was with news – with hope, and perhaps even a new confidence.

Still, what did Jean mean about my blood?

Thomas joined Elisabeth at the window, Jiro beside him. Norman sighed and rose to man the periscope himself.

Outside, across the hardened earth, waited a row of steam cars. Two deep and a dozen wide, they blocked the trail leading up to Alita's Shell. *Just as Sergeant Wilkins' scout promised.* Most of the force seemed to be garrison soldiers from Last Castle, but they were joined by Warrick's men with their green and black flags.

In defiance or desperation, the kingdom blockade stood beneath the hot sun in their black flak jackets and helms, rifles and small cannons at the ready. Was it a doomed effort? The Sand-Hog would have no trouble breaking through... which suggested a ploy. *It has to be. Is Warrick even part of the formation?*

"I wouldn't have given Warrick's men this much credit for bravery, nor condemned them to be so stupid either," Norman said from behind them. "We'd shatter that line and have little trouble running down the survivors."

"It's a trap. Has to be," Thomas said.

Elisabeth glanced at him with a raised eyebrow. "Doubtless, but *what* is the trick?"

"Well..." He pointed to Williams' men. Though the soldiers stood four lines deep behind the steam cars, numbering in the hundreds, there was no way they could face the sand-steamer at full speed. And though they blocked the path, there was too much open ground. "This can't be the best place for an ambush. They don't have enough firepower to stop us... it's like they're bait without knowing it."

"I wouldn't stand against the Hog like that unless I thought I had something big up my sleeve," Jiro agreed.

Elisabeth glanced back to the soldiers. "They could be this arrogant, if Warrick is directing them."

"You know him better than I," Thomas said. "But I still think they could set up a better ambush elsewhere and instead, leave a token force here to gather information only."

"I'm wondering if Warrick *will* have some surprise planned – yet he himself might not actually realise that he's wrong about its strength. Or maybe daddy is feeding his men some lies, sending them in to help Warrick on a fool's errand?"

"It's hard to tell from inside," Thomas said. "I think I need to get closer... or maybe just out of the Hog. I can't make sense of what I'm feeling in here."

She gestured beyond the window. "You could try one of the rifle positions if you're certain there's no trigger-happy magnifier sneaks out there."

"Better than walking around in front of the line."

"Then see what you can manage," she said, leading the way to the ladder.

Thomas climbed after her, the steel rungs firm beneath his grip.

If the past few months had shown him anything, it was that his mysterious affinity with steel and iron had grown beyond anything he'd first imagined. He could just as easily rip the rungs free as climb them, have little trouble tearing through the very walls of the hog itself and even – if given enough time – it seemed, cast the pieces away or draw them to him, as he had with the guns, pins and buckles during his last visit to the Shell.

So far, he hadn't needed to use his power again, but that would soon change. *And according to Jean, my blood is important too. Did Silas... feed me something as a child?* The question was not going to disappear any time soon.

Light and heat poured into the shaft as Elisabeth opened its hatch. She climbed free then reached down to pull Thomas up the final steps. Together, they knelt at the Gatling by the railing, peering down to the line. "Any better?" she asked.

"Let's see." Despite the mountain of steel and iron around him, it *was* easier to sense the steel waiting at the enemy line – it seemed almost to call to him. All the guns, rifles and twin-barrels alike, the bullets, the buckles and helmets, and the steam cars especially – it all washed over him in a discordant wave.

Thomas closed himself off to it as a test – it was easier to dim something from afar, just as he had been doing for the Hog itself.

But there's something closer...

A *lot* of steel rested before the line of troops. An illusion? *That doesn't make sense.* Thomas squinted but it made no difference. Instead, he closed his eyes and focused on the invisible steel.

"What do you feel?"

"There's something in front of them..." He opened his eyes. A row of hidden steel waited before the Hog, considerably closer than the soldiers. And deeper too – buried!

It's like a pair of mighty jaws.

"Thomas, what?"

"They've buried mechanical jaws of steel in a massive trench; I think it's meant to trap the Hog. At worst, it would slow us considerably. We might actually be trapped."

Elisabeth pursed her lips. "Not bad."

"So, how do we deal with this?"

She grinned. "Well, you know we can't circle this place – there's only one path into Alita's Shell."

"I don't know if I can move that much at once," he admitted, despite his earlier confidence.

"Then just move enough to let us through. Make a nice wide bridge, perhaps."

Thomas stared at the hard earth before the enemy line, where a sandy topsoil *did* seem to suggest a trench, now that he was looking for it. *This vantage point probably helps too.* Elisabeth's request was possible, most likely, but at what cost? *That's a lot of steel.* But failure probably meant risking the crew, and more, Mia and Ethan too, since Elisabeth would charge ahead one way or another. *Blood I refuse to have on my hands.* Williams' men were a little different. *They chose to stand with Williams.*

She slapped him on the shoulder. "I'm going to get everyone ready – do what you need to do, Thomas, then let us know when we're clear to attack."

"All right," he said, still frowning over at the enemy line.

"And once we're done with these fools, tell me whatever it was Mia dreamt about too."

"Fine."

Thomas focused on the trench, trying to both open himself up to the line of steel, while at the same time block out the Hog. The more he relaxed his guards, the louder the humming began, swiftly rising to a buzzing in his ears.

His body responded – like before, as though he were a bell chiming in response, only he made no actual sound.

Is it my blood?

Whatever the reason, the trap seemed near enough to pull toward him, now that he'd focused in on it. Sweat ran down his temples as he called to the metal. The sand quivered, but the jaws remained in place where they were buried. He growled. The sheer volume of the steel was not an insurmountable factor – that much he could feel – but he needed to be closer.

"Damn it." Thomas tried once more, but again, won only minor movements for his efforts – perhaps not even enough for the steam cars to notice. Thomas knelt by the hatch to call down. "I need to get closer."

"Tell us when," Elisabeth called back up. "And remember, I need enough room to make at least a modest run-up."

The Sand-Hog rolled a little closer, causing shouts to rise from the enemy line. Thomas kept his connection with the hidden trap as they moved. His grip solidified. *This is it.* He called down, then stood as the Hog ground to a halt.

"Come on," Thomas said.

He pulled at the steel and almost without meaning too, he held out his hands, making a lifting motion. The jaws resisted him but he fought them, grunting at the effort.

It shifted again, the very earth trembling now.

"Got you!" he cried as sand burst forth.

An enormous row of steel teeth rose from the earth – only one half, by the looks, but it was working.

Cries of shock and horror rang out from the Kingdom soldiers.

Sweat began to trickle down from Thomas' temples, but

he lifted the trap higher, sand trailing, and made a twisting motion. The jaw snapped in half and the crack echoed across the plain, obliterated another shout of effort. Below the now floating halves of the trap, the line of soldiers threatened to buckle.

"Watch out." Thomas dropped one half. The jaw struck with a boom, dust and sand flying forth.

And now the soldiers did flee, heading up or out toward the plain, while some took shelter behind the line of cars... but it wouldn't be enough.

Thomas hesitated a moment, straining to keep a hold of the mass of steel – a lot of people were able to die. *And yet, each one had made a choice, each one chose to stand with Williams.*

He swung.

Sparks exploded. The jaw smashed through the line of cars, scattering steel and soldier alike. They flew to tumble across the road in a cacophony of screeching metal and screams, some crashing into the stone walls, others simply disappearing from his line of sight.

Thomas fell to one knee, chest heaving.

But he wasn't done.

The depth and width of the trench was still a problem.

His limbs shook, but he lifted his arms again, focusing upon the piece he'd dropped before. It rose easily enough, though his breath rasped as his strength continued to wane. *I can do this.* Warrick's forces had scattered, leaving behind weapons, packs and vehicles – but they were not his target this time.

Thomas swung the steel around behind several of the steam cars, those few that had evaded his first strike, and swept them back toward the trench.

Metal scraped against the stony earth, wheels buckling then snapping but he kept on, dragging in lungfuls of air, not letting up until the mix of steam car, debris, supplies and bodies alike had been swept into the trench.

"Done," Thomas said with a gasp and a faint sick feeling in his stomach. *He had just killed a lot of people, enemies all, but nevertheless...*

And maybe it hadn't been much of a final gesture, making sure Warrick couldn't use those cars, but if Elisabeth wanted to cross the trench with any heavy equipment, then this would be faster than building a bridge.

But he'd done it – somehow, he'd broken the line with his power.

A flicker of horror crossed his mind. Just what *else* was he capable of? But he could not even hold on to the fear; his body gave way and he collapsed to the grated floor, metal warm against his cheek, no longer able to move.

Chapter 25.

Thomas stared up at the clear sky and its scattered clouds of grey and black as the rumble of the Sand-Hog faded. Little drops of rain struck his face now and then, almost as though the sound of the Hog shook them free.

Or maybe it was the occasional bump or jostle from Captain Donovan's men that did it as they carried his stretcher up the slope.

"Sorry about that," the lead man said.

"It's no problem," Thomas replied. "I appreciate the help."

He lifted his head slightly – even that was an effort – to look around. The pale grey and yellow of stony walls rose up around them in granite streaks, all obscured by Donovan and his men, along with Mia and Ethan ahead. Beyond the limits of Thomas' view would be Elisabeth, Jiro and the Queen too.

And that's all I've got in the way of energy. He slumped back with a sigh.

Dealing with the barricade had left him kitten-like, with

no strength to speak of. Staying conscious had been hard enough, until he was carried back inside the Hog for one of the medics to check him over. And despite everyone's worry – even Elisabeth's concern seemed genuine – he grew no weaker at least.

But he could not stand let alone walk, nor move his arms much at all, and each movement came at a cost of further exhaustion.

But Ethan's idea of a stretcher solved one problem, leaving the larger force to undertake the final climb, while Wilkins and the skeleton crew chased down Williams' men as they searched for Warrick.

Elisabeth was banking on meeting a reduced force at the gate, though Mia had not sensed anything amiss. Nor could Thomas be sure of the source of all the steel he sensed ahead; a mass of vibrations that were mixed in with the chiming resonance of what he assumed was the Orichalcum. *I couldn't sense it last time.*

Figuring that out could wait; he had to recover, had to be ready for whatever waited at the Gate. Ethan was betting that Warrick would simply wait for them do all the hard work before springing from some hiding place to attack. *Equally likely.* Thomas clenched a hand – or tried to. *Not that I'll be much use either way.*

It wasn't all bad, as Mia had Ethan at her side. And Elisabeth was no fool, nor was the Federation Captain. *None of them, really.* They'd all be watching... but it was hard to accept that his weakness would endanger the two Westerners who were forced to carry and protect him. *So it's impossible for me to stop worrying about everyone. Or let go of control?* If he could manage to let the others take care of things until he recovered, hopefully soon, then he'd make up for being a burden.

"All right, set up camp!" Elisabeth called from ahead. "Get the transports built too. And triple the watch!"

Thomas was placed somewhere out of the way to rest more, while the bustle of work began. And while he could see little but stone walls of the large opening, even when he turned his head, in time, Jiro and another man arrived with something made of steel.

"We reassembled this for you," Jiro said. "It's a wheeled chair – made it up for Nhial when he broke his foot with the two-man wrench."

Thomas lifted his head – a far easier task now, and saw a steel frame supported by four wheels, the two larger ones at the back. A canvas seat stretched across the chair, two stirrup-like fittings for his feet included.

"That's great," Thomas said. "Thank you both."

"Happy to do it," Jiro replied. Together, the two soldiers lifted and carried Thomas into the chair. He settled in, quite comfortable, and found himself able to look around and move his torso and arms a little too. *Strength slowly returning? Good.*

The broad opening before the gate was half-filled by soldiers and their weaponry, or the skeletons of large platforms and their serious-looking wheels and mighty axels. Hard to say whether it would all be strong enough for the Orichalcum but his eye was quickly drawn to the giant gateway.

Set into the mountain, the gate towered above everyone, the double doors four-storeys tall. The runes and markings supporting the Gatehouse symbol were still unclear but the age seemed just as strong as his last visit. *Like the metal can tell me exactly how long ago it had been carved.*

The row of head-sized, triangular alcoves still spanned both wings, twenty openings waiting patiently at the bottom of the gate. Within would be the grooves for the Royal Mechanical Birds but for now Mia was still speaking with Ethan, not too distant from where Elisabeth was waving her men closer.

Each pair carried a heavy chest between them, four in total, with the first being unlocked as Thomas watched.

"I can take you closer if you want?" Jiro asked.

"Yes, please."

Jiro started wheeling him across the uneven earth, a rough ride even with the Sergeant taking care, but people made room for him without complaint – he was, after all, a hero twice over for those upon the Hog and now the Federation soldiers also regarded him with a touch of awe, even trepidation.

Awe was one thing, but the ones who seemed nervous... *If I wasn't so useful, would I be called 'freak'?*

Once Jiro had him on the more even ground near Elisabeth, who wore a smile of anticipation, Thomas glanced up at her. "You're enjoying this, aren't you?"

"Very much."

"And if it doesn't work for some reason? Do we have a back-up plan?"

She shook her head. "Won't need any."

"What about Warrick, then? Anything from the scouts?"

"Nothing. I think Ethan has the truth of it, Thomas. The weasel will be hiding, waiting for us – or you – to finish the heavy-lifting."

"Then we've got plenty of time to come up with something while I recover."

"I hope so."

"I'm ready," Mia said as she approached the gate. Once the final birds were placed into the alcoves by kneeling soldiers, she clasped her hands together and started to sing.

The familiar words and melody filled the air as sound died away, hammers and voices alike coming to a halt – everyone stopped to listen. Mia's voice did not ring out across the ranges but it was clear and confident – Mia knew the birds would respond. *I just hope the Bird of Light doesn't appear too.*

But it did not – only the royal machines, their chirping rising quickly to a crescendo, light glowing within the sharp beaks.

Mia raised her voice to compete and beams of light shot from the birds. The beams ran up, within the actual steel, setting the runes to blazing. Thomas shielded his eyes as a grinding rumbled beneath the song.

When his vision cleared, a dark shadow in the stone stood before them – the mighty gate stood open, revealing a smooth, gleaming floor leading into darkness.

Mia let the lullaby fade. "It's clear. I don't sense any threats in there."

"Brilliant work, Mia," Elisabeth said. She turned to those gathered. "Finish up here and we'll be back with some airship fuel before you know it, everyone."

A cheer rose as Elisabeth moved around to take the wheeled chair from Jiro. "Now it's your turn, Thomas."

"Let's see what's in there first."

Elisabeth pushed him into Alita's Shell, the others following. His wheels encountered no resistance from the seamless floor. Like the walls, it was made from the same faintly luminous, almost golden metal – or, more accurately, Orichalcum.

They'd not traversed very far before he straightened in the chair. "I feel a little stronger in here."

"Strong enough to walk already?" she asked.

"No, but better."

The walls were lined with more engravings, this time pillars of stone – both stalagmites and stalactites. As they slid by, an illusory sense of depth was revealed, perhaps aided by shadows cast from the lamplight. It was a magnificent work of art – on both walls, and stretching on into the shadows. Perhaps the ceiling was the same, but it was beyond the limits of the light.

"I don't imagine Gatehouse have time to spend on these carvings," Ethan said from nearby, lamp in hand where he walked beside Mia.

"The palace does hold some few incomplete records of earlier times, times well before the Turmoil," the Queen replied. "Such early generations maybe have been responsible for this place, along with the ruins on the islands to the north west, though I had not the chance to visit it before it sank."

Generations before the Turmoil. Hard to imagine a time so long ago. *Were they the Forefathers that Jean told Mia about?*

The broad hall continued, resonance from the Orichalcum surrounded Thomas, almost like an invisible cloak of warmth. But it was not quite like with the coffin, since he had not struck it – did the sound linger from the opening of the gates?

Perhaps it did not matter. More importantly, his limbs

were growing lighter. *I* am *getting my strength back... slowly.*

"There's something ahead." Elisabeth slowed to point, then looked over her shoulder. "Be ready."

"We are safe here," Mia assured her.

Not much was visible, just a large... shape.

But once Elisabeth wheeled him near enough for the light to reach the object, there was no doubt – the Thorn of Souls, as expected.

The cannon rested upon a low, stretching altar, which was in turn flanked by twin doorways that led into darkness. But the weapon seemed to devour most of the light, its surface gleaming. As Mia had described, it was adorned by engravings of thorns, the faintly-orange tint to the Orichalcum warm and soothing compared to the cool of the mountain.

Up close, huge fittings for mounting the weapon were clearly visible, as was the muzzle – which was not a round opening, but rather a narrowing point. Almost like a mighty needle.

Or thorn. Obviously.

But it was not narrow in every sense; Thomas could have fit his head inside.

Elisabeth wheeled him closer. "Take a look while I search those rooms."

Jiro and Captain Donovan joined her, leaving Thomas with Mia, Ethan and the Queen. When he twisted in his chair, he caught a glimpse of Felicity standing rear guard, her rifle pointed toward the distant square of white. *Prudent, but probably unnecessary since Mia has already said we're safe.*

"How does this fit in with your blood, Thomas?" Ethan asked From where he stood near the Thorn now, though he had not touched the cannon – instead, the rebel leader moved around to lean against the wall. There, he peered behind.

"I'm hoping I get to keep it," Thomas said with a smile.

"Perhaps it refers to your lineage," the Queen suggested.

"Did you know our parents, Your Majesty?" Thomas asked – and he could have kicked himself. He should have asked her about it long before now. She was the perfect choice, after all. *Not that you've had much time together to simply stop and chat.*

"Unfortunately no. Perhaps the Alchemist did, however."

"We will ask him," Mia said, firmly.

Thomas hesitated, despite a surge of hope at Mia's apparent change of heart. Hope and perhaps even gratitude? She'd been so vehement for so long… not that he blamed her. *She was only protecting herself from more pain.* And a change in heart now shouldn't be surprising.

Maybe finding the truth could now become just as important as escaping.

Focusing on the cannon had to come first, either way. Once they united the Thorn with the *Clara*, and once Williams was cooling on a slab somewhere, then it would be time to find the Alchemist.

"There's a large conduit back here," Ethan said. "It runs through the wall."

"Everyone, come and see this," Elisabeth called, her words almost falling across Ethan's.

Ethan wheeled Thomas into the next room, where additional lanterns had been lit and placed upon neat stacks of rectangular blocks of Orichalcum, some reaching up beyond the light, and others far smaller. But all of it gleaming bright – beautiful, really.

And each piece lent him just a little more strength, somehow. Not enough to walk, or even rise yet, but it was better than nothing.

"Not that," Elisabeth said. "Here."

He turned, and Ethan wheeled him closer to where Elisabeth and the others waited.

It was a huge chamber of crystal... or maybe diamond? Whatever it was, it certainly caught and refracted the light in pleasing little rainbows. By size alone it was impossible to value – twice his own height had he been standing.

A pale fire more silver than white swirled within – as though being stirred very gently by an invisible breeze, sparkling in lines that wavered from grace to uncertain shapes, distorted by the case.

"I can't be sure but it looks like this chamber was once filled with Orichalcum," Elisabeth said as she pointed up and to the side.

There, a mechanical arm and claw hovered above. It was poised as if to deliver something to the diamond chamber, perhaps by funnel or hatch, but it stood empty now.

"No boiler or similar, however," Captain Donovan said. "So we cannot be sure it isn't incomplete."

The arm seemed near as smooth as everything else in the chamber, as though free from ravages of age, but also, unlike the mechanical cranes in the cities, Thomas could not find evidence of nut or bolt, and the seams at each join were so perfect as to be a hairline, if anything.

"Can you take me closer?" he asked Ethan, who obliged.

The crane rested between the diamond case and the towering stacks of Orichalcum. Above, there seemed to be a few regular gaps, as though a block was missing – and it would have rested in the swing zone of the crane. *But how does each block reach the zone after the previous gets taken?*

Were pieces truly transported to the diamond case?

If so, why?

He looked back to where the others were still examining the chamber and its mysterious, soft flames.

"It's connected to the pipe, surely," Ethan said as he pointed. "Something is fed through the chamber wall and into the Thorn of Souls."

"Then is it safe to remove it at all?" Donovan asked. "We do not understand any of this is, remember?"

"Sealed away for a reason, right?" Ethan said.

Elisabeth rapped her knuckles upon the diamond. "Well, we have to find out one way or another – I'm not leaving the Shell without it, gentlemen."

Chapter 26.

Once more, Thomas lay upon his stretcher beneath the warm sun. He was actually able to doze while both Elisabeth and Donovan's men and women hammered and shouted to each other while completing the transports for both the fuel and cannon.

The work was nearing an end, it seemed – it had taken longer after Elisabeth ordered everything reinforced further, the afternoon wearing down swiftly now.

At least the floor in there will make for smooth sailing... at first.

But would the transport be able to support the cannon's weight? Would wheel and axel hold? *And I have to recover first too.* Especially considering what the Thorn of Souls was made from. *Can I even move it at full strength?*

Thomas rose. Hopefully, he had time to relieve himself before... he stopped.

I just stood up.

He took a few steps – and did not falter; his entire body was restored!

"You can walk again," Ethan said as he approached, Mia beside him. Behind them, soldiers in their black and blood red were now working to remove obstructions from the path to Alita's Shell, the great doors still open.

Elisabeth stood at the base, speaking with Queen Marianne and Captain Donovan.

Thomas nodded with a smile. "I think it was the Shell. Being surrounded by the Orichalcum… maybe. I don't know for sure, but I do feel better."

"Good," Mia replied. "Because we'll need you – there's something familiar nearby, but I can't pinpoint it."

"Familiar how?" he asked.

"I don't know. It's probably just the fact that I *know* Warrick is probably out there somewhere – just, watch for me, Thomas."

"I will." To Ethan, he said, "What about the Thorn itself – can it be freed? What happened when you removed it? Was that flame or mist dangerous?"

"I'm pleased to say it wasn't. Once we disconnected it, there was a self-closing valve that…" Ethan paused. "Mist… It *was* like mist, wasn't it? Mia, the diary mentioned something about the Mist of Dawn, didn't it?"

"Yes, but I don't think Alita's Shell is the Thunder Forest, is it?" She lowered her voice. "Where did it lie upon the map?"

"I thought a little further north west. We can check once we get back to the Hog," he said, before explaining to Thomas about the diary entry. "Whatever it is, it's something else Gatehouse wanted to keep from the Williams dynasty.

Maybe it's the diamond chamber, or maybe it was just another name for the Thorn of Souls."

"Thomas!" Elisabeth waved from the entrance. "Ready if you are."

"Let's find out," Thomas murmured as he led Mia and Ethan back to the opening, joining the others inside.

"The transport will follow, but let's see if you can move the cannon first." Elisabeth lifted her lantern and started along the spacious passage.

"I'll try – I'm feeling stronger in here, at least."

"Surrounded by the Orichalcum?"

"I think so," he said. The faint resonance had not faded and it continued to banish his weakness. "Any word about Warrick? Or Wilkins?"

"He'll be here – I've sent Lawrence and a team to signal, they'll certainly have a good vantage point to do so."

"How many men would Williams' son have remaining at this point?" Captain Donovan asked. "The garrison from Last Castle perhaps took fewer casualties before they broke and they may have called for reinforcements by now."

"I don't know if they'd want to leave the town so vulnerable."

"Against what threat, however?" he replied.

Elisabeth grinned. "Us, of course. They might assume that we've joined forces and plan to strike through to the Kingdom."

"I see. That seems possible."

"And they've had a taste of the Hog too," Jiro added. "That will keep them cautious."

"Mia dear, any concerns?" the former Queen asked. Unlike before, she now had a rifle of her own slung across her shoulder.

"I think we need to be especially watchful – something will happen, Warrick hasn't given up," Mia replied.

"Anything specific?" Elisabeth asked when they reached the Orichalcum cannon.

"Yes – stone."

"Stone?"

Mia had folded her arms. "I know we're surrounded by it, but that's all I have for now."

"Keep trying," she said. "Thomas?"

He reached out to touch the Thorn of Souls – more energy flowed within him, and the cannon seemed more expectant now. *Like it's ready for something.* Thomas braced himself against it – giving it a push to test, and the Thorn began to slide upon its platform. Not a lot, but enough that if he put more effort in, he'd surely be able to get it onto the transport. "I think I can move it after all."

"And your strength?" Captain Donovan asked.

"Feeling pretty good."

Elisabeth smiled as she turned to wave her men closer, wheels crossing the smooth floor and nearing swiftly.

The flatbed transport was impressive considering the time they'd spent on it, offering plenty of room for the cannon and even bearing a small rail – and it did look sturdy, with twin axels at both ends, and a set of three axels in the centre.

Once it was close enough, Thomas moved around to slide the Thorn into position, doing his best to be gentle.

The transport groaned the moment the cannon touched down, but Thomas caught a hold of the metal, gripping firmly, and somehow; kept the platform together. Points of stress appeared as he manoeuvred the cannon closer to the centre, but Thomas found and fortified them too. *If I can tear steel apart, why not this?*

Oddly enough, while the enormous weight of the Orichalcum was a threat to the tray, it was the Orichalcum itself that lent him the extra strength to hold everything together *and* push the cannon forward.

"It's working," Jiro said, excitement in his voice.

"So far," Thomas said.

"Give him room," Elisabeth called, and the soldiers spread out.

Thomas started forward, and while he wasn't exactly charging along, he managed a steady pace. It took some effort, but he was also able to correct the steering with the cannon, both where he gripped fittings and with his gift.

But once the smooth passage ended, he had to work a little harder through the camp. There, Elisabeth and Donovan's men continued to work on transports for the blocks of Orichalcum. *Some pieces are pretty large; I'll have to help them after this.*

"How's it going, Thomas?" Ethan asked.

"Getting harder but I'm still feeling strong enough." Sweat was beginning to form – and it definitely wasn't the still-warm afternoon, the slowly setting sun half-hidden by the walls, but the effort of holding the cannon and managing the occasional large bump, all on a downhill slope.

"Are you sure?" Elisabeth asked.

"I am."

He didn't have breath for any more words.

Yet somehow, he reached and then passed the half-way mark. It helped that troops had spent time clearing some of the worst of any debris but his limbs were aching now. He glanced below; the carnage he'd caused earlier was visible at last. Streaks of blood and gouges in the stone, fragments of glass and steel scattered before the makeshift bridge.

No Sand-Hog yet, but surely it was close.

His shirt was now soaked in sweat as he lurched forward in uneven bursts, half dragged downward, half holding the Thorn of Souls back.

Elisabeth and Ethan called after him, and Mia too, but he still had control.

Level ground was so close!

Thomas ground his teeth, gripping the Orichalcum so hard that his fingers sunk in a little – just like upon the Saint's Bridge.

But he did not seem to be harming it, and so Thomas dug his heels in and slid down the final slope. The platform scraped hard at the bottom, where the ground levelled out, but he managed to wrench the transport to a stop with a gasp. "Made it." He glanced back to where the others were jogging after, a trail of dust marking his path.

Was Mia waving at him? And Ethan pointing?

Rumbling rose from nearby.

Thomas spun.

A not-too distant rock formation was crumbling apart, dark sand filtering down as pieces tumbled to the earth.

Something large, gleaming orange in the setting sun, had lurked within.

Steam burst from several points as it straightened, finally revealing a steel and glass cage in its centre, where a pilot sat, hands upon levers, looking tiny within the three-storey monster. Bulky arms held mighty, twin hammers the size of steam cars and huge steam cannon rested above the pilot; a beak-like head and nose, ready to strike.

The Colossus.

Chapter 27.

Williams' beloved Colossus had undergone some improvements.

The boilers concealed somewhere beneath the iron cladding were probably a little smaller than those on steam cars, though powering the machine would take a lot of fuel... and no doubt several engineers too.

The Gatling guns positioned on small platforms beneath the pilot were unmanned, but the giant carried some serious weaponry without them.

Thomas fell back against the Thorn of Souls.

So, Warrick makes his move at last – this is bad. Thomas squinted but could not see into the cage well-enough to make out any clear features of the pilot, no sense of Warrick's rat-like face and burning eyes.

Either way, we need the Hog.

The Colossus lifted a foot and started forward. The first step landed with a boom; vibrations spreading out to reach

Thomas. The Colossus was starting for the Orichalcum cannon. *Shit.* Thomas scanned the horizon but still no sign of the Sand-Hog. *How can I stop that thing?*

As the machine walked, the head-cannon swivelled toward Mia and the others.

"No!" Thomas roared.

He charged forward, senses shooting forth to the mass of metal. There was so much to choose from, with so little time to settle on a section – even as he ran, Thomas was cursing himself. *I should have sensed that thing before!* Had the sheer force of the Orichalcum clouded his senses? *Just do something.*

Thomas clawed for the cannon with his gift and shoved as hard as he could.

The barrel rocked as its blast rang out.

Thomas stumbled, twisting to follow the heavy shot – and it flew wide! The cannon-ball crashed into the wall. A shower of stone fragments exploded beyond Mia and the others, but everyone had already scattered.

Thomas sighed, relief setting his limbs to trembling. He hadn't been able to do much from a distance, but it was enough.

Yet the Colossus had not stopped.

Its steps continued to rock the earth and when the car-sized hammers swung, they whipped up dust and sand.

Thomas rose, giving ground, only to falter to a stop.

My legs.

"Come on." He couldn't move.

Worse, his knees were buckling, and suddenly he couldn't even lift his arms to break his fall as he tilted over. "Gods be dammed!"

Thomas slumped to the ground with a grunt, his strength spent. He lifted his head, panting now, as the Colossus thundered closer. The pilot was visible at last – and it *wasn't* Warrick; this man bore a shaved head and an unhappy expression, but he was pulling new levers to raise the mighty fist.

This is it.

Thomas pushed back against the Colossus with what little he had left, but it was like hurling a feather into the wind.

Sparks screeched.

The great machine rocked back. A huge dent was now visible in its side. A cannon blast? Inside the cage, the pilot tore at the levers, mouth moving as though he shouted. Thomas tried to pull himself back but still his body failed him.

Another blast – this time Colossus' own cannon returning fire.

It's Wilkins in the Hog, it has to be.

A mere moment later and a second shot struck the Colossus; steam and sparks exploded as the ball tore through one of its legs. The machine toppled but one arm swung out and the hammer struck sand, keeping the thing mostly upright.

Another return volley from the Colossus followed, but it did not seem to be harming the Sand Hog. A third concussion rocked the air right after.

This blast smashed through the Colossus.

Steel and glass shattered in a fountain as the machine spun away, crashing to the earth with a shockwave that rattled Thomas right down to his bones. He exhaled, hard

– a puff of dust following. *If that thing had fallen the other way...*

Yet he could not stand to warn Wilkins or the gunner.

Raising his head again was too much.

But he did not pass out, at least.

Instead, distant cries and the rumbling of the Sand-Hog eventually reached him. A taste of dust and sand lingered all around him; his ears were ringing too but his limbs were like stone... though the weakness was almost welcome. *A brush with death will do that, I suppose.*

"Thomas?"

Footsteps thundered close – Mia or Elisabeth? Hard to tell.

"Here," he said, barely managing a whisper.

"Thomas, answer me, can you?" It *was* Mia. A hand fell upon his shoulder. "Thomas?"

"I'm fine."

"Thank the heavens."

"My strength... must have used it... getting the cannon here."

"It's fine."

"Check the wreckage," Elisabeth was shouting, though the Sand-Hog no longer rumbled across the earth, it was idling nearby and the great hissing of steam remained something for her to compete against.

"You're... not hurt?" he asked.

"No," she replied as she rolled him over, then clung to his chest. "Ethan has a few scratches from shards of stone, but we're all fine."

"Good."

"*You* nearly weren't."

"I know."

She gripped a little harder. "I saw it fall both ways, you know. Toward you and away from you... I'm still not sure what tipped the balance."

A chill ran through Thomas. "Oh."

"This one's alive!" A call from Captain Donovan, his accent clear above other voices. A moment passed. "He's asking for Thomas."

"What?" Mia rose.

"I'll go," Thomas said.

"Let me get Ethan," she said, and moments later, Ethan and Jiro arrived to lift and carry him to the Colossus.

The pilot lay within the half-crushed cage, covered in shattered glass and blood. A steel beam had pinned him and his eyes were barely open, but he was still breathing, though it caused him pain by the way he grimaced.

"I am Thomas."

"Good," the pilot said, his voice soft. The dying man's eyes did not seem to focus very well, though his head tilted to the sound of Thomas' voice.

"Why ask for me?" Thomas asked.

"Because... I am... you," he managed. "Before."

Thomas frowned. "What?"

"I am.... a failure. Silas... made me. Like you."

"Take me close," Thomas said to Jiro and Ethan, who obliged. Nearer now, Thomas saw that the man was a little older – or so it seemed beneath the dusk and blood, but no-one he recognised. "What did he do?"

Blood spilled down the man's chin. "Not enough... for me, I guess."

"Hold on!" Thomas urged. "What did Silas do to us?"

"It's... our blood," the man gasped. "He fed... when... babies."

The pilot of the Colossus fell silent.

Chapter 28.

Lamplight from the door did not quite reach Thomas where he sat within the Sand-Hog, slouched low in the seat of a steam car, which was in turn, one of several surrounded by stacks of Orichalcum.

The rumble of the mighty Hog's engines seeped through the walls of the hold – to Thomas it could have been labouring a little, considering the extra weight, but it was moving. And the sound had been joined by the almost musical, bell-like tones as Orichalcum stacks clinked against one another faintly – not that anyone else would have heard the ringing, even when the Sand Hog hit a larger bump. *The sound must mean something – is it connected to what happened with the coffin? Maybe Jean can explain it.* Yet so far, Mia had not been able to contact him despite several nights trying.

And even though Thomas had recovered, the spectre of Silas haunted him still. *What had the pilot meant? What had Silas fed them both?*

He glanced around the room – no answer forthcoming, same as every other night he'd visited. The Thorns of Souls gleamed faintly orange from the opposite end of the hold, but it was not resonating, not like the stacks at least.

Footsteps approached the doorway.

Thomas straightened.

Sergeant Wilkins entered, then turned to survey the room a moment. "Thomas?"

"Here, Sergeant."

The man approached. "Any luck this time?" He stopped at the bonnet of the car, leaning against it.

"None," Thomas said. "But maybe the sound doesn't mean much at all? I probably won't know what it means until we try to use the cannon."

He nodded. "Hmmm."

"Are we nearing the coast?"

"Later today," he said, and then hesitated a moment. The man stroked his moustache then pushed himself off the car. "Thomas, something troubles me."

"Captain Donovan?"

"No. I can see why the Federation would want him to accompany us; they need to see what the *Clara* can do, after all."

"To determine what sort of threat it could pose."

"Exactly," he replied. "But it's not that."

"Warrick then?" Thomas suggested. "He's probably running east, tail between his legs."

"Not Warrick either. And I agree with you there; I drove him off myself after all. His gambit failed and he'll be on to something else by now." Wilkins smiled now. "You know, if you let me tell you what's on my mind, you'll find out."

Thomas laughed. "I guess I've figured it out now. You're worried about Elisabeth."

"Aye, I am." He glanced to the Thorn of Souls. "What is a cannon save for a weapon? It's an obvious thing to say, I know. But I'm worried about it and I worry that the Lady is less focused on escape and more on vengeance. Once I take the Hog east and you are both back on the ship…"

"She's looking for vengeance *and* freedom, isn't she?"

"I think so. But we don't know what this cannon can do… and if she had to choose…" Wilkins trailed off, then shook his head. "I should not speak of this, even to you."

Thomas leant forward, resting his forearms upon the steering wheel. "Then who else?"

The sergeant grunted. "I suppose you're right. Here is my fear then, in plain words. I fear that if My Lady has to choose between escape and revenge, that she might not take the right path. I want you to make sure she survives whatever happens, Thomas."

"You've asked me this before, you know."

"And you've kept your word then. I ask it once more, now."

Thomas frowned. *I didn't precisely promise anything last time, did I?* "I don't want her to come to harm but Mia comes first, Sergeant. I can't put Elisabeth above my sister."

"Mia has Ethan now."

"That's no reason for me to abandon her," Thomas replied. "She's my sister."

"And that's not what I'm asking." Wilkins jerked a thumb to the Orichalcum weapon. "If that thing is so powerful that it had to be sealed away, then we don't really know what it is capable of."

"Right. But are you saying that Elisabeth might use it so… recklessly that she'd endanger herself? Us? Everyone?"

"I am," he said, his voice weary. "What if that thing can

level cities? What if it starts another struggle for resources, like the Coal War? Or worse."

Thomas met the man's eyes, doubt softening his voice. "Is revenge really so important to her?"

Wilkins nodded. "She hides it, Thomas. But it still burns. You must have caught hints."

She'd spoken so little of the palace... but there had been one time, after the slaughter of the bandits. It had been clear then. "Maybe."

"I will not share what she may not have, but Williams is due whatever she metes out to him."

"I imagine that's true."

"It is. And you've got a right to vengeance too, especially after what Williams did to you and your sister. To so many others."

"Not if it brings harm to Mia. Or the city," Thomas said with a small frown, but it might have been aimed at himself. "We don't know what she's going to do. And none of us know what the Thorn of Souls is capable of."

"Exactly," Wilkins replied. "And that is why I worry. Promise me that you'll steer her to the right path, if she's faced with the kind of choice I fear."

It was still difficult to imagine Elisabeth so enraged – she was always in control, was always thinking ahead... and more, the Thorn of Souls, could it truly be so dangerous? It *had* been sealed away, true. But Gatehouse obviously felt, at one point at least, that the cannon was worth the risk.

Sergeant Wilkins was waiting.

"If it comes to that, I will." *Somehow.*

Chapter 29.

A cold sea-breeze sliced at Mia's skin as she started to climb the ramp, one hand on Ethan's shoulder as they boarded the *Albion* in the dark of night, no stars, no moon above, but plenty of lamplight visible in muted patches beyond her blindfold.

"You're late, Aiden!" Elisabeth called from ahead.

"Shut up," he replied. "I'm here now, aren't I?"

"Just help them get everything loaded, will you? I need a bath," she said.

"Ha. You think I'm like Thomas? No-one else can help with that thing."

"Pretending you don't know about the smaller blocks, I see – are you truly so afraid of some honest labour?"

A snort. "As you slink off for a bath?"

"You've got me there," she said, her voice already fading.

Marianne's words followed. "Our gratitude, Aiden. It is heartening to see you and the *Albion* relatively unscathed. I take it you were able to fend off the *Whale* and others?"

"Took some doing, but we did. *The Iron Whale* is heading

back for repairs, and *White Wave* is playing escort instead of chasing us. Sank the final ship. We can expect more trouble when we return, I suspect."

"Then we must plan for that," she replied. "And I believe your strength could still be of use when it comes to the Orichalcum you know."

"Of course, Your Majesty."

His footsteps seemed a little petulant to Mia, but that might have simply been her *wanting* it to be true.

Once she reached the top, she let Ethan guide her toward their cabin after only a minimum of words for the Queen and Felicity.

"You seem tired," he said when they eventually lay beside one another in the dark.

"All the waiting wore me down."

He sighed. "I know what you mean. I spent half the time thinking Warrick would attack again, but I guess Wilkins really did chase him off."

"He won't give up – he was always more stubborn than Julian."

"We won't be giving up either."

"I know."

He kissed her check. "Let's get some rest then."

Mia murmured her agreement, already drifting off to a warm dark but when she woke in the *chromata*, this time sitting upon a huge tree stump beneath an orange sky, it seemed she was not going to get rest right away.

Jean sat beside her in his leathers and grease-stained shirt.

"Sorry it's taken so long for me to return," he said. "I felt you searching, you know, but I couldn't work out how to get back here."

"No need to apologise, Jean," she replied. "Do I need to ah, hold your skull again?"

He grinned. "I'll let you know. So far, I think – now that we've met again – I can find you without too much trouble."

"We have the Thorn of Souls."

"So I saw, well done. But I do have a warning, something you would have realised for yourselves, but don't try to take the Thorns overland, Williams will interfere. Fly the *Clara* to the *Albion* and affix the cannon here, at sea."

"Is that possible?"

He nodded.

"I'll tell everyone tomorrow," Mia said. "Thank you, Jean."

"Of course." He stood then, and collected a handful of acorns from the grass. "So, in case I have less time than I thought, any questions?" He began to juggle them then, pacing as he did.

"Yes, we do."

"Fire away."

"What *is* the Thorn? A weapon? We didn't understand the diamond chamber either, it seemed to contain burning mist."

"That's as good a description as any," he said. "We found something else there, you know, Stella and I. A message from those who came before us; I'm not sure how many centuries. But you've seen the place, right? It's nothing we could have made ourselves."

"Nor us," Mia replied.

"Well, whoever did – we called them the Forefathers, not very specific, I know – claimed that something grave was happening, but that they had a solution. The only problem was that it would take hundreds of years before it was ready."

"The cannon?"

"Partly. That diamond chamber was more important though. The cannon just delivers what's inside, but we could never figure out what *it* truly was," he admitted. He tossed one of the acorns off course, letting it fall to his feet, where he kicked it back into the loop. "There was obviously Orichalcum in there with whatever else had been burning down to feed the Soul for a long time, but we don't know the full recipe, I guess you could say. Orville estimated that it would take another fifty to one hundred years to finish, which is why we sealed it away."

"You gambled."

"We did; same as the Forefathers, to be honest. As a bit of insurance, we tried to pass down the song. And the birds, well, we got lucky when we found them."

Mia straightened. "Wait, my mother taught me the lullaby... does that mean..."

"You and your brother could be descendants of Gatehouse," he said with a smile. "Maybe Helena, or Vincent but I'm not sure."

"Can I ask you about them, sometime?"

"Of course."

Maybe I should ask now, since who knows how many times I'll be able to speak to him... but we need information about the Thorn. "So, did the Forefathers ever describe the threat?"

"They did – you might be a surprised."

"All right."

"Because of some calamity in the past, one that's still lingering now, everyone is dying sooner than they should and it gets a little worse with each passing generation."

Mia opened her mouth to reply, but found no words at

first – it wasn't what she'd expected. *It's not an urgent threat. Or maybe it is and I'm just not looking far enough ahead?* "How could they be sure?"

"Let me ask you this, then. If I asked you to describe an 'old man', how old would you imagine him to be? Generally."

"Fifty or sixty years, I guess."

Jean nodded as he tossed the acorns aside. "Perfect. What would you say if I told you that, in my day, people could live to seventy fairly easily? And that the Forefathers, in extreme cases, could live to over one hundred years."

Mia blinked. "One hundred years?"

"We had little reason to doubt them, considering their technological advancements for one."

"So, where does it end?"

"Well, your generation might average forty to fifty. Any children you bear? Maybe only thirty years old, before the ancient poison takes them. It's accelerating, Mia, and that's why using the Thorn of Souls is so important. It can reverse all this."

So young? Mia struggled to speak at first. "Are you sure about all of this?"

"I am."

"So..." Mia spread her hands. "How does it work?"

"Try not to laugh, but you fly over each city, each settlement, crops and lakes, and fire the cannon – the mist will fall like rain."

Mia frowned. *It doesn't seem comical, just inefficient; prone to weather and... well, roofs.* "But won't that–"

He raised a hand. "I know what you'll say – and yes, it has to reach both the crops and water systems to make sure people ingest it, and then it can begin to reverse the traces of poison that is carried within every man, woman, and child."

"And people will live longer?"

"A little," Jean replied. "But according to the instructions, this final gambit is more about protecting future generations. So, children of today but especially of tomorrow, will begin the climb back to a more natural lifespan."

"And if we fail?"

Jean sighed. "Hard to say. Maybe life cycles here are reduced even more... maybe people never reach adulthood."

"But how?" Mia asked as she stood. "How could this have happened, and no-one is aware of it?"

"You and I are," he replied with a small smile. "Thanks to warnings from the past. And as to how, I don't know. The calamity is not recorded."

"Is it just us?"

"You mean other nations? I always wondered about that. Even during my day we didn't easily or often travel so far. And we weren't really welcomed when we did."

"Then we'll start at home, with the *Clara*."

He nodded. "One more thing, Mia. The Soul cannot fall into the hands of Williams – it's still a weapon, no matter that we use it for a noble purpose."

"More powerful than the cannons on the Sand-Hog? Or the ships?"

"A single blast could flatten city walls."

Chapter 30.

The sea was not particularly calm in the days that followed. Mia found herself dividing her time between visits to Jemima, careful discussions with the Queen and the others about what she'd learnt from Jean, and time with the Thorn of Souls, trying to sense something about its future – some way to be sure that affixing the cannon to the *Clara* would be possible.

At least the nights were usually afforded to her and Ethan alone.

But now Jemima had asked to see her, and so Mia was again following one of the sailors, who guided her below decks to the older woman's tank.

Inside, the wave of lavender had been replaced by something from the west – lemon myrtle, perhaps? But a welcome scent in any event. "Jemima?"

"Hello, dear," she replied, her voice echoing.

Mia counted her steps to stop before the tank. "Is everything all right?"

"I believe so but I wanted to share something with you."

"About the Thorn of Souls?"

"No, this is about Ethan, dear. It may not come to you – that's how it is sometimes when you are close to a person, as I'm sure you know. But I sense a threat when you reach the city."

Mia tensed. "We weren't planning on returning there." *Or are we? I don't know anymore. I want answers but what if it's not possible?*

"What I've seen might not come to pass at all, of course," Jemima replied. "It's something vague. A lock of hair, almost pale purple, but it poses a danger to Ethan."

Not something associated with Williams, then. But it was not bright news either. "Thank you, Jemima. I'll warn him."

"Copper has been asking after you and Thomas, you know."

"Oh?"

"He must have something he wants to show off." She chuckled. "In fact, I wonder if I hear him approaching even now?"

Footsteps *were* nearing, someone moving at a jog. Mia thanked Jemima again, and started for the door, where the sailor was now speaking to someone – it was indeed, Copper. "Is she in there?" the boy asked.

"I'm here," Mia said as she neared.

"Mia, Hawkins wants to see you," he said, a little out of breath. "He said he has an important question."

"Of course, lead on, then," Mia said with a smile.

Together, with one of Aiden's sailors in tow, they made their way forward to the brig, where Captain Hawkins would be waiting.

As with her previous visits, Mia was allowed to see Hawkins without fuss. No doubt he'd been teaching Copper enough to satisfy Aiden's expectations and so maybe some suspicion toward the prisoner had eased.

"Thank you for joining me, Mia," the Captain said when she sat within his room, his deep voice filling the space. This time, the cell did not smell so closed-up, as though he'd spent less time imprisoned.

"Is it something I can help with?"

"I am hoping so," he said. "I would ask that you use the *Clara* to deliver me to the new world."

"Truly?"

"As much as it pains me to give her away, I suspect that the *Albion* can do more good in the hands of the Queen than in mine."

Mia struggled for words. "I didn't think I'd hear anything like that from you, Captain."

"Nor I to say such words. But at least I'll be free. I have friends beyond this nation and even now, I hold no hope that Aiden and the Queen plan to offer me any more than the role of captive engineer, useful to have on hand in case of emergency."

"But–"

He raised a hand. "I've made my peace with the decision, Mia. Will you help me?"

"Of course."

"Excellent. Now, I do have some good news."

"You do?"

"Well, it should be. Based on what we've seen and our estimates, the Thorn will be simple enough to affix to the airship, even if we have to make something ourselves to get the whole of the job done."

"Like something to fire the cannon from the cockpit?"

"It could be one problem, but I don't think the *Clara* has given up all her secrets just yet."

"But you can leave that to us," Copper said. "We've got a few ideas ready to test. It won't be that hard, I think."

She found a smile, despite her concern over Hawkins. "Your confidence is quite welcome, Copper."

"Something troubling you?" Hawkins asked.

"Other than your request?"

"Yes."

She sighed. "Something that poses a threat to Ethan, if we go to Birnhale."

"Ah."

"It's not specific enough to worry me yet – not too much... but I don't know."

The Captain shifted where he sat. "And you're not sure whether to tell him or not?"

"Right."

"Care for some advice?"

Mia nodded.

"Ethan's a thoughtful fellow – he'd be hard to surprise. He's probably got half a dozen contingency plans for all manner of things, as I did, as all must when they defy the Dirt Kings. If you add an unknown threat, something he *cannot* plan for, I wonder will that aid or hinder him?"

"That's my fear. Until I know more... maybe I will say nothing, for now."

"Aye, probably for the best."

"Right," Mia said. *At least, I hope it is.*

Chapter 31.

Thomas stared north across the wasteland toward where the *Clara* waited – hopefully. Beyond her resting place would be more desolation and eventually the marshes, where Adam, Edwina and their people waited.

Beyond that in turn, the hills of Birnhale and then the dark city itself – Williams was suddenly awfully close. *And he's probably closer than that, hiding in the cavern with hundreds of men.* Warrick too, if the man had made better time overland. The weather on the ocean had not offered swift sailing... but whoever reached the *Clara* first did not matter.

The real question was who would *leave* with the airship.

Once we walk into that cavern, everything anyone would need to fly the Clara *will be in one place.*

"We're not ready," Thomas said.

"Is that so?" Elisabeth replied from where she was loading water into the back of their steam car. "If only there had been some way to offer a suggestion earlier."

He kicked at one of the stones. It clattered over hard earth to roll into the grey undergrowth, thin branches and old leaves swallowing the rock. "I know we're doing the best we can with a force this size, with no way to get the Hog close enough to the entrance, but Williams will have half his army there, I'm sure of it."

"Is that what Mia thinks?"

"No."

"Then guess who I'm going to trust, Thomas?"

He sighed. "Sometimes she doesn't know right away. I just don't want surprises now – we're *so* damn close."

"True," she said. "And we'll be leaving with the *Clara*, I promise."

"Who can predict the future now?"

Elisabeth shook her curls. "No visions, just a promise."

Thomas hesitated. Was it the right time to ask her about Williams? Instead, he said, "Then I hope there's another entrance."

"If there is, your sister will find it." She rested a hand upon his shoulder. "We have all the advantages except numbers, but Williams cannot match us in any other way, we just need to get Hawkins and that kid inside and then we'll be unstoppable."

"Let's hope so."

He turned back to the others. Mia and Ethan were loading their car with Jiro, Aiden and the Queen nearby at their own vehicle, one of his heavily armed sailors already standing at the Gatling. The hiss of steam signalled another car was ready – Captain Donovan and two of his men.

It was not a large force but against ground troops, the

steam-cars were an obvious advantage, yet if Williams or Warrick had established cannons with fortifications... maybe it wouldn't matter. The cars were as much for travel as anything else, at least until they neared the entrance, when it would be time to switch to foot.

With plenty of places available for ambush during our approach.

A secret entrance or exit would solve our problems. "I'm going to check with Mia one more time," he said.

"Thanks for the help, then," Elisabeth called after.

Mia, Ethan and Jiro were finishing up.

"Thomas?" Ethan paused where he was settling into the driver's seat.

"I wanted to check, one more time."

Mia shook her head from where she sat in the passenger seat, rifle beside her, expression troubled. "Nothing, Thomas. But I'm trying, believe me."

"I do."

"Wait." She straightened. "I *do* have an idea, but it might be dangerous."

"How?"

"Dangerous for you, I mean. What if you use *your* senses – you can sense steel and iron from a distance, right?"

Thomas paused a moment before laughing softly. "I am a fool."

"Maybe, maybe not. Won't it only work if you're not surrounded by us?"

Was she right? The weapons and the cars... they made for a strong vibration, definitely enough to make it harder to sense any lurking enemies ahead. But not impossible either, since he'd definitely honed his senses further when he found the trap before Alita's Shell. *And that had been while standing on the Hog itself.*

The danger would come from scouting ahead, alone.

Especially without the cars. He'd be exposed with only what cover the hills afforded. Cover Williams' men would also enjoy.

But it was still a good idea.

"I'll convince Elisabeth," he said as he started back toward their car. "Stay safe, you two."

"We will."

Elisabeth waved him over when he neared. "Finished?"

He climbed into the passenger seat. "Mia had an idea – I'm going to be the forward scout once we can't drive any further."

Elisabeth nodded as she fired the engine. "Sensing their weapons as you go, of course."

"Right."

Elisabeth started along the old road, bumping down a slope, then increasing the pace once they levelled out, dust pluming behind them. Thomas was still able to see Mia and Ethan in one mirror as they travelled beneath the bright sun.

The plains were dotted by mounds and grey trees, their leaves a green so dark as to appear black. Others bore bell-like pods. Ahead, one was actually opening, spreading seeds like a blanket, though the breeze scattered them only to dry earth.

The great craters, those he and Mia had hidden themselves within so long ago now, were not yet visible. It would take the rest of the day to reach them. He glanced to the boiler, where one of the men from the Hog worked on the fuel.

"Do we have enough fuel? And water, for that matter?"

Thomas asked. "I've never travelled from this side of the craters."

"Enough to reach Turnor River, at least," she replied. "I took on a barrel of salt water too, in case we get desperate enough to risk the boiler."

"Right."

The bleak but sadly familiar terrain rolled on, not precisely flowing, since Elisabeth had to slow frequently to detour holes, nor could they race ahead with their modest load of Orichalcum, but she seemed unperturbed by the delays, something that would have raised her ire before.

"You seem pleased enough," Thomas said.

"That's because I am."

He gestured ahead, to where the hills rose dark in the distance – where so many unknowns lurked. "We've still got to deal with a few problems, you know."

"I do. But this close, I'm thinking ahead."

"To Birnhale."

"Among other places, yes."

"And Williams?"

"What of him, Thomas?"

He tried to read her expression. Again, she seemed in a perfectly fine mood. "You looking to take some revenge on the way out?"

"One can hope."

"What if he's not there?"

She shrugged. "Then he can die another time – why, you think it should be you?"

"Why not?"

Elisabeth slowed to avoid yet another uneven depression in the road. "I'm not saying you don't have plenty of cause, but I thought you had other priorities?"

Mia's safety *was* more important.

"Your sister, as we both know," Elisabeth said. "Now, I want to ask you something – what do you think about the Queen's plans?"

"Ah, I'm not sure. It's possible, I suppose..." *Why ask me? I don't know anything about the other nations.* "But she mentioned using the *Clara* or its fuel as a bargaining chip. That's concerning."

"Agreed. With the Thorn of Souls, we don't need an army."

Thomas glanced at her. Everyone, from Wilkins to Captain Donovan saw the Thorn as a weapon as well as a tool to save the nation – and it was, it was a mighty cannon, but what Mia had revealed was chilling.

All of it.

Elisabeth returned his gaze a moment. "You doubt me? Come, nothing built or hidden in such a manner would be trifling."

"You know that from the books you stole?"

"They strongly hinted as much."

Something else she held back. "And the Queen would know this too?"

"Surely."

Thomas checked the mirror once more, this time seeking the Queen's vehicle but it was obscured by Mia and Ethan's car. "Then the call for aid from another nation is... a farce? Cover for something else?"

"It could be. How long has she been seeking to overthrow Williams? How long have she and Aiden been working together, sailing around, making who knows what sort of promises?"

"Could she simply be sincere?"

"Maybe, and that would mean she *is* who I thought she was."

"But you still doubt her."

"I doubt everyone."

Somehow, the words stung a little. "Including me?"

Elisabeth chuckled. "Yes, Thomas. I can easily envision a time when you choose Mia over me. You have promised me as much."

She has a point. "But our goals align now. Restore the *Clara*, use it for our freedom, crush Williams. There is no need for doubt."

"Just add one more thing to your list."

"What?"

"Keep the *Clara* – and the Orichalcum – out of the Queen's hands. I don't know if she and Aiden can be trusted and I don't want to be taken by surprise."

"And Captain Donovan?"

"Believe it or not, I trust he has been clear with what he seeks for the Federation. *Bareo* would be the one with hidden agendas, but he probably wouldn't have mentioned those to a straight arrow like Donovan."

"Then it's the Queen and Aiden we need to watch?"

"I believe so."

"Assuming everything goes exactly to plan, how do we stop them?"

"That's something I haven't figured out yet, admittedly," she replied. "But we have to get the *Clara* airborne first, right?"

"Yes, we do."

It was growing dark by the time they reached a point

in the road where the steam cars could no longer be used, Elisabeth ordering everyone on foot from there – leaving the cars unguarded. All agreed; they couldn't afford to leave behind even a single gun.

And now, Thomas led them between the stones, eventually coming to a halt again where he pressed himself against yet another stone column. Like the others, it had retained plenty of warmth despite the heavy dusk. He paused to listen, letting his senses seek more steel. Anything beyond his own rifle and helm, the knife on his belt, or a dozen other smaller items, would be enough.

But still he found no sentries.

They have to be out there somewhere.

He peeked around the stone, looking up. Uneven ridges, taller pillars and other uneven, shadowy shapes surrounded the *Clara's* hiding place. No hints of movement between or upon them, just the same old darkening purple sky above.

It made little sense.

Why leave the approach unguarded? *They know we're coming.* At the least, sentries should have been in place... now, he'd be able to lead the others directly up to the southern end of the hills that protected the airship without any trouble.

Is it a trap after all? They know we're coming, they know what I can do...

Thomas signalled to Elisabeth, who in turn waved everyone else after. She kept some distance but Thomas urged her closer again. There were no threats.

Beyond, and beneath the earth, the wealth of metals from the *Clara* was clear, and beyond it in turn a camp of soldiers – *many* of them, but no-one had slipped south to post watch, that much he could tell quite easily.

"It has to be a trap," Thomas said when Elisabeth brought everyone closer, weapons in hand, expressions of wariness common. "Why fail to watch for us, right?"

"To lure us in – only, they'd *have* to suspect that you can sense steel," Mia said.

"Exactly."

Elisabeth frowned. "Then it's a taunt. Williams is aware that we're heading here and is betting on numbers to carry the day. We need a secret passage, something from the south."

"Can we climb the ridge?" Ethan asked. "The skylights could be an entry point."

"Maybe I could force the lattice into a ladder," Thomas said as he glanced up to the dark line. Steep indeed. Few paths upward, vague indentations for foot or handholds, but maybe it wasn't impossible... hard to say in the failing light.

Captain Donovan shook his head. "Won't there be troops stationed within also?"

"Hmmm."

"Then we must circle back, and assault their forces," the former Queen said. "Can you guess at their numbers, Thomas?"

"I think they number in the scores. Maybe a couple of hundred."

"Then we are out-gunned here."

Elisabeth folded her arms. "Ideas?"

Mia nodded. "I have one – just let me sleep on it."

Chapter 32.

Falling asleep 'as fast as possible' had not been easy, despite their march across the uneven terrain, but Mia woke to a pool of clear blue water lined by stone. The place rested beneath the shade of lush greenery – broad, long leaves that held sparkling dew drops and bright pink and white flowers too, vines hanging from trees above.

Sunlight seemed to glow where it bounced off the water – a scene of beauty, and one that still gave her pause... something was not right.

A shadow waited.

It rose up from one corner of the pristine pool – and even before the horned skull broke the surface, Mia knew what had come to her. She clenched her fists. *I beat you once and I'll do it again if I have to.*

"Nyath."

She tensed, ready to strike, but the red-cloaked figure did not exit the water, instead spreading muscled arms across the stone and leaning back. "After a fashion."

"What?"

"Following my diminishing at your hands, I have returned in a new, quite different role."

She did not lower her guard. "Which is what?"

"Protector still, only this time more of a negotiator, perhaps. And I can offer you exactly what you seek; a way to win through to the airship that you seem to value so much."

"Are you saying the *Clara* won't be of help us?"

"I'm saying such a thing can hardly compete with the *chromata*, now can it?"

She folded her arms. "How?"

He shrugged. "Let's say I visit each soldier in their sleep and ensure they remain in that state – say, until dawn?"

"Why would you do that?"

"Because the *chromata* is not a playground for any and all to simply visit and take or create whatever they need – you do not operate here via sanctioned means; I have told you this before."

Sanctioned? By whom? He's not making a lot of sense – I need the guide. But she had to forge ahead without aid. "And if you help me now, that teaches me what?"

"Nothing," he replied. "It is actually the *price* you must pay to receive my help, not a lesson."

"Tell me."

"Banishment."

"From the *chromata*?"

"Of course."

Mia nodded. "So be it." If that was the price then she would pay it to make sure the *Clara* could be theirs, to make sure the Thorn of Souls could be used.

"My, my. Such confidence."

"I don't need this place."

"Even to solve a pressing mystery? The truth about the lock of hair that threatens Ethan?" he asked. "After all, your Foresight is not cooperating, is it?"

Mia ground her teeth. "What do you know?"

"That if you agree to my terms, you will have the airship by the dawn – providing you can restore it in time."

"Fine." Mia pointed at him. "But you had better keep your end of the bargain, or nothing will stop me returning here to finish you off."

"I *must* keep my word, all threats aside."

"Then do it," Mia snapped, and turned from the pool and strode off into the... nothingness that surrounded the tranquil place. "Bastard." Asking her to pit Ethan's life against the lives of so many...

But I don't *need the* chromata. *My Foresight will be enough.* It had to be.

But a splinter of doubt lingered when she woke to the faint glow of shielded lamps, reaching for Ethan. She found his arm. "It's done. We have until dawn."

"Brilliant," he said, taking her hand. "What did you do?"

She lowered her voice. "Nyath was there – he's going to deal with the soldiers."

Ethan took her by the shoulders. "Wait, how? You defeated him, didn't you?"

"So I thought. He claimed to be changed. And he didn't attack," she said. "I didn't actually feel the same threat now that I think on it. He truly did seem less powerful in a way."

"But can we trust him?"

"I'm not sure," she said. *Nyath had never seemed to be lying about wanting to keep me out.* "He offered a bargain –

he'll take care of the camp but in return, I can't access the *chromata* again."

"Oh. That's... unexpected."

"I'll pay the cost, gladly. I still have my gift and we *need* the airship."

"You're sure about this?"

"I am."

"Well, that does reduce one threat, doesn't it? If you can't return, and he doesn't want you there, then we don't have to worry about him seeking you."

"I'm hoping so."

"Though I have to wonder, what will Nyath do to the soldiers?"

Mia swallowed a callous remark about those who sided with Williams. "He said we have until dawn. Sounds temporary."

"Then let's tell everyone that we can make our move."

"But we might as well keep Nyath to ourselves for now – only Thomas knows."

"Right."

Mia accepted Ethan's help to join the others, where she explained that their path was open – that she's seen them reach the *Clara* without interference, only they had to leave by dawn.

"How can you be sure?" Elisabeth asked.

"I put them to sleep," she replied. *Surely not the worst guess, considering Nyath's dawn deadline.*

"As you dreamt?"

She nodded. "I called for help – like at the *Esmeralda*."

"I see." Elisabeth's tone lost some of its doubt, replaced by a faint trace of unease.

"Meaning?" the Queen asked.

"Mia can call a great Bird of Light," Elisabeth replied. "It blinded my men, most for weeks and some permanently."

"Hmmm."

Queen Maryanne did not ask any further questions, but her curiosity was not lost on Mia. *Does she know something about the Great Bird? Or does she just seek a powerful 'tool' for her plans?*

"Let's not waste time, then," Thomas said. "Everyone ready?"

"I am," Copper announced, the cheer in his voice almost out of place. And yet, it was a welcome sound too, taking the edge off her discomfort.

Ethan led her after the others as they circled toward the camp, traversing the rock-strewn ground with some trouble, but the night was still young by the time he stopped at the enemy camp.

Tension was rebuilding within her limbs. Light from camp or cook-fires waited before her, at least a dozen of them. Yet as they neared, other than the crackle of the fires, the camp was hushed. Only the sound of steady, even breathing from the soldiers. Many had seemingly fallen where they stood; so it seemed based on the odd path Ethan took her along what was probably an ordered campsite.

"There's another tent pole to your left," he whispered.

Mia stepped lightly, even though it seemed likely that no soldier would wake before dawn. No snoring or uneven breathing surrounded her, no sounds of shifting or anything other than a deep, unnatural slumber.

Nyath will keep his word – he truly wants me out of the chromata *for some reason.*

That was its own mystery.

And hopefully one unconnected to the *Clara* or restoration of the people. *It can't be.* There really was no reason. *Keeping me away is about his ego, since I defeated him.*

Ethan led her onward and from behind, a soft curse from Elisabeth.

"What?" Thomas asked, his own voice quiet.

"I stepped on someone's hand," she said. "It was gross."

"Mature."

"Quiet now," the Queen said, though she too, did not seem concerned, this deep into the camp.

How close are we to the entry now?

Barely half a dozen more steps and Ethan came to a halt. "There are guards inside – asleep like the others. We'll need the lanterns from this point on."

"Light them up, then," Elisabeth said, and the excitement was clear in her tone.

And by the butterflies in Mia's own stomach, it seemed to be rubbing off.

Chapter 33.

Thomas paused when he stood beneath the *Clara* once more – moonlight falling through the mass of latticed skylights above and into the great cavern, where it hit the giant balloon with its old graffiti.

Jean's name caught his eye. *Does Mia still carry his skull? We'll need his help again, I'm betting.*

The cables of steel still supported the balloon, long rails with Gatling guns and rifle docks; the sleek hull and silent propellers, the sealed portholes and more – every inch of the airship called to him as he craned his neck to stare up to it.

Soft gasps came from behind but he did turn to see who… there was something familiar about the airship, something he hadn't recognised the first time.

Orichalcum. I feel it now.

Something was responding to the pieces he'd carried – with some effort – through the sleeping soldiers.

The *Clara* was at least partially made from Orichalcum.

"We are truly blessed by someone or something," Elisabeth said from beside him, eyes alight.

"Maybe we are."

"I won't deny our own strengths but for Gatehouse's gambit to have paid off, for the *Clara* to thwart the Williams line for so long, to have gathered all the pieces, for Silas' research to have succeeded in you, for Mia's gift to have opened the way here – it is miraculous."

Thomas frowned at being described as 'research' but her point stood. "Then we'd better not waste our good fortune."

"Agreed." Elisabeth directed Jiro and another soldier to search the cavern as she started for the building and its elevator. That too was a mass of metal that called to Thomas where it rose to the waiting ladder. To reach that ladder, they only had to cross the arched walkway then climb up to the lower platform, and that was it. They'd be aboard and ready to work on getting the ship underway, racing their dawn deadline.

"Let's search the building too," the Queen said.

"See if you can locate the controls for the skylight," Thomas added as her men scouted ahead.

Inside the dust-covered reception area he found the same set of steel stairs waiting off to one side. Fresh footprints led up, the muffled sound of their soldiers above.

The steel cage of the elevator waited nearby, ready for use. It also bore evidence of recent use, doubtless Williams and his men had searched the place again. It did not seem as though they had tampered with the box or lever either, and surely the chains and pulley system were also in working order.

Everyone who wasn't already searching, squeezed into the cage and Elisabeth pulled the lever. Many still had hands near their weapons as they waited for the rattling journey to complete, but Mia did not appear at all concerned.

She fully expects that the soldiers will stay asleep.

Meaning, so should I.

"A thought," Captain Donovan said after a time. "Should we take advantage of the enemy's weakness and inflict some casualties? Prince Warrick may be among those sleeping, perhaps even the King himself. We would have to search the camp, of course."

"If we end up having time," Elisabeth said after a moment's hesitation, as though she were tempted. "We don't know how long it will take up here."

"I doubt my 'former husband' will have come here himself," the Queen added.

"Then get the airship afloat first," Thomas said. "No matter who is here, they won't be able to stand before the *Clara*."

The Captain nodded as the lift slowed, coming to a stop level with the walkway. Elisabeth opened the cage doors and once again, Thomas found himself passing through what was no doubt a sitting room, with leather seating scattered around and an ancient clock hung high upon the wall.

"Lead on, Thomas," Elisabeth said with a gesture. "You and Mia know the ship, right?"

"It's simple enough," he replied as he took the lead, climbing swiftly now as growing excitement lent his limbs extra energy.

When he reached the hatch, it opened as easily and he pulled himself up into the dark, pausing to ask for light. When Elisabeth passed up a lantern, he lifted it to reveal giant rivets and beams large as his arm span. *The Orichalcum feels closer now that I'm below decks too.*

"Last time, I just went straight up that other ladder," he

told Elisabeth, who moved aside to let the others join them.

"Straight to the engine or pilot's room, I think," she said. "We can explore the rest of the ship later."

"Right." In the passage above, he passed closed portholes, including the one that he'd opened before. *Suggesting that Warrick has definitely searched the ship.*

"What of these doors, Thomas?" Elisabeth asked.

"They were empty last time."

"Could soldiers be hiding within?" the Queen asked from further back.

"They'll be sleeping if they are," Mia replied. "So long as we get airborne before the dawn."

Elisabeth nodded. "We'll do a proper search once Jiro and Lawrence return."

At the third ladder, Thomas took them up several floors and finally to the silvery decks, and the gleaming rails. Moonlight from above cast the bloodstains left by Julian's men in a deeper darkness, but the bodies had been since moved, probably a long time ago now.

He did not notice any bullet holes on the way to the bridge, though they would have been there too. At the ornate door, with its cloud-like engraving, he gained entry with ease, the metal almost too light beneath his grip.

My own gift keeps growing stronger. Was it the passage of time or exposure to the Orichalcum? Impossible to know why, but as the others filed into the room – Copper with excited murmuring – and spread their lanterns, there was enough to wonder about a possible orange tint to the metal.

"Anything changed?" Mia asked him as the others looked around.

"Not that I see. Same seats at the back and stools before

the console. I forgot that it curves around nearly the entire room – Copper's nearly climbing across it."

Mia smiled and Ethan chuckled.

"There are a *lot* of levers and buttons here," Captain Donovan said from where he bent over the controls. "Can we really expect the lad to do handle everything alone?"

"It will take a few of us to actually pilot it," Thomas said. "Like those twin handles or the keys, and that's not to mention the wheel itself. And the boiler room if it has one, we never had a chance to check last time."

"We'll take care of it, not to worry," Hawkins said with a grin. He too, seemed just as awed and excited as Copper.

Mia was now at the steering wheel with Ethan and Elisabeth.

Fresh iron chains had been fitted, the ruby heart closed once more. Mia ran her hands across the links and to the lock, where she fitted the key into the heart-shaped lock. It clicked open and she let it thud to the ground, and together the three freed the steering shaft from the chains.

"Let's take stock of everything here," Elisabeth said. "Captain Donovan, can you keep searching and everyone else, take heed of Hawkins and Copper."

Thomas drifted back to the door at the rear of the room – which he'd first taken for the Captain's quarters, but it seemed more likely a place for the pilots to catch some rest. It did include a wardrobe and desk along with the bed, and old charts.

But it was the decaying journal he sought – and it had not been taken.

He lifted it to turn each surviving page gingerly, seeking the words at the back. *And so I hath pulled the ruby-red heart from Her and bequeathed it unto Arthur, Vivian's eldest and sent the lad away with all my knowledge… such is my shock at her betrayal that this is all I can manage, now that they are coming. But let them try and fly her without it.*

Jean's words, surely… though the writing was more formal than his speech, according to Mia.

The mystery was still just that, a mystery.

Were the seeds of betrayal lingering somehow? After all, if Arthur's descendants had somehow reached David and the others, would the traitor have left behind more than just whatever ill-gotten gains they won for their betrayal?

"Thomas, let's head below. Find that engine room."

Captain Hawkins stood in the doorway.

"Good idea." He set the journal down – the truth behind what seemingly broke Gatehouse apart would have to wait.

Chapter 34.

Thomas set the slab of Orichalcum down with a clink, resting it before the cold furnace they'd found within a spacious but windowless boiler room.

Located almost directly beneath the cockpit, there had been no direct path at first, the silence of the airship seeming to magnify their footfalls as they searched. But once Thomas had wrenched the heavy door open – without much trouble – they found a ladder and hatch that might have led up to the pilot.

However, it seemed the radio was the main method of communication.

A different exit waited at rear of the room, this door wider than it was tall, and Thomas found himself drawn to the moving platform there. It currently sat unmoving, but it was probably connected to the ship's hold.

"See the cylinders?" Hawkins said as they examined it. "They let the belt roll, bringing up fuel from the loading bay, I'd wager."

"Then it's stored in these shelves, I guess," Thomas said.

The shelves were like narrow alcoves, almost sized like... the handle of an axe. The piece of Orichalcum he'd carried from the *Albion* was probably twice as large but when he glanced at the windowed hatch on the furnace, it became clear that the piece would fit *quite* easily.

But how much Orichalcum does it take to achieve flight? Is it the only fuel source?

At least any pieces that would fit the alcoves would be small enough that they could be moved by anyone, rather than just those who had been experimented on by Alchemists. Thomas glanced back at the slab he'd carried. *Or maybe two people per piece?*

"This isn't that different to what we found in Alita's Shell," Thomas said as he knelt before the furnace. There was a slot for the Orichalcum to be fed in, separate to the diamond-like window on the hatch. *Where the mist would be visible?* The furnace – if that was truly its purpose – was also lined by four gauges and a pair of levers. One was marked Boost and the other Cut. Mighty screws suggested the entire front of the furnace could be opened if needed.

"No ignition method?" Hawkins asked as he, too, examined the chamber.

"I don't think so." There didn't seem to be any button, switch or lever labelled as such. *Is it more like the set-up used for the gate in Silver Rock?* Opposite the storage slots waited the radio, its speaker and mouthpieces mounted on the wall. One had the word 'Pilot' written overhead and the other, nothing. "I guess we just have to load it up and see what happens."

"I'll leave that to you, then," the man said. "Let me test the radio."

Thomas knelt by the Orichalcum. To fit in the furnace, it probably needed to be torn in half. He rapped the surface with his knuckles, letting the sound resonate a moment before striking it a few more times. With a breath, he lifted it to grip both edges. "Come on now."

He pulled at it, muscles in his hands, forearms, elbows and shoulders – and then even his back, taking up the strain.

And the mythical metal tore soundlessly.

He now held two halves in a reasonably even split.

Thomas let out a small gasp of effort or relief, then set the slightly larger half into the slot. He gave it a nudge – and like the silent conveyor belt, cylinders rolled the piece inside and out of sight where it clinked its way down to land in the chamber.

There, it sat without changing, but a needle from one of the gauges flickered.

"We have to assume it's working," he said.

"Well, the radio isn't. I think we need to check from above," Hawkins said.

"Let's search more of this floor first."

He nodded. "Think we'll find any soldiers?"

"I don't know. They've obviously been here and the ones outside outnumber us..."

"It's higher ground too."

"Right," Thomas said as he took his lantern and started back down the passage, passing another row of portholes, these also bore space for gunners. "So they *should* be here but we haven't found a trace yet."

He checked each door as he walked, finding only cots, storage, or the occasional bathroom. But by the time they reached topside once more, it was without a trace of any hidden rats. Thomas still searched the decks again, heading to the prow where a small room waited. It bore no actual weapons, but a large handle and trigger was affixed to the wall.

He sighed. Nothing. No trace of any soldiers. It should have been good news but he couldn't stop a little doubt, worry. *Time to focus on the* Clara *again, then.*

"Something wrong with good news?" Hawkins asked. "We might be alone here, after all."

"Seems like it could be. If the others come back with similar news." Thomas gave a shrug. "How about the ship itself? I know it's early, and it's not like the *Albion*, but are you confident that you and Marcus can get her airborne?"

"Hard to say right now. There's a lot to learn."

"What if you had more help?"

"Such as?"

"Advice from the original pilot," he replied, but did not explain. *Not before I'm sure it can happen.*

"Were there notes you had in that old book?"

"No, but there might be more hidden somewhere," Thomas said as he shook his head. And that was probably true in any event. "Or maybe there's another way entirely; I'm going to look."

Hawkins chuckled. "Anything you can come up with is worth a shot."

Thomas returned below decks, this time drifting to the starboard where he found more empty rooms, some with narrow beds or packed with ammunition, a mess hall which had recently been searched by the others, not too far from more sleeping quarters. There was a series of glowing, pale blue lights and another thin gauge above the rows of stoves...

"Powered by the Orichalcum?"

Just that one piece?

He lifted a ladle. Could that single piece drive the ship *and* power a kitchen? More? It was a sobering thought.

The next room of note was a hall for training, containing both standing dolls and targets for shooting drills, but he moved on quickly – the next room was marked Library and warm light escaped from beneath its door.

Inside, he found Jiro and Lawrence standing over a long table where they'd spread documents across the surface, lamp light also reaching rows and rows of book spines in tall shelves.

"Thomas, I think some of this will be useful," said Jiro.

He joined them. Many of the documents were diagrams but they'd also gathered notepads, written in a range of hands. Thomas lifted one of the old pieces. Lines that seemed to connect different pieces of the console were labelled, but the words were not quite what he expected, with 'f' used in place of 'ph'.

"And this," said Lawrence as he handed a thin, leather-bound book over.

"Interesting," Thomas said as he flicked through. It seemed to contain instructions for mounting something called a 'navigation globe'. He handed it back. "Collect anything else that could be useful and get it to Copper and Hawkins right away, I'll keep looking."

"Good idea."

Thomas searched the shelves as they worked quickly, passing over gilded spines and tattered scrolls, unrolling or pulling only a few. They mostly seemed to be works of fiction, and histories. But one blue-bound book bore a title that caught his eye – *Calamities?* There was a sub-title too, something a little poetic. "A Nation Adrift on Dark Oceans."

It went under his arm and he found two more volumes that could be of use before pausing to check the *Calamities* book, setting it upon the table and sliding a lantern closer.

The text was extremely small, and precise – very cleanly applied to the page, and no language he understood. But pictures of giant, dark clouds of flame swallowing cities were troubling enough.

Will Jean himself have to solve this mystery?

Thomas continued his search through more unassuming rooms and another armoury. Again, he found no hidden soldiers in a deep slumber, only abandoned tools or weapons, helmets and jackets too, and soon circled back to the furnace to check on the gauge.

A faintly golden mist *was* slowly filling the chamber, as though being extracted from the piece of Orichalcum. *Different but similar to the Thorn of Souls here.* Impossible to judge the pace, but if luck held, it would fill the chamber enough to fly. *Maybe it's enough already, after all, isn't it a powerful fuel source?*

This time, he used the rear door and took a passage deeper toward what did end up being the ship's cargo hold. Entry was barred by a thick lock and chain, again, a ruby-heart sealed the way.

"Sorry, I'm in a bit of a hurry," Thomas said as he drew a fist back.

He swung down and the chain shattered.

The lock clattered to the ground and he pushed the doors open to step within, raising his lantern as he did.

Orichalcum gleamed in response.

Chapter 35.

Mia smiled as Copper tugged on her sleeve. "And these levers here, if we could connect them, they're the ones that controls the stabilisers. The horizontal is blue and the vertical is green."

"And they control the fins on the back?"

"Exactly," he said. "But there's a piece missing from each – just two cogs, but they've been removed and we can't find any replacements the right size."

"Another way to sabotage Williams, it seems," Captain Hawkins added. "We're still looking but dawn is pretty close."

"Let me try to contact Jean again," Mia said. If she returned to one of the leather chairs, smooth and quite comfortable, maybe she could drift off quickly. Her eyelids were already heavy from the enormous day they'd already been through.

"Here he is," Ethan said, and she reached out to take the skull once she'd taken a seat; a now-familiar weight. *Jean, can you hear me?* Only silence for an answer. At least, from the skull. Even with her eyes closed, turned away from the others, in the chair, the click and murmur of voices was enough to break her focus.

"Let me try just outside," she said.

Using the shapeless glow of lamps, Mia moved from the pilot's room and into the hall for some quiet. In the dimmer space, she stumbled over something, but caught the wall and steadied herself, managing to keep her grip on Jean's skull too. With a sigh, she moved a little further away again, voices fading now, and sat against the wall to hold up the skull. She faced it with closed eyes. *If you can hear me, Jean – we just need one more answer.*

Mia took a deep breath and slowed her breathing, letting the somewhat fainter sounds from the other room recede a bit further, then spoke. "Jean?"

A golden glow appeared, shaped as the skull. *Hello, Mia.*

No *chromata*, exactly as Nyath promised. And so this time, there was no strong sense of Jean's presence, no shape of his figure this time, just the glow and his voice. "Jean, we need your help again."

Don't worry, it's simple enough – the cogs are probably still hidden in a compartment beneath one of the food bins. Potatoes, I think.

"And all we need to do is reconnect them?"

Exactly.

"Thank you. What about the Thorn?"

Let's make sure you get airborne first. The glow faded and she tried to keep a hold of the sense of him, but it was not like within the *chromata*, and Mia lowered the skull when he disappeared. He was right, but a surge of hope had not been dampened either.

"Mia?"

It was Ethan.

"Here," she said as she stood. Her movements weren't as energetic as she'd have liked – the long night was not going to get any shorter. "The cogs are hidden in the kitchens, there's a false bottom on one of the food bins."

"Truly? That's perfect, I think we'll make it."

"Is it dawn?" She smothered a yawn.

He took her hand. "Not quite. Do you need to rest?"

"Not yet, not until we're in the air," she said. "But I wouldn't mind some fresh air, if we could call it that. What about the skylight?"

"Already open, so we're in the clear there," Ethan said as he led her out to the deck.

There, Mia glanced up to where a very faint hint of growing light suggested the new day approaching.

"I'm going to help them finish the *Clara*, will you be fine here?" Ethan asked.

"I think I can stay awake that long."

He kissed her cheek and then his footsteps thumped across the decking.

Mia sighed. The closer they came to taking flight, the sooner they'd have to face Birnhale and Williams. And Jemima's warning.

Even though she did not sit, it seemed she dozed while standing, for when footsteps returned – she wasn't sure how long after – she flinched into wakefulness. "Ethan?"

"We're all set and it's not fully dawn yet," he said.

"Good." She smiled, though it did not last. "Ethan, I want to speak to you about something."

"Is something wrong?"

"That's what I'm not sure about."

He took her by the shoulders, but his voice was gentle. "Something you haven't told me, right?"

Mia took a breath. Wouldn't revealing her fear create a deadly doubt in Ethan? *I can't do that to him, I can't have him second-guessing himself once we get to the city.* It was too risky, surely?

"Ever since you spoke to Jemima that last time, you've been quiet."

"I have?"

"Tell me; we'll face it together."

Again she hesitated, but the tone in his voice... he sounded calm, strong. *I don't want to bear this alone.* "She said that you'd be in danger once we reach Birnhale... but all she had was the sense of pale purple hair."

A new voice spoke. "You're in danger now too, Mia."

Warrick.

Chapter 36.

Thomas gripped the radio's mouthpiece, eyes upon the chamber where dissolving orange and silver of the Orichalcum swirled. The gauges were not full but they were nearly half complete – would it be enough to launch?

Dawn had already broken, but the final cogs were installed and now he was just waiting for the call.

"Have they woken?" Thomas asked.

After a moment, a crackling voice replied – Hawkins. "Not that we can tell."

"Then we'll make it," he said, tapping his foot now, a smile breaking. The drag of the night, the frantic search and final adjustment and everything before the night had paid off. "Right?"

A chuckle. "If that lever does what it should, then I think so."

Thomas glanced to the opposite wall. Twin levers stood waiting – Boost and Cut. According to the plans they'd found, all he had to do was pull one and then reload the fuel chamber. He already had a new piece of Orichalcum at hand.

A faint rumbling shook the airship. Not enough to upset his balance, instead, it sent shivers across his limbs. *It's working! We're going to make it – finally!* Even their luck was holding; Warrick and his men were still asleep.

Everything had been far easier than expected, if he thought back on their time on the airship. *Thanks to Mia. And Jean.*

"We're going to make it," he murmured, clenching a fist in triumph.

Another rumble and the *Clara* shifted again. This time it was joined by creaking from below and above, but for a furnace room, things weren't so noisy that he'd have to shout into the radio. Just another small piece of evidence to suggest that the *Clara* pre-dated Gatehouse.

Within the chamber, mist was being drawn up and out of sight, disappearing at a steady rate as different parts of the ship became active, most likely.

"Are you ready down there, Thomas?" Elisabeth asked.

"I am."

"Let's lift off," she said. Then she lifted her voice. "Well done, everyone. Take a hold of something – we're about to fly."

Thomas replaced the mouthpiece and strode to the lever where he paused. *Free at last.*

He pulled the one Boost.

The furnace room rocked and muted roaring from outside followed. In the chamber, the golden orange deepened to a dark red, spreading quickly before being sucked away as the bar of fuel withered.

That fast?

The light was already fading to a pinkish flame – and then the last of the mist was sucked up into whatever pipes delivered the fuel to the engines and the balloon itself, too. At least, according to the schematics; the burning air would help keep it afloat.

And the *Clara* was rising steadily – even swiftly.

A sharp lurch to the left followed, but the airship steadied and continued its ascent – even with the chamber empty now. "Shit." Thomas leapt across the room and ripped a bar of Orichalcum from the alcove, then shoved it into the chamber.

The bar flashed into a riot of reds and pinks, dwindling far too quickly and he swore again.

The Boost!

Thomas wrenched the lever back up, then dashed across the insert a third piece of Orichalcum into the chamber.

Success! The coppery mist returned as he slumped against the wall with a sigh, shaking his head.

"We did it, Thomas," Hawkins called from the speaker. "Come up and see."

"On my way!" he called back, though the captain wouldn't have heard.

Thomas charged from the room and ran along the passage – spinning the handles on all the portholes as he did. He took a moment to stop at one where sunlight poured in, causing him to squint. *No good.* He moved on, coming to a halt at a ladder and trying that porthole, and this time his eyes had adjusted, and he peered out to see the pale waste of the southlands below.

The skylights on the *Clara's* resting place stood open, and a few soldiers, like black-clad figurines stood below, waving their arms. He grinned. *Too slow, boys.*

Though his view was restricted, he could still see the warm horizon and distant mountains like shadowy sentinels. An even better view surely waited above. Thomas climbed the ladder and stepped onto the decks, where he ran around the pilot's room... and froze.

Warrick and another soldier stood only a dozen feet from the door, wind whipping their dark uniforms as they waited, revolvers trained on their captives.

Mia and Ethan.

Thomas reached for his own rifle with a growl – but he carried none. He strode forward.

"Be careful, Thomas," Warrick said from where he stared across at Elisabeth, Donovan and Aiden, all who held their own weapons ready, glaring back at the weasel of a prince.

He looked back to Warrick, jaw clenched. *Where the hell where they hiding?*

Williams' remaining son had not changed much; his face was still rat-like, the same sunken eyes as his father, an almost dull cruelty therein. Different to his brother. "Any mistakes and Ethan here will die," the so-called prince said.

"What do you want?" Thomas spat.

"Your unconditional surrender. All of you, after which, you will fly the *Clara* directly to Europa. Once there, I will release you – providing you obey me in all demands instantly."

Thomas glanced at the others, none of whom looked ready to respond.

"Join your friends, Thomas," Warrick added.

Thomas moved at a steady pace. All around, hunks or

strips of steel hummed with a sort of readiness. If he chose, he could hurl anything he wanted at Warrick and his goon, but with Mia and Ethan held captive, it would probably be impossible not to hurt them too.

"If we surrender you free us all?" Thomas asked. "Your father no longer seeks Mia?"

He sneered. "I care not for what my father desires."

"Then how do we trust your word?"

"Have I ever lied, Thomas? I have always told you that you were beneath me, I have always told you that is *exactly* why you deserved every piece of violence and ridicule that I sent your way. I didn't pretend there was any other reason."

And it was true – each time he'd knocked Thomas down, arms laden with trays of food or drink for the nobles, costing Thomas a beating, the man had seemed to take little pleasure in it. *It was just 'normal' for him.* But the strange logic of the claim was hardly assuring.

Before Thomas could answer, Elisabeth spoke. "I remember things a little differently, Warrick."

He narrowed his eyes. "And what does that mean?"

She laughed. "You were just passing it along, like the shitty little coward you are."

The man's grip tightened on his gun, which he pointed directly at Elisabeth now, Mia still caught in one arm. "Listen, bitch. This is not the time to play at being a hero. Be smart for the first time since you left."

"Is that why *Daddy* favoured Julian? You weren't as smart as your brother, were you?" Elisabeth raised an eyebrow. "Is that why he beat you, Warrick? Tell me, do you still have that pretty purple scar on your back? From the time with the wrench?"

Thomas caught her arm. "What are you doing?"

Warrick's face had turned bright red, and he was trembling now, though Mia was still ensnared. She'd caught his arm to keep him from choking her. "One more word! One more word and you're dead!"

Almost before Elisabeth spoke, Thomas was moving.

"One more word, Warrick."

Shots rang out, shouts echoing with them.

The bullet slammed into his chest – a second right after. Before he could even *feel* the thunderous impact, a third struck his shoulder. He fell to the decking, clutching his chest at spreading pain. His ears rang and the chaos of movement was unclear, as more shots fired and figures struggled above him.

He gasped for air as he rolled to the side, but the fight had already ended, leaving a hush filled only by heavy breathing.

Thomas gasped out a curse. The pain in his chest was already easing and when he raised his hands, they were not covered in blood. There was not even a hint of red.

"Thomas!"

He looked up in time for Mia to crash into him – he caught her in his arms. "Mia."

She pulled back and ran her hands across his face and chest, and he winced at what was no doubt extensive bruising hidden beneath his clothing. "Are you... you're not bleeding?"

"It still hurts."

She squeezed his face in-between her hands. Tears had dampened her blindfold. "You idiot."

"I know. I guess it's like before, with Julian."

"Take him below," Aiden was calling, and as Mia settled beside him now, Thomas saw the Bruiser dragging the body of the other soldier away, and Ethan standing unharmed beside Captain Donovan.

Jiro and one of Donovan's men were binding Warrick, who was still shouting, frothing at the mouth. Elisabeth's approach blocked his view then – her expression bore traces of surprise. She crouched beside him.

"Thomas. Thank you."

But he frowned, and at least half the expression was aimed at himself. *I didn't think I'd do that for her.* "That was your plan, wasn't it? Goad him into something and trust me to be your shield?"

"It was. And I only did it because I knew you would survive – your gift is stronger than ever."

"Luckily," Mia said, and her voice did not bear much warmth.

"Well, that's understandable," Elisabeth said as she stood. "I'll be interrogating our friend if you need me."

Chapter 37.

Thomas stood at the prow, beside a large cannon and its empty rack, doing his best to keep still in the shadow of the balloon. Even small movements enraged his bruises, which seemed to be deeper even than he'd first thought.

The alternative was worse. And Elisabeth, for all her callousness, was right about the strength of his gift. Would it change again? Would he grow stronger still? Even more resistant or more connected to steel? Hard to imagine. *I'm already a little too different to everyone else.*

The morning was wearing on as they charged through the clouds, beneath a bright sky – the visible blue so vivid that it seemed almost unreal. Cries from birds somewhere *below* added to the strange nature of their flight.

In fact, everything about sailing through the sky was strange – and beautiful too; there was just no way even a single person could find or bother him here. Freedom merely a question of time, if he wanted it, since there was plenty of Orichalcum in the hold. They could reach any corner of the world, any time.

"Hard to believe," he murmured. *But it was real – all of it is.* Despite Warrick's interruption, the *Clara* was certainly airborne. "We really did succeed." Next would come the Thorn of Souls and Williams himself. *And then, finally Silas.*

Despite his relief, there was a lingering concern over Warrick. How had the man avoided Nyath's strange spell of sleep? Had he simply found some overlooked spot upon the airship and fallen asleep there, remaining so until dawn?

Or, more troubling was Mia's suspicion – Nyath had betrayed them.

As yet, the prince had not offered any explanation.

Footsteps approached.

Thomas winced as he turned. Ethan was jogging across the decks, worry clear in his eyes. "Thomas, something's wrong."

Thomas straightened. *Not more bad news, please.* "With the *Clara*?"

"We're having trouble setting a course. Come on, we'll show you."

Ethan led the way back to the cockpit and its pale blue light, where Hawkins sat before the wheel. Copper was flitting from dials and buttons for the thrusters and then the levers for the stabilisers, while the Queen and Aiden stood nearby, the Bruiser with arms crossed.

Mia sat upon one of the leather chairs, Jean's skull in hand.

"We can't change course," Hawkins explained. "Everything seems to be functioning well enough but we can only make minor adjustments."

"But we're not falling," Copper added.

"No. It's as if our destination is pre-ordained. Watch."

Hawkins turned the wheel and the *Clara* tilted to the right, but although Hawkins kept the pressure on, the wheel returned to centre as though possessing a mind of its own.

Thomas frowned. "How?"

"It could be one of the settings here," Copper said from where he stood before a large sphere set in the console. It was almost like a ring around a black sun, the featureless globe had never moved before. It *could* have been for navigation but when Copper slid the ring with a steady clicking, it swung back. "I think it can set a course, without a pilot, but I can't change it."

Aiden spread his hands. "You should let me try again."

"This isn't a job for brute force," Hawkins replied.

Elisabeth cut over the Bruiser's reply. "It's probably something put in place by Gatehouse. Maybe a final gambit to prevent the *Clara* being used by Williams."

"Can we guess where we might be headed?" Thomas asked.

"We're hoping Mia can work her magic once more."

"So far, I'm not having any luck," she said. "He's getting harder and harder to reach."

Thomas glanced back out the door to the empty decks. "It might be time to start making sure the weapons work, just in case."

"Good idea," Elisabeth said, then turned to the Aiden with a grin. "Why don't you get right on that for us, since you're so eager to do something?"

***

Mia still hadn't been able to reach Jean by the time the *Clara* began to slow. The airship had moved at quite a speed;

making it dangerous to go topside and Thomas had spent half of the time in the furnace room, just to be safe.

But the Orichalcum continued to be true to its reputation for longevity.

And when he returned to the decks it was to yet another surprise – he paused before a small crowd, every single person aboard stood around staring, even Copper, who clung to the rigging.

A floating island of shining steel drew near.

There was no forest of balloons above and no hint of engines anywhere... no reason that it should be so! Clouds swirled gently beneath it, but since part of the trip to reach the place had been a climb, the island would hardly have been visible from below.

"What is this?" Jiro asked, voice hushed.

"A dock?"

Thomas wasn't even sure who responded, but they were right. A long platform extended out from the island, and it wasn't the only one. Four others were gleaming before the buildings – smaller, box-like shapes lined up before what must have been a 'hanger', according to the books they'd found. A huge building to house airships, these appeared to be built for slightly smaller ships.

Still, there was enough space for the *Clara* to dock.

"This is one of the sky ports from the *Aviator's Guidebook*," Copper cried. "Wow!"

Maybe this isn't the only one?

It obviously pre-dated Gatehouse and probably the Williams dynasty. *The Calamity too?*

Without guidance, the *Clara* docked herself, engines fading to a murmur.

"Spread out as we search," Elisabeth announced as she motioned to Jiro, then leapt the rail and strode along the platform.

No fear, as usual.

Thomas followed suit, after making sure Mia was fine – Ethan helping her climb down, and then continued to the floating dock.

Elisabeth had already stopped at a large pedestal, its round top bearing engraved images of land masses, mountains and rivers leading down to oceans... the world. Even worn by time, the details were clear. Yet perhaps more impressive was the globe set in the centre. Faintly aglow, it seemed to contain a similar scene, only with vivid greens and blues – and clouded by a coppery mist.

"A navigation globe," he said.

"Yes, but locked in place," Elisabeth replied.

"Let me try." Thomas placed both hands around the globe and lifted – but it was stuck fast. Trying to pry it free with a bar or something similar would risk shattering it, which left the podium. He switched his grip to the steel and applied some pressure, it began to bend easily enough.

He folded it down from one end and the globe shifted, rolling forward as he pulled the steel further.

Elisabeth caught it with a smile. "Perfect, Thomas."

Hawkins and Copper had reached them now, and the boy's face was alight. "It's really here!"

"Want to see if you can fit it to the console?" Elisabeth asked.

"You bet I do."

She handed it over – to Hawkins, who chuckled at Copper's sigh – but when they headed back to the ship his gait seemed excited enough.

Yet when Thomas began his own search of the docks, there seemed nothing much beyond the box-like rooms to be found. They faced the stretching rail at the air-dock and seemed to have nothing but bed frames within.

"Why don't you try one of the doors?" Elisabeth said. "Wouldn't hurt to have another airship or two."

"Good idea."

The wind pulled at his jacket and hair, which had grown a little longer than he preferred, as he neared Ethan and Mia. Both already stood before the enormous golden doors and their rigid, grid-like pattern. Did another airship truly lurk within? He gave one wing a push when he reached the doors, but it did not budge.

"Hmmm." He leant into it then and even tried to warm up his hands first, tried to get a sense of the metal before him but it did not seem to be iron, steel or Orichalcum. It was something else. Something flat or empty seeming, as though, even when he gave it a thump, *could* not resonate.

Would all hangers be the same?

Mia and Ethan joined him.

"It must be sealed by another force," Thomas said between breaths.

"Still more surprises for us, then," Ethan replied.

Thomas kept his voice low, even though no-one was all that close to them. "This is one of the locations on your map, isn't it? We flew northwest, right?"

"It has to be," Mia said. "But it still doesn't answer that many questions."

"The globe? Or the hangers – we might find another airship."

"That's one, yes," Ethan said. "I'm wondering, if the *Clara* had been set to dock here and Williams *did* manage to get it airborne, then that navigation device would have been lost to kingdom forces. Obviously not any other ships, I suppose, but it was probably a gamble, on Gatehouse's part."

"But if they assumed that allies would end up finding the globe instead, what of the sealed doors?" Thomas asked. "Even I can't open them."

Mia was nodding along. "It could be the Mist of Dawn, but we still don't know what it is. I wish I could ask Jean."

"You can't reach him at all anymore?"

"That might be true. Each time it takes longer and longer now that I can't access the *chromata*." She gestured to where she carried the skull in her pack. "I'll keep trying."

"I think we're going to have another problem soon too," Ethan said. "Once the cannon has been fitted to the *Clara*, the same arguments will rise about where to proceed next."

"Everyone will agree, surely? The next step is using the Thorn to cure everyone."

"But after that?"

Thomas leant against the door. "Well… selfishly, I want to take down Williams first. To find Silas. Other nations can wait, since we still don't know if we can trust them."

"Or the Queen and Aiden," Ethan added.

Mia exhaled. "Maybe so. And they might decide that using the Thorn is an easier way to destroy Williams, especially if it can shatter city walls. No real need to call in a foreign army then."

"Meaning, we're siding with Elisabeth if it comes to a stand-off?" Thomas asked.

They both hesitated.

"If it comes to that, we'll probably need her and Donovan," he added.

Ethan glanced at Mia, whose mouth was pursed. "If so, we need to be careful – especially you, Thomas."

"I know I protected her before but she knows who I'd choose to if it came down you and her."

"Sorry, Thomas," she said. "I didn't mean to doubt you."

"Then we've made a decision," Ethan said with a nod. "I just hope we don't have to act on it."

"I've been thinking about something else, you know," Mia said, facing away from them. "We haven't really talked about it yet, either. I know I haven't allowed myself... it's never seemed worthwhile."

"What do you mean?"

"Our future," Thomas answered first. "I understand." Her reluctance was a familiar, almost comfortable one. Why think about the future at all when everything was impossible? *But that's actually changed now.*

"Right."

Ethan drew Mia close. "I'll make it happen, Mia. Whatever you want it to be."

Thomas wanted to add his own voice, to put his arm around her shoulders... but maybe that wasn't his place anymore. *She has Ethan now, and he'll fight just as hard as I did, I know that.*

"A big promise," she said.

"It is."

She turned to where Thomas stood. "We never thought very far ahead but now... well, suddenly I feel like escape isn't enough. Maybe not unless I know the nation will be left in good hands."

"Then we have to make sure that the Queen has noble intentions," Thomas said. "It *seems* like she does but I don't know how we'd prove it."

Ethan snapped his fingers. "We unravel the secret that ties her to Aiden."

"Think that'll be enough?"

"It's a starting place," he replied. "Give me some time and I'll try to figure out a way to do it."

"All right, then." Thomas pushed himself from the door. "If we don't find anything else, I think I'm going to try Warrick. We could use something on his Father."

"What's your plan?" Mia asked. "No-one else had any luck."

He glanced back at the *Clara* and its graffiti like lingering cries of defiance beneath the bright sun. "I don't really know – he's fended off pretty much everyone by now."

She smiled. "Going in with confidence, then."

"Or at least stubbornness," he said with a chuckle.

Chapter 38.

Warrick sat against the wall of his cell in the dim light, a cup of water and empty plate nearby. Blessedly, his bucket had been emptied recently but the fellow's face was sour enough to taint the whole room.

"I'm still not going to betray my father," he grunted. His face was covered in cuts and bruises, one eye swollen. "No matter how many times any of you visit."

Thomas leant against the wall opposite, the thrum of the Orichalcum pleasant – especially after the strange emptiness from the hanger door. "So I hear."

So far, the King's son had been unfalteringly loyal. *Almost admirable.* No matter who came to speak, threaten, cajole or beat him, he did not offer anything beyond his own plans for escape. *Hard to know what to even try.*

Warrick glared across the small room. "Well?"

"Well what?"

The man snorted. "You think you can *annoy* me into talking?"

"We're talking now, aren't we?"

"About nothing."

"Then you're consistent," Thomas said. "But I've been remembering our past too."

"Pleasant memories, are they?" the prisoner said with a smirk, contorting his rat-face into an even less appealing picture. *It matches what's inside, which isn't always the case.*

"Not at all, but I'm going to replace them today."

"I'm too valuable to the others, Thomas."

He shrugged. "They'd forgive me in time, if there was an accident. I'm the only one who can work with the Orichalcum, after all."

Now Warrick shifted a little. "You won't do a single thing."

Thomas drew closer. "Remember when you shoved me into Lady Patrice's wedding cake before it was finished, down in the kitchens? I can't imagine that back then, you would have spent any time on this future."

"What do you mean?"

"That you lived in a comfortable little world without consequences, and that right now – now that you're about to experience some, you should be more afraid. The reason you *aren't* is because you don't have anything to compare. You don't actually know what a consequence is, do you?"

The man's jaw was clenched now. "I'm a valuable hostage."

"Are you?" Thomas said. "We all seem to remember someone else as the favourite in your family. Remember when you tried to shoot Elisabeth, not too long ago now, for saying something similar?"

"That's between me and the King," he said, leaning back against the wall with a shrug. "And you aren't saying anything Elisabeth and the Queen haven't already tried, slave."

"That's probably true." Thomas moved closer again – but only stared down at the King's son.

Warrick sneered. "I've struck a nerve, it seems."

Thomas sighed. There was only one thing left to do… his gift. "No, but I'm going to try that myself."

"What?"

He took a step back. How to use it exactly? A mistake would be costly. *Do I have enough control?* Warrick *was* a useful hostage, even if Williams had preferred Julian as a son, he'd react strongly enough. *After all, Warrick is probably like a piece of property to the bastard. He'll want 'it' back.*

"Out of ideas, Thomas? Give up like the others and leave me alone until you're ready to make your demands of my father and hand me over."

But Thomas did not answer.

Instead, he reached out to the steel cladding, to the flooring that surrounded Warrick and lifted. Rivets popped free, clinking across the room. Warrick flinched, but chained as he was, could not escape. "What are you doing?"

"Just going to wrap you up." Thomas eased the pressure and the slabs of steel began to curve more gently – it seemed they'd wrap around Warrick easily, but was that enough? Enough to *really* put some fear into the man?

"Hey!"

Thomas lifted his hands – best to mime what he wanted from the metal – and now, still slowly, everything moulded a little better. *It's actually working!* The steel was not quite becoming liquid, but mixed as it seemed to be with Orichalcum, it seemed more malleable and it settled upon Warrick quite nicely, like a close-fitting suit of armour.

Warrick let out a shriek.

Shouts from the guard echoed but Thomas flung a hand back with a twisting motion, and the entire door *and* frame bent out of shape enough to seal the room.

Thomas stalked closer, leaning down beside Warrick's face, which was now the only piece of visible skin – even the man's hair had been covered by steel. "Anything to say before you suffocate?"

The whites of Warrick's eyes were clouded by tears. "Yes! Get me out of here!"

"Then you'll talk?"

"I will, just please – please free me."

"Answers first," Thomas replied. "Starting with your father's forces. Does he have any other surprises like the Colossus?"

"No! You ruined the only completed one."

"Then what is his plan, without the *Clara*?"

Warrick's eyes were still wild. "He's been creating cannons, giant cannons. He calls them Ogre-cannons; they're probably big enough to take down an airship. One takes up half the Arena – please, I can barely breathe."

Thomas loosened the grip. "How many and where?"

"There's one in the palace too," he said, his voice losing its shrill edge.

"And they're both ready?"

"Yes."

"And if they fail, will he attempt to negotiate?"

"I don't know," he said.

Thomas narrowed his eyes.

"It's the truth! How would I know? He's probably mad enough to fight until the end. You know him."

"Sadly, I do." And Warrick's words *did* bear the ring of

truth. The King would shoot down the *Clara* and risk being unable to repair it – that was his style. To prevent others from having something he could not, as triumph was more important than the future. Thomas straightened, glancing down at Warrick as he let the steel ease, sliding back to its proper form – wall and floor. "Tell me something else."

"What?"

"Where were you hiding? Before."

He blinked, and it took a moment to answer. "What do you mean?" Warrick was frowning as he caught his breath. Then he shook his head, and it seemed his resistance was not defiance but confusion now. "We climbed after you."

"You saw us board the ship?"

"Yes." Again, there seemed to be no guile in the man's gaze. "We barely caught up to you in time; only the two of us from those who'd given chase actually made it aboard. None of us would have made it if it weren't for someone raising the alarm."

"A sentry?"

"Right. Why does it matter?"

"Just answer."

"Fine. It was a sentry. A new recruit, I suppose, since I didn't recognise him. He might have been from the garrison, since we don't wear that much red."

False memories and *a sentry in red... Nyath did help, after all.* "Fine. Whoever's after me, I hope you'll speak to them."

"I will."

"Good." Thomas returned to the door, where he shoved it back into shape – not the best job, and spoke to the wide-eyed guards. "He's alive. Sorry about the door, but we need to get everyone together; I have some news."

One of the soldiers ran ahead, while the other, Lawrence, went into the cell to give Warrick water. Thomas kept his own steady pace. The news from Warrick was serious enough. The size of the cannons alone... it certainly dwarfed anything on the Sand-Hog or the *Clara*.

He slowed. The *Clara* was tilting, nothing too strong, but it did seem that they were slowing too. *Have we reached the* Albion *already? How long was I in there with Warrick for?*

When Thomas started up the final ladder, he was already planning an infiltration of the Fortress. The C*lara* could be used to divert ground troops, allowing him to sneak in and destroy the so-called Orge-cannons. Then, Williams would be far more vulnerable and—

Gun fire echoed, close by.

Something's going on above and I'm down here again, damn it.

Thomas scrambled up the final rungs to fling the hatch open. It clanged against the decking, bouncing back but he shoved it aside again and leapt free, only to freeze, barely out of a crouch.

Aiden lay slumped over the rail, blood dripping through his fingers, face shadowed.

A second shot punched into his back.

The former Bruiser flinched and the movement was enough to send him slipping over the edge. He grasped after rail but his hands found nothing but air as he plummeted toward the ocean with a hoarse cry. The splash that eventually followed echoed in silence.

"And so vengeance is served."

Captain Hawkins stood nearby, revolver in hand, eyes ablaze.

Chapter 39.

"Hawkins?" Thomas stumbled as he rose. "What..."

"Don't worry, Thomas. That is all I required." He still stared after the bruiser.

All that remained was blood, dripping down the steel to add to the red pattern on the deck. The revolver clattered across the wood then, and Hawkins simply stood still, breathing calmly beneath the hum of the engines.

Calls from below neared – Elisabeth and the Queen burst up from below, followed by Felicity and one of Donovan's men. All held weapons ready but their bearing eased when they found the calm scene.

"Are we under attack?" the Queen asked, though her tone suggested she did not think it possible.

Hawkins shook his head. "We are not."

Thomas glanced between them, then met Elisabeth's gaze. Her frown of confusion had shifted as her eyes narrow, an instant wariness – she'd noticed the blood.

"Aiden was working on the cannons up here. Where is he?" the Queen demanded.

"Paying for his crimes."

Queen Marianne began to tremble; her own revolver shaking in her grip. "What did you say?"

"I'm telling you that he is dead," Hawkins snapped.

Colour drained from her cheeks.

Thomas leapt forward, but this time, the distance would be too great. The Queen's arm flashed up and even Elisabeth was not going to be fast enough.

But Felicity caught the Queen's wrist. "Please, My Lady."

The Queen was breathing hard. "No!"

"We need him; Copper can't pilot the *Clara* alone," Felicity said. "We've come so far."

"He must pay," the Queen ground the words out, eyes glistening with tears.

"Oh, spare me your tears," Hawkins roared. "Aiden was scum – responsible for murdering every single member of my crew! Every last one, do you hear? Every last one like a brother and he killed them all to get his grubby little hands on my ship."

She did not reply, and though her face did not reveal shock, she did seem conflicted as she continued to fight Felicity. But her maid's grip was like iron.

The Captain pointed a finger at the Queen. "And if you expect me to continue helping you, I'll have none of your false righteousness. Be sure to keep her away from me," the man said, then strode back to the cockpit, where the short figure of Copper watched with wide eyes.

Maryanne collapsed, sobs bursting free. Felicity crouched at her side, speaking softly, as Captain Donovan and several other soldiers arrived.

Thomas left to Elisabeth explain, instead following

Hawkins with a frown.

The loss of Aiden was... troubling from a logistical standpoint at the least, and certainly for more reasons. Someone else would have to command the *Albion* and lead its crew, since none would accept Hawkins. *The bruiser had known more about our past too.* He'd obviously been *very* important to the queen after all, and who could guess what impact his death would have on her in the long run.

But above all, how would Hawkins' revenge change those aboard the *Clara*?

The control room was quiet. Copper was making tiny adjustments to the thrusters, aligning the airship to hover above the *Albion*. Hawkins had already returned to his own seat at the wheel but he sat with his hands in his lap.

"I'm not sorry to see him go," Thomas said. "But everything could change now."

"He wasn't going to set foot on my ship ever again," the man replied without looking over his shoulder. "I promised myself I'd do at least that much for my men."

Thomas exhaled. "I'm going to put someone by your side – both to watch and protect you."

"I have what I wanted, Thomas. I'm not going to sabotage my own future; I need the *Clara* too. But I don't object to what you've said."

Thomas held back a retort. "Good."

Captain Donovan entered. "Lady Elisabeth seeks you, Thomas. Can I be of assistance here?"

"Yes. Please watch Hawkins for signs of any threat."

"From or against?"

"Both."

The Federation soldier nodded, even as he raised a hand.

"I will say that this is not a role I expected to take on."

"I didn't think we'd need you to do this, to be honest. But I suppose you can think of it as another way to safeguard the Federation's interests."

"Indeed."

Thomas joined Elisabeth where she paced outside. Neither the Queen nor Felicity were to be seen, only Jiro at the rail with a bucket and mop.

"Where the hell did he get that gun?" Elisabeth asked, still shaking her head.

"Who knows? It wouldn't have been difficult. And once Hawkins became as important as he is to the ship, I guess Aiden let his guard down."

Elisabeth came to a stop. "I sent Donovan to watch him – I assume you picked up on that?"

"I did. Do you think the Queen will retaliate?"

Elisabeth spread her hands. "Who can say? I didn't realise the full extent of their relationship. Seems clear that they were lovers. Perhaps she'll wait, like Hawkins did."

"Has Mia mentioned Hawkins' request?"

She nodded. "It might be for the best, once we're finished here."

"Should we gather everyone together? Explain what happened and remind everyone about our goals?"

Now Elisabeth chuckled. "Becoming quite the leader, aren't you?"

"Not by choice," he said with a smile.

"It's a good idea, in any event – we'll figure out a way to keep Hawkins out of it, and see if the Queen is ready," she said. "I'm sure it's far too soon, but leave that to me; you get ready to help with the Thorn. I'll send Felicity and

Lawrence to manage the *Albion's* crew. We can't have them staging a revenge attack."

"Can we keep it from them? What if they saw Aiden fall?"

"Hmmm. We have to deal with that somehow. It was the far side of the *Clara*, maybe it wasn't clear who or what fell?"

Thomas scratched at his stubble. "This could get out of hand."

"I know that – so be ready for anything," she replied.

"And do what?"

"I don't know, Thomas. Sink the *Albion* if you have to. Use your gift."

"What?"

"Nothing is more important than the *Clara* – you know that as well as I."

She was not precisely wrong... and yet, *if* such a thing were even possible, that didn't mean he wanted to drown an entire ship's crew. "I'm hoping you and Felicity can come up with something better than that."

"Just be ready in case we don't."

Thomas nodded as he turned to head below decks again, striding through circles of light from the portholes – she was right, he had to be ready but not having a plan... well, when Elisabeth decided to make things up on the fly, that usually meant he ended up getting shot.

Is our alliance going to hold together?

Common goals definitely still existed but there seemed a real chance that they'd be forgotten. Could the Queen set aside her grief and rage? Could the rest of the group fight off the threat of doubt? Aiden's body probably wouldn't be found but even without it, his death was going to hang over the *Clara* like a pall.

Chapter 40.

At last the work was complete; the grunts and cracking thump of rivet guns, their boilers puffing away, or the grinding of the huge wrenches and coordinating shouts, it had all faded and Thomas could release the Thorn of Souls.

Even with his gift, even 'charged' by the Orichalcum, helping to stabilise the massive cannon while everyone worked had his limbs burning – he barely made it to a nearby box to sit without his legs buckling. *We'll be in trouble if something happens and Elisabeth is still counting on me to use my gift.*

But whatever Felicity had told the *Albion*'s crew seemed to have worked. Did that mean she'd lied to them? Claimed Aiden was working on the airship for now? Had she described the falling body as someone or something else? After all, everyone would have been crowded around to stare at the *Clara* as it descended.

Yet none of the men and women seemed to be harbouring any ill-will and none who'd helped with the Thorn of Souls seemed to be concealing murderous rages either.

Could it be because Felicity and the Queen are planning something? Is everyone playing calm and waiting for their own time to strike?

He groaned. *Exactly what I was afraid of before. Paranoia.*

But if he began to doubt everyone at every turn, the whole gambit would fall apart and that couldn't happen. The *Clara* had to finish its flight. Better to believe everyone was still working together, to move forward as if it were true, while still watching... *That's just distrust again, you fool.*

By the time ladder returned to take him back up to the airship, someone working the winch above, Thomas could barely keep his eyes open. His responses once aboard the *Clara* again were vague but apparently the ones expected, and so when he finally collapsed upon the bed set off the cockpit, it was with a long sigh.

And when Ethan woke him hours later – it seemed an entire day or more had passed, since the airship flew bathed in silver light from a giant moon, not a single cloud in its path. "Think you're up to some more metal magic?" the man asked.

Thomas laughed as he rose – his limbs *were* feeling lighter now. "What do you have in mind?"

"The cannon's ready but no-one can actually test the trigger."

Thomas rose to follow Ethan through the cockpit, where Copper, Hawkins and Captain Donovan were still hard at work. "Gatehouse set things up so that only someone like me could use it?"

"Either that, or it was meant to be a mechanical process – we've had to improvise for now."

Ethan led him to the cabin at the prow, where Mia

waited before a large viewing window that rested within the floor. Was it diamond or some unusual glass too? It seemed that it had always been there, hidden beneath a sliding panel.

A shining lake waited far below – a deserted place somewhere within a mountain range.

"We're testing it here, just to be safe," Mia said, anticipating his question, then explaining that Copper had worked to connect the Thorn of Souls to the control panels. And while the lad had impressed as usual, there was a clear problem – from the pilot's room there was no way to see exactly where the cannon would fire. Not until the search turned up a second set of controls in the forward cannon room, where once again, the young engineer had poured over instructions from the library until he had everything working.

Except for one item; the large handle and trigger-piece that had been affixed to a panel on the wall. It bore an inscription, but the language was nothing Thomas recognised.

"We think this is the original device, but whether Gatehouse was interrupted before finishing it, or whether it was never intended for this room, I can't say."

"What about these dials?" Thomas asked, resting his hand on the wall beside the trigger.

"To aim. Horizontal and vertical. Push them down to activate."

He did so, and a modestly sized but bright red cross appeared in the centre of the viewing window. And when he turned each dial, the target moved. "Well, this could be easier than I thought." He aimed the cannon at the centre of the lake, switched to the trigger and nodded.

Ethan lifted the radio and checked in with Copper, who was busy arranging the thrusters to compensate for possible aftershock that could send them off course.

"We're ready, Thomas," Hawkins' voice crackled from the speaker.

"All right. Tell everyone to hold on to something, I guess."

Ethan repeated the warning, his voice echoing across the decks and no doubt below too.

Thomas took a breath, glancing at Mia, who had braced herself where she sat.

No instructions for the trigger itself; if he squeezed it, would one... lance of mist shoot forth? Was it going to spray in a cloud if he held it down?

"Thomas?" Mia asked.

"Sorry. Here we go." He squeezed – a little hard perhaps.

The *Clara* rocked and a bare second later, a gigantic fountain of water exploded up from the lake – crashing down across the treetops in a beautiful but terrifying display.

"I almost emptied half the lake," he breathed.

Proving that a test-run was important indeed.

"What happened?" Hawkins called from the speaker.

"It worked," Ethan replied. "The cannon seems *extremely* strong. Too strong – I don't know how we can use this to cure people."

"Hold on," Thomas said with a groan. There was a switch on the handle. "I missed something."

"What?"

"There's a switch here. Maybe it's a second function?"

"Find out," Mia said.

"Right." He flicked it over as Ethan gave another warning over the speakers and then Thomas squeezed the trigger again. This time, the resistance was serious, even with his gift.

But he *did* move it, and below the still settling lake had not exploded again.

"Thomas?" A new voice crackled on the radio – Jiro from the boiler room. "The mist gauge for the Thorn is moving pretty quickly now."

He released the trigger.

"How much is left?" Ethan asked.

"More than enough, I think... maybe the cannon was built for a much larger population?"

Thomas nodded. "Where to first?"

"We're probably closest to the north western nomadics," Mia replied. "But anywhere is good, so long as we leave Birnhale until last."

"Think you're both ready for that?" Ethan asked after a moment's silence.

"I don't know," Thomas replied, leaning against the wall. "I don't want to count on getting answers – who knows if Silas even lives?"

Mia adjusted her blindfold. "We have to deal with Williams first either way. And it won't be as simple as destroying the walls on the way in, surely. He'll know we won't want to crush innocents in the rubble, he'll know we want to speak to Silas."

"Any feelings?" Thomas asked.

"Nothing yet."

"What about Nyath?"

She shook her head. "Nothing from him either. Maybe getting Warrick aboard was some final gambit?" Her tone grew firm. "I won't let him interfere again."

Ethan set the mouthpiece down. "What about 'pale purple hair'? The threat Jemima mentioned?"

"What's this?" Thomas asked, unable to prevent a frown as Mia explained. "You think it could be connected?"

"There's a chance, I suppose."

"We're going to have to sneak in at one point, aren't we?" Thomas asked.

"If so, it might be worth bringing the Queen along," Ethan said. "And we need to find out a way to safeguard the *Clara* from both enemies beyond, and the desires of those who might remain aboard."

Once again, a quiet fell across the room.

"Is there a chance Williams could be convinced to surrender? If we threaten something he actually holds dear?" Mia asked.

"I assume you're not thinking of Queen Maryanne there?" Ethan asked. "Or Warrick."

"No. I meant his arena or workshops... but they're in the Fortress, along with a lot of innocents. It's the same problem."

"He sought me as a pilot but the Colossus is finished," Thomas said. "You, he wanted to pass down your gift."

"Then, should we offer some sort of false negotiation?" Ethan asked.

Mia frowned. "Maybe. Let me think – if I could reach Jean, that might help somehow. I don't know."

Thomas placed a hand on her shoulder. "Well, you've got some time while we spread the mist, at least."

Chapter 41.

Thomas eased the pressure on the Thorn's trigger as the *Clara* strafed the river system and bright mangroves above the Drinking Village, north of Birnhale. The mist fell across the isolated homes and the water alike, faint glittering of orange gold difficult to see through the window. This time, no-one came to point and shout as they had in other places over the days since the successful test.

Now, the grey pall that hung over Birnhale was not so far, the *Clara* would soon reach and pass over Saint's Bridge, and then it was time to strike.

It had already been decided that 'cleansing' the city would come first but without a rainstorm from which to work an advantage, the *Clara* would be vulnerable to the giant cannons. Elisabeth seemed convinced of taking at least one of them out with the Thorn of Souls, but that would still leave them vulnerable to the second.

A problem no-one had yet been able to solve.

Implying that someone would have to abandon the

relative safety of the airship and infiltrate the Fortress, not just to take out the second cannon and deal with Williams, but to locate Silas and to free other prisoners.

Not a simple task – and one reason using at least one sort of diversion remained a popular idea.

But there were so few options. *Even with Wilkins out there, we wouldn't be able to draw most of the troops away.*

But when Thomas returned to the dining hall to meet with Elisabeth, the now stoic Queen, Ethan and Mia, it was to a new idea.

"There is one obvious place we might have overlooked," Queen Marianne said. "The Arcana Mine."

"Of course," Elisabeth said. "Williams would have to respond."

"Hard to outfit a conquering army without steel, right?" Ethan said with a grin.

Mia straightened. "Tell him not to pass the Pigeon's Watering Hole."

"You've seen something?" the Queen asked.

"No. But I know that way spells disaster," she said, and raised a hand. "There's something hidden there... I can't be sure what it is. But I do see something in the city. It's a seamstress with a crimson gown in the window."

"Can you describe anything else?" Ethan asked as he leant closer.

"Maybe... an older man wearing glasses."

He snapped his fingers. "It's Francis; it has to be,"

"Who is that?" the Queen asked.

"A funnel Silas used to send me funds," Ethan said. "Maybe he can lead us to Silas or offer a way to infiltrate the Fortress."

Mia shook her head. "I don't know one way or another yet... but he's important."

"What of other nations?" the Queen asked. "Is it too late to seek their aid?"

"I sense nothing about them," she replied.

"Shouldn't we strike while momentum is in our favour?" Thomas asked.

Elisabeth nodded. "Agreed. Wilkins can reach the mine by evening if we send word."

"How long before we can strike the arena?" Ethan asked.

"If Thomas fires, any time," Elisabeth said. "What did Copper say about the new firing machine?"

"It's due to be completed before midnight."

Thomas rested his elbows on the table. "Then all that's left to decide is who goes where, right?"

No one spoke at first, only the sounds of boiling water from the stoves and their pale blue flames.

"I think nearly all of us want to get down there," Ethan said. "But we might need two or even three groups."

"Two for the city and one here? Or do you have something else in mind?" Elisabeth asked him. "I don't think Wilkins would need any further support."

"One to safeguard the airship and two for the city – we need to deal with the second cannon before it threatens the *Clara*, if we want to use her to threaten Williams. The other group will infiltrate the palace itself if the sabotage group is held up," he suggested. "That's if we want to attempt something basically simultaneous, to cause as much confusion as possible."

"Or we form one larger group below," Mia said. "We won't be able to empty the city of soldiers so a small party might be vulnerable."

When no-one objected, Thomas rose. "Who's coming with me, then?"

Another moment of silence. *No-one's willing to make a suggestion – Hawkins has definitely sown seeds of doubt.* If anyone suggested that another stay behind, or urged them to take part in the infiltration, it would be impossible not to read some underhanded motive into it. *And be honest, you're not sure what the Queen will do if she's left alone on the ship.*

"Ethan and I will accompany Thomas," Mia said. "Give us Jiro, Felicity and someone from Donovan's force and we will succeed."

The Queen straightened; she did not seem too pleased. "Is that what you have seen? Or what you suggest?"

"It is what I've seen."

Elisabeth sighed. "Fine with me."

Thomas glanced at her – she leant back in her seat, appearing no more concerned than usual. *I thought she'd fight for a chance to get at Williams personally.* But what seemed best about Mia's words, was that a potentially difficult situation *upon* the airship was also managed.

With the Queen, Elisabeth, Hawkins and Donovan, everyone who had a potentially conflicting stake in the airship was countered by the other. And no-one had too many 'more' supporting troops on hand, since Mia would be taking some below.

Queen Marianne motioned Felicity closer. "What do you say?"

"I will do as you order, Your Majesty."

"Then, I agree. We will destroy the cannon in the arena while you strike the one within the palace," the Queen said as she stood. "Let's prepare, then."

Thomas started from the room with a little spring to his step. Not only was he able to keep Mia close by, but they were finally striking back at Williams; Williams who had hounded them for so long.

And more, Silas would finally have to provide some answers.

He moved to Mia as the Queen motioned to Ethan, but Elisabeth appeared at Thomas' side. "Thomas, I have a request. Outside, though."

He followed her through the cockpit, onto the decks and into the soothing moonlight. "I think I can guess."

"Oh?" Her eyes were narrowed now, but she was not 'out of control' by any stretch. "Do so."

"It's about Williams. You want to come with us but you want to keep an eye on the Queen more."

She folded her arms. "I don't know about 'more' but since I'm not heading down there, I want you to promise me something."

"What?"

Elisabeth took his face in her gloved hands. "Promise you won't leave the city until Williams is dead. No matter what anyone else says; kill him at all costs, Thomas."

"I..."

"Do that and you can ask anything of me."

He caught her hands. "I have no love for him. None, he is a fetid stain on our nation, you know that I feel that way. But as much as anything, I'm returning for answers from Silas. I might have to choose between–"

"Take both, Thomas, or I will make sure."

Thomas frowned. "How?"

"I will level the Fortress."

"What if we're trapped down there?" He hesitated – the next question could be too revealing. "What if *I'm* in there?"

She released him and her expression was unreadable. "Kill the King and you won't ever have to find out."

Chapter 42.

Mia followed Ethan, his grip firm; the heavier tread of Thomas close behind as they passed through the quiet streets of Birnhale, sticking to the shadowy back alleys for the most part.

Lamps and warm glows from the windows of late-night bars provided stark contrast from the side streets, enough that it seemed a busy night. *Probably because they don't know what's lurking above them – or at least, not until we give the signal.*

"We're close now," Ethan said as they paused before the mouth of the alley, where the sweet scent of flowers lingered from somewhere.

"Give me a sense of the city," she said. "We haven't had to hide much – are there many soldiers?"

"Not really," he said. "Plenty of drunks and a few powder-rats but I've only seen a few pairs – they're usually inside, drinking. That first time they were breaking up a fight."

"Can we assume that numbers are thinning down here because of Wilkins?" Thomas asked.

"I'm hoping so."

Mia pulled Ethan back as he started forward again. "What about the hair? Seen anyone like that yet?"

"Nothing."

"All right." Together they moved forward and now she gripped his hand a little harder; the tension was growing again as she followed.

"I'm watching too," Thomas said.

She nodded.

But when they came to a halt once more, she still had a good grip on Ethan. *Why have we stopped? Have we arrived? Is it Williams' men? Something worse?* She clenched her jaw. *Calm down!* Being unable to see properly... things weren't getting easier.

"That's Francis' shop over there," Ethan said, giving her hand a quick pat. "Now we just need to wait for the others."

"Think they succeeded?" Thomas asked.

"Jiro and David certainly look the part," he said.

Mia settled against the wall of whatever shop or home sat nearby. At least the street was quiet; a single steam car rumbled along from somewhere but was not nearing. *I still don't want a long wait here, come on.* Whether Felicity and the others had been able to locate the exact location of the second Ogre-cannon was not vital, since Thomas would be able to sense it easily; he'd already mentioned the one in the arena being like a crushing wave within a city overflowing with steel, but any scouting they could do was important.

Guard numbers, positions and rotations, the gate, the streets near the Fortress and most of all, any possible hint that Williams was up to something else.

"What's the plan inside?" Thomas was asking Ethan. "I

don't remember our tailor friend being all that helpful."

"He won't want to be revealed as a funnel, so we should be able to blackmail him easily enough."

Footsteps approached.

"It's them," Ethan said.

"Not much to report," Felicity said. "It doesn't seem like much is going on beyond those giant cannons. The one inside is where the barracks used to be and there are still plenty of troops left. Once the arena is hit, we'll have less people inside, but by then we'll be inside ourselves," she finished with a shrug.

"Let's see what Francis can offer," Ethan said.

Mia followed him across the street and paused when he did. After a moment, a lock clicked open and Ethan led her into darkness, where the scent of dusty floorboards and... something unpleasant lurked.

"Jiro, take Felicity and David out back and upstairs," Ethan said. "Wake Francis and bring him down if he's home – I want to check on that smell from the workshop."

"Right."

"Be careful."

"We will," Felicity said and the sound of a revolver clicking followed her words.

A door squeaked and Thomas murmured.

"What is it?"

"Too dark to tell, but the smell is worse here – it's blood and maybe worse."

Fabric rustled as Ethan knelt to light their lamp. Once he'd lifted it, Mia moved forward to join Thomas, one hand outstretched to gauge the counter. She wrinkled her nose at the door.

There was a dead body within, no doubts lay in her mind.

And it was important to know who. There was a... trail to be found; that much her gift was telling her.

"It's Francis," Ethan said next, and his voice was a little shaky.

"Who would do *that*?" Thomas breathed.

"Tell me," Mia said.

"I'll spare you some details," Ethan said, "but it's troubling also because it's either something *very* personal for the killer, or someone utterly unhinged and I don't know how that changes things for us."

"All right."

"To put it crudely; he's been transformed into a pin-cushion," Ethan said, voice heavy. "I... there's not a needle or pair of scissors that haven't been used. Mostly his torso, but his eyes and ears too. He's sitting in a chair that's black with blood... do you need any more?"

Mia swallowed. "Maybe. The killer might lead us into the Fortress."

"Using the same path Silas smuggled drugs *out*?" Ethan asked. "As we hoped?"

"That's what I'm sensing... but I don't know if we can find it without some other clue."

"I'll check on the others upstairs," Thomas said. "Anything I should look for?"

She straightened. "Actually, yes. Now that I'm here... A blue crane." *Feels good to know that my gift is still working, even if I can no longer reach the* chromata.

"Like, embroidery?"

"It could be."

"On my way," he said as he left.

"Ethan, what about the rest of the room?" Mia asked.

The light shifted as he lifted it higher, then moved across the workshop, his silhouette one among several. Many of them seemed to be torsos on stands, or maybe ball-gowns and racks?

"Here," Ethan said.

"What is it?"

"Star-dust. Smeared all over the place." He returned with the light. "It's on the handles of the scissors too."

"Then, was his murder about drugs only?"

Ethan did not answer at first. "I think I know how we can find out."

Chapter 43.

Ethan was pacing, passing back and forth before the lamps where they'd gathered downstairs, having closed off the room containing Francis' body.

Mia shifted where she sat, rolling her shoulders and stamping a foot.

The waiting was sapping her alertness but it couldn't be rushed. Jiro and David were out trying to round up Ethan's contact, Boots; the kid was probably working the harbour. That was their first, and probably most direct lead to follow when it came to hunting down Lina. The star-dust dealer was the obvious possibility for the murderer, since she'd worked with Francis and had been a powder-rat herself for a long time.

The question is, did she want to cut out a middleman, and has she been to the palace already to find Silas?

There was no guarantee that Lina was involved at all.

And speculating on her purpose... it was probably better to find Lina in case she was the killer and now knew of a secret entrance or path into the Fortress. *Especially since the blue crane hasn't revealed its secrets.*

But it was important; that much her gift made clear.

"Thomas, can you describe what you found again?" she asked.

"The ransacking upstairs?"

"Sorry, just the blanket."

His outline changed as he lifted the small piece – perhaps for a babe – though no evidence of children had been found. "It's beautifully made, and it is a blue bird but it looks more like a sparrow than a crane to me. Anything new come to mind?"

Mia shook her head. "No. Just keep it on you, for now."

"I will."

Footfalls approached the shop. "Found him," Jiro announced from just outside. He and David seemed to carry someone between them, though it was not a struggle.

"Hello, Ethan," a cheerful voice said. "Welcome back to the city."

"Where is Lina, Boots?"

"She left for the palace a few days ago. No-one's heard from her since."

"And she did this?" Ethan said, no doubt referring to Francis.

"She did." Some of the cheer had left his voice now. "She's become a real greedy bitch. That's what did it, I think."

"How did she get inside?"

"No idea."

Ethan moved closer to the boy. "You have some idea, right?"

"Well… not really. I thought you'd know, yourself. Didn't the old guy tell you?"

"You don't believe he was that stupid. Tell me *something*, Boots – whatever you're hiding; I'll make it worth your while."

"Ah, I know that she took her two thugs with her to the smelters."

"Really?"

"Yes," he replied. "That all you need?"

"For now," Ethan said. "Go to the Little Bear Fountain – there's a loose stone in the rear. Take what you find within."

"Really?"

"Yes. And when you see fire in the sky, take shelter."

"Ah... what does that mean exactly?"

"Exactly what I said," Ethan replied. "Off you go."

"Thanks, Ethan." The sound of two smaller boots touching down preceded the sound of swift but not panicked flight.

"We'd better check it out then," Ethan said. "I think I have an idea of what to expect, actually."

***

Yet when they arrived, it turned out that no-one actually needed to enter the still-operating smelter at all – Ethan took her arm where they stood in an alleyway across the street. "I see a blue crane."

"Where?"

"It's one of the waste carts from the palace," he said. "Malcolm and Sons Sort and Disposal."

"Then Silas sent the powder out disguised as rubbish and Francis had someone collect it from here?" Thomas asked.

"So it would seem."

"What about this Lina, and our path now?" Felicity asked.

Her voice carried a hint of excitement. "What if we hijacked two of the carts?"

"We could fill one with gunpowder," Mia said. "Use it to create another diversion once we're inside."

"That would help," Thomas said. "We still don't know how many soldiers have left the city to confront Williams, or how many will rush to the arena."

"Let's see if we can borrow a car or two, then," Ethan replied.

"How do we convince Malcom and his sons?" Thomas asked.

A pause. "I'll borrow David's uniform, minus the red goggles, and take Jiro there. We'll tell them something about needing the cars for the attack on the mine."

"Is the attack public knowledge?" Mia asked.

"Good question," he replied. "If not, 'Lord Pryor' will threaten them."

"And if that fails?" Felicity asked.

"I'll think of a third thing," he said. "Or maybe Thomas will distract them with his power?"

"I could manage that."

"Perfect."

Once the clothing had been exchanged, Mia turned to Thomas's larger silhouette. "Can you describe for me, Thomas?"

"I will."

"Do we intervene if they're attacked?" Felicity asked. "I have my magnifier rifle if nothing else."

"I can probably overturn most of those cars if we get any sort of signal," Thomas said. When he next spoke, it was to describe the meeting. "They've hailed someone wearing the grey and blue disposal uniform… they're talking. No-one seems tense – whatever Ethan's saying seems to be working, the fellow is nodding."

"What about the others?" Mia asked. *This is harder than I thought it would be.* Whatever apprehension anyone else might have been feeling, it seemed she was drawing it all in as her muscles tightened.

"They're just loading and unloading at the rear of the smelter while others are sorting through the cast-off objects and the trash," Thomas said. "Some pieces go to an armed guard but he doesn't seem too interested in Ethan or Jiro."

"It's working," Felicity added.

"They're taking them to one of the empty cars," Thomas said. "And sending Jiro to a second. Ethan's climbing into the driver's seat; it worked, they're being waved from the lot."

"Good." Mia let her shoulders slump a little and there was an extra release – her gift seemed to be urging her too. The blue crane was going to grant them easy access to the Fortress.

It left the mysterious pale, purple lock of hair to be resolved, but for now at least, they were on the right path.

Chapter 44.

Thomas drove along shadowed streets, the pools of lamplight narrower but brighter than he recalled as he neared the Fortress Gates at a steady pace. Felicity and Jiro remained concealed within the rear of the mostly empty wagon-part of the car. As they passed each gate, the light gleamed on the Orichalcum bracelets he wore on each wrist, lending him strength and obscuring his tattoos.

He called back to them. "Everything ready?"

"It is," Felicity replied. "We've arranged the powder so that there shouldn't be any need for a direct hit."

"How about the bow strings? And the oil?"

"Still fine, Thomas," Jiro said. "We have rifles too."

"Not sure bullets always cause sparks," Felicity said.

Thomas diverted around a snoring drunk who lay sprawled in the quiet street. "I suppose Ethan and Mia have their own too."

"You're worrying too much," Felicity said, her voice not unkind.

"Maybe I am," he said. *And it's hard not to; I just hope*

Mia's going to be fine. She and Ethan, their own steam-wagon following close behind, and were in charge of both signalling to the *Clara* with their own burning arrows and clearing a path for Thomas to strike at the Ogre-cannon. *Which should keep them out of direct danger.*

As for the Ogre-cannon, its location was fairly exposed but at least it was close to the walls.

"I've been thinking more about our escape," Jiro said. "We'll be pretty exposed on that ladder when we try to get back up to the airship."

"Didn't Ethan suggest using the uniform trick again?" Felicity said.

"He did but what if that only gets us out of the palace and not the city? We're going to destroy at least one of these cars, and we don't know what will happen with the other."

"We can hide underground if need be," Felicity said.

Thomas waved a group of slaves to cross before him, their expressions listless as they hauled hand-carts laden with fruit. Behind them, an overseer kept a close watch with his rifle. *Too bad I can't ram him.* "Underground?"

"Her Majesty told me of several sites we can use in the city."

"We'll take it," Thomas said as he continued on, the hiss of the boiler rising as he pulled the lever to accelerate. "Jiro, can you signal to Ethan? We're close enough now."

"Can do."

The walls around the Fortress blocked much of the light from the palace and grounds but there a bright pool surrounded the towering gate itself, revealing heavily armed soldiers. A dozen rifles and twin-shots gleaming. Anyone approaching would also be clearly visible to guards in the towers, and though they themselves were concealed, the thin sense of their weapons remained obvious. *To me at least.*

As was the almost painful buzzing from the Ogre-cannon.

Similar to the sense of the Sand-Hog, the power of it poured from the right – the direction of the barracks, confirming the information Boots had offered.

Which means breaking in and charging there immediately.

But no matter how swift, the palace would respond to the threat. The question was, in what numbers? How many troops would have left to face the threat from Sergeant Wilkins? *They have to respond; there's no way Williams would give up access.* But nor would the old monster leave his own Fortress undefended.

What I need is a way to protect everyone while I attack the cannon. Giving them a chance to fire the signal was just as important.

"They've noticed us by now," Felicity said, a note of urgency in her voice.

"Take the wheel," Thomas said.

"What?"

"I need to concentrate – I think I can do better than just blasting the gates open."

Felicity dropped her rifle and reached across him to take the wheel. "Got it."

Thomas let his senses quest forth, opening up to the riot of metals surrounding him, that he'd been dampening as a matter of habit, blocking the clean scent of Felicity's hair so he could narrow in on the gates.

The soldiers were shouting, demanding a halt, some with weapons raised but Thomas waved his hands apart and tossed the weapons aside. Half the guards went clattering across the streets, thrown by the force of his gift.

Next came the gates.

One should be enough?

Careful not to jostle Felicity's grip on the wheel, he mimed a punch. One half of the gate flew off its hinges in a shower of stone. Shouts rose from the remaining soldiers as they fled, and cries echoed from above too.

Thomas caught those rifles and twisted each with a flick of his wrist before gripping the other gate and lifting.

It snapped free and hung in the air a moment as they bore down on the entry. He mimed a folding motion and created a huge wedge, one large enough to serve as a giant shield. "Stay within its protection," Thomas shouted over alarms that echoed across the palace grounds.

The effort of holding up the gate wasn't too much... yet.

"Slow us down," Felicity said, her eyes a little wide as she steered.

Thomas used his elbow to ease the lever and Felicity took them into shelter cast by the floating barrier.

Even with plenty of lamplight, the palace grounds were not clear beyond the folded gate. As they headed east, Felicity hugging the wall to make room for the flying gate, only glimpses of the palace walls, stone or glowing glass, were visible.

The occasional crack and ringing would follow the sound of gunfire but it did not last. *It's working.* Jiro did occasionally return fire, from rear pursuit, but Thomas was able to shield them from the vast majority of the still sporadic counter-attack.

Shock was doing its job.

The car thumped onto grass now, slowing a little. Thomas

nudged the lever again to compensate as they neared the barracks.

Or would have, if the buildings remained.

But ahead, caught in glimpses as he juggled the gate in and out of position, Thomas saw an open space dominated by a monstrous cannon-platform. The barracks were gone, even the outbuildings where he'd sometimes hide from nobles as a kid, lamps now lit only the weapon.

Stone crunched and glass shattered as the gate swung closer, but Thomas kept a firm grip. The Orichalcum felt warm against his skin. *I'm drawing a lot from it already.*

"What was that?" Jiro called.

Rubble was already falling by the wayside. "I think we clipped the palace itself."

"I don't see that many guards," Felicity said.

"They must have been relocated when Williams installed that thing," Thomas said.

She glanced at him with a grin. "Looks like you've got a clear shot – you tired yet?"

"So far, so good."

"I just had an idea about our eventual escape," she said. "I'm going to turn around so we're facing the wall."

"You want to use the gunpowder?"

"In case you don't have enough strength to smash through with the gate," she said. "I don't think I really understood what you could do, you know. Seeing this..." she turned the wheel.

"Ethan's signalling to us," Jiro shouted.

"Wave him closer if he can," Thomas replied.

Felicity slowed the steam car now, bringing it to a halt but not cutting the boiler, leaving it facing the Fortress wall and half-concealed by both the Ogre-cannon and the gate.

Thomas stepped free and swung the giant hunk of steel around to protect one flank, letting it strike the ground with a boom. Ethan and Mia were already approaching.

"What's the plan?" the rebel-leader asked, and his own eyes were alight with a little excitement. Mia had her head tilted, as though listening.

"Fire the signal shots," Thomas said. "I'm going to deal with the air-cannon and then Felicity wants us to blow a hole in the wall as an escape path, if we need it."

"Perfect," he said. "But let's take things a little further. What do you think of this? Crush the cannon and blow the wall but make the opening wide enough for a steam-car. Jiro, you lead anyone who follows away while we four hide in the rubble and wait for a chance to continue on."

"I'll do my best."

Shouts and whistles were growing near now.

"Hurry," Thomas said as he drove the gate deeper into the earth, enough to stand as cover on its own, then charged around the edge.

The air-cannon was like a two-storey inn and from the look of the twin platforms on the base, able to swivel to fire from more than one angle. The rough, unfinished surface was dull beneath the torchlight, befitting its name perhaps. Rungs climbed to the top where a gunner's dome waited... it seemed to bear a faint gleam of glass but had been concealed beneath a thick grate, like steel saplings.

Can I actually smash this thing?

It was going to be like striking the Sand-Hog.

Shots rang out. Bullets thudded into the earth nearby, but he ran harder, flinging an arm back. "Come on."

Thomas leapt the final paces and swung.

His fist crashed into the base. A jagged split ran up and along the body of the weapon. *More.* Thomas swung an overhand blow now, slamming down hard enough to buckle the plate, driving it into the earth. *Enough to jam up its movement, I hope.*

Then he leapt up and climbed the ladder, hands a blur.

Something bounced from his back as he worked – more bullets? The pain was fleeting and he did not stop. When he leapt onto the walkway that ringed the dome, he didn't bother seeking an entry; instead, Thomas kicked his way inside with a shower of glass, leaving behind twisted steel.

Something lit the sky, only half-realised from behind his eye, hopefully the signal.

But he was crashing his way through the square control panels, a huge lever and twin wheels and their handles next – leaving only the cannon itself to destroy.

Thomas paused to catch his breath, glancing at the bracelets which almost sang in time with his raging pulse. *I'm not slowing down.* He smashed through the dome again, and leapt onto the shaft where he quickly rubbed his hands together a moment. Heat built quickly, far swifter than usual, and so he knelt and plunged his hands into the steel.

Yet he did not find the inner tube – it was several feet of metal that he had to almost dig through. Sweat formed but he did not slow; he had to render the Orgre-cannon useless. The *Clara* would be on the move and below, Mia and the other could already be under threat.

He glanced over the side as he worked.

More gunfire rising from below, but it did not stray near – he was obviously a harder target in the shadows, and concealed by the cannon itself. Troops were approaching the enormous gate, some with portable cannons, others with steam-cars but none were so close to threaten Mia and the others. Yet.

She and Ethan had already sent the loaded car toward the wall, using his own car as cover, Felicity and Jiro watching from either end of their shelter.

Thomas tore at the cannon's shaft with a new frenzy.

While Williams' men were approaching slowly, no doubt unsure of exactly what Thomas could do, they would encircle everyone before long.

He tore deeper into the cannon, flinging hunks and shards of steel aside now, some so hard that they smashed into the palace walls.

Creaking came from below.

Thomas tore free more strips, widening the gaping cavity he'd made until the cannon's nose began to dip. Then he stood back and spun. *There.* A slab of the console would be enough. He stepped inside and lifted it free, wrestling it outside, then swung it like a hammer.

The crash hurt his ears but it worked.

The nose of the Ogre-cannon shuddered down with a groan, falling to the sound of cries from below. The shaft crashed into the ground with a boom, scattering cobbles and huge clumps of dirt alike.

Thomas let out a shout of triumph.

But a second cacophony roared across the sky, burying his own cry, and strong enough to buffet him where he stood.

Thomas spun.

The *Clara* blackened the moon and half the night sky – or so it seemed from his vantage – where it hovered above the city like an avenging cloud of darkness. Below, the towering walls of the Arena were now smoking piles of rubble.

He exhaled.

The area around the arena didn't seem *too* damaged... so hopefully no innocents had been hurt, and it was hard to be sure in the dark, but it was heartening to see that the Thorn of Souls could be fired with precision.

Now all we have to do is deal with Williams – before Elisabeth loses her patience.

Chapter 45.

Hiding within the cold steel wreckage of the Ogre-cannon had not been unnerving – in fact, Mia found herself fighting off the urge to tap a foot while guards organised their search-party, chasing after Jiro in his steam-car.

And nor did she feel so concerned after as Ethan had led her into the palace, a firm grip on her hand, everyone whispering directions as their footfalls landed on marble floors, muted echoes whenever they were forced to run.

Familiar scents of musty tapestries and plants – sleeping now, no doubt, their flowers closed. And somehow, it was worse than a clammy hand upon her shoulder, or the slime of the sewers against her bare skin. *I'm not going to need that memory soon.*

Above all, it might have been the door they'd stopped before.

It led to William's workshop – Ethan had not bothered with the throne room or any 'royal' chamber, Mia *knew* where he'd be. And it didn't matter what Williams had; the old prick was out of tricks now.

There was only one surprise left – the purple lock of hair.

Soft footfalls approached.

"Felicity," Ethan said softly.

She was returning after having set a false trail for pursuit. Whether it would work completely was unlikely, but any delay would be useful, even with all the chaos beyond the walls. So far, it still seemed to be pulling away soldiers, but that didn't mean the Fortress was completely unguarded.

Yet the room beyond contained... not danger, but something unknown.

Mia straightened. "It's safe to enter."

"Perfect," Thomas said.

No-one greeted them when the door swung open on silent hinges, revealing an equally quiet room. The only light seemed to be that which Ethan carried, but two sounds caught her attention.

Ticking.

Two clocks, one further away, a deeper sound. The sharp scent of steel, oil and something else... apple? Old apples? The cores? *It's like he hasn't finished eating before setting them aside to turn.* Something was gritty beneath her feet, metal shavings and tiny screws?

"Are we alone?" Mia asked.

"So far," Thomas said. "The workbenches are all empty... there's a door to the back but I don't remember ever using it, even when we delivered trays here."

"On we go then," Ethan said.

She followed him with one hand on his shoulder as they wove between benches, which she imagined were covered in cogs, tools and springs. It did not take long for him to come to a halt again, then he called for Thomas. "Would you do the honours?"

"Right." The sound of snapping steel followed. "Just a dark passage."

"Felicity, can you close up behind us?" Ethan asked.

"It's not perfect but looks closed, at least."

Light seemed to grow as the sense of walls narrowing surrounded Mia as she walked on. "Any webs?" she asked after a time.

"None," Ethan replied. "Williams must use this passage pretty often... or maybe I should say, 'passages'. There's a three-way intersection."

"Left," Mia said after a moment. To the right, the corridor led to his bedchamber and the centre to a network of other passages, eventually exiting the fortress but to the left waited Williams himself.

I can actually sense him – like a waiting poison, rotting from his soul.

And something else. The unknown thing. Something very clearly important, very present in the room they sought, but which... confounded her gift.

"I sense Orichalcum there too," Thomas added.

"Left it is, then," Ethan said.

This passage was far longer but just as unobstructed – the only time Mia had to stop was when Felicity hissed a warning from her position of rear guard. "I hear footsteps – a lot of them."

Faint thunder drew near. From within a nearby passage? Or the palace hallways? Mia reached for the revolver she carried, even though a better choice might have been trying to summon the Bird of Light. *Maybe.* Softly, she started to hum, just in case...

The crowd was loud enough to believe they were just a few feet away, separated by the stone wall.

And then they began to fade.

"Let's keep moving," Thomas said. "Hopefully they're on their way outside."

Once again, Mia kept pace by resting one hand on Ethan's shoulder, the glow of light bright through her blindfold. With each step the sense of the unknown... thing, grew. And it wasn't the threat of the lock of pale purple hair either.

It remained nothing she could fathom.

Or – more concerning, again – it seemed to be nothing her *gift* could fathom. Nothing like this had ever happened. She'd been unable to sense certain specifics, or she'd been unable to sense anything at all, plenty of times in the past.

But nothing had been so... blank. *Thomas feels Orichalcum there but I haven't reacted like this to the* Clara *or at any time in Alita's Shell, so it's something else.* She frowned. *Maybe something to do with Nyath? Is my gift linked to the chromata after all?*

"This is interesting," Ethan said.

Mia blinked. "What?"

"There used to be a door here." He paused. "Actually, several of them. Maybe a dozen. But they've been cut through."

"Who was keeping who out of where?" Felicity asked.

"This last one is Orichalcum too," Ethan added.

Thomas had drawn nearer, and now placed a hand on her own shoulder. "There's more farther along."

"What's it mean?" she asked.

"I don't know. And... now that I'm this close it's not quite the same. There's something more to it."

"You sound worried," Mia said.

"Maybe."

"We still have the advantage of surprise here," Felicity reminded everyone.

"Let's use it then," Ethan said and set off once more, yet he had not travelled so far before coming to a halt once more. "Voices."

Mia froze. Muffled as though from beyond a door, and over the breathing of the others, she heard the familiar rough voice of 'King' Williams. He was shouting in what seemed like frustration as much as his usual rage.

"It has to be now – you've had weeks to figure this out; there must be a way!"

"We're trying, Your Majesty," one voice replied, an older man too, by the rasp. "There is only one final element that eludes us."

Footsteps stomped across stone. "Work faster! They've already infiltrated the Fortress. I need whatever he's hiding in there."

"Yes."

Ethan lowered his voice. "This is our moment, everyone. Ready?"

Chapter 46.

Thomas lifted a leg and paused before the steel door, a tingling spreading through his body. *Is that actually excitement? Idiot.* There was a little, but so many unknowns lay beyond. What if Williams *did* have troops in there?

Some new machine?

But when he kicked and the door exploded from its hinges with an echoing crash, he was grinning. *Wish I could do that again.*

Thomas charged through the empty frame, everyone else on his heels, and skidded to a halt before a huge sphere of an unknown metal. It filled an entire wall. Part of the floor and roof had even been re-shaped to fit the globe too.

A faint sense of Orichalcum emanated from the smooth surface, but its tint was a deep and rich blue rather than orange. As though something else made up the majority of the sphere. Part steel, part Orichalcum and part something else.

Something that did not resonant or hum like other metals, but which seemed to *take* or draw in sound and light from its surroundings.

Another powerful weapon?

Three figures stood before the sphere, two of which wore tool belts where they had frozen, half-leaning over what might have been a control panel on a podium. *That looks a lot like what was up at the sky port.*

And Williams.

The self-styled king wore a singed and tattered apron over his red silks, a revolver at his side. Yet he held no weapon, instead a cup. His expression seemed irritated, rather than shocked. Still unshaven, the grey stubble covered his cheeks and obscured deep lines too.

But the furnace of his eyes had not dimmed.

"Before you speak, let me promise you that I planned for this occasion," he said with a growl. "You are in fact here to concede and hand over the *Clara*."

"No." Thomas said.

Williams sneered. "And let me tell each of you why — even young Felicity there, it is nice to see you again, dear — but it is because I have a steady supply of hostages."

"We will destroy you and your weapon, if that's what you mean," Ethan said.

The old man glanced back to the globe. "Isn't it lovely? But I thought I would start with something more personal." He gestured to one of his assistants. "Bring in the first two."

"Wait!" Thomas snapped. "Who are you talking about?"

A leer. "Friends of Ethan there, I believe."

"Show me," Ethan said, his jaw clenched. "Just one of you."

"They are not far," Williams replied, nodding to one of the servants.

The assistant shuffled out through a side door, and soon

returned with two familiar figures, each led by a stony-faced guard.

Thomas stiffened. Genevieve and Carlo stood with hands and feet bound by heavy ropes, but worse was the wooden cage built around their torsos. Sharpened stakes were poised at their chests, connected to a lever held by each guard.

"Ethan, we're sorry," Genevieve said, her voice hoarse.

Carlo didn't seem much better, his cheeks bruised – one perhaps even broken. "Nearly everyone's been captured."

"As I'm sure you've noticed, one misstep and they die," Williams said. "All it takes is for my men to pull those levers and believe me, the hardwood jaws are designed to operate without any hints of metal."

Thomas ground his teeth in the silence.

Williams had thought ahead – that much was true; Thomas couldn't simply break the jaws apart but there had to be *something* he could try. The globe was too large to simply crush Williams with, it would endanger everyone, but more, it didn't seem like something he could get a firm grip on.

"Let them free, all of them," Mia said.

"And why would I do that?"

"To survive."

He narrowed his eyes, stalking forward a few steps as he did. "That is what I'm offering *you*."

"Clearly we have a stand-off," Ethan said.

"Then you wish to negotiate? Very well. Your lives and the lives of your pitiful rebel force in exchange for the *Clara*. And, Marianne is to be delivered to me."

"Never," Felicity said.

"Those are my terms."

Thomas did not take his eyes from the poser-king.

Williams would not honour any agreement he made. *We need a distraction... or something to break this stalemate. Mia probably can't call the Bird of Light fast enough, or warn us if her gift lends her a vision... it's up to me.*

The guards weren't wearing any steel either – but Williams was.

"So, what will it be? Who will speak for this little band of heroes?"

Thomas pointed. "Free them and I will turn you over to the Queen for a trial and life in a cell. Refuse and you die here, and then your men die too."

"Quite the claim."

"Answer me," Thomas snapped. Almost before the words left his mouth, he had ripped the revolver from Williams' belt with his gift. He shoved the barrel up against the old man's stomach then.

The trigger was so light...

Williams fell back a step, eyes wide. Thomas pushed the gun along, keeping it jammed against the man's apron.

"Free them or bleed out here."

Williams gestured to his guards and both complied, quite swiftly. Once they'd removed the wooden cages, Carlo and Genevieve looked to Ethan.

"Go to the others," he said, a smile on his face. He tossed his revolver across the room.

Genevieve caught it. "Right."

This time, it was the rebels who 'accompanied' Williams' men.

The Dirt-King was frowning. "It seems you have the upper-hand but don't think it will last. Even if you kill me now, you will not escape the Fortress."

"Didn't you see what I did to your Ogre-Cannon? This entire place will look like that if I decide it."

"Too many innocents here, yes? The yellow, the white and black... the red."

Thomas folded his arms. "Any soldier holding a weapon will have it wrapped around his throat, or shoved through his stomach."

"Or will they?" Williams asked. His gaze shifted beyond Thomas, relief visible.

Lina stood behind Ethan, twin-shot pointed at his back.

The powder-rat wore the same corset, bare arms revealing her tattoos but her face had grown a little more corpse-like in its pallor, the missing parts of nose adding a grotesqueness to an already marred face.

And in the uncertain light of the chamber, it seemed her hair had taken on a pale, purple tint.

Chapter 47.

Thomas shifted, so he could keep the revolver pressed against Williams while at the same time, watch Lina and her dead smile.

Mia's jaw was clenched – she knew, and it seemed fury rather than fear that caused her to tremble. Felicity had lifted her rifle, keeping it trained on Lina.

Ethan stood with his hands raised. "You smell a little better than usual," he said. "New perfume?"

"Thank you for noticing, Ethan," Lina replied.

"It masks the scent of powder fairly well."

"That's just about enough, I think." She glanced to Williams. "Do you need them all alive?"

"Not truly. Ethan is yours to do as you wish. Felicity could serve as bait, I believe but Thomas and Mia are precious, still."

"I appreciate that," Lina said, and though her ghoulish grin stretched in anticipation, a trail of saliva visible, her arms bore a faint tremble. Symptoms of the drug?

"Hear my counter-offer, Lina," Ethan said without turning.

"Help us kill Williams now and you take the entirety of Silas' stockpile, not just whatever he's offering. You'll be the richest drug lord in the city. Probably the nation."

Williams tried to take a step forward, but the revolver stopped him. His voice still rang out. "Don't be a fool, girl – our arrangement will see you live a life of comfort."

"Fool?" Lina narrowed her eyes, and something flashed behind the haze... Williams had made a mistake.

"These people cannot deliver upon their claim."

Lina strolled across the room now, weapon raised. "Then triple what you've offered me."

Williams snarled and veins bulged in his neck. "Triple?"

"Why not?"

"Because that is obscene," he said. "Surely even someone like you can see that?"

She levelled the gun at him, stalking closer. "Even I? Meaning what exactly?"

Thomas glanced between them. Williams' eyes were darting about even though his posture remained firm, but Lina did not seem to have the best grip on her anger as she continued to tremble, knuckles white on the weapon. "I only meant –"

Lina spat as she came to a halt before him. "What?"

Shit, she's going to do it. What then? Lina was almost standing on top of the tyrant now. Thomas reached out to her weapon with his gift and twisted the barrels.

Lina pulled the trigger.

The twin-shot exploded with a boom and a flash of gunpowder, blasting both figures to the ground. Shot ricocheted but did not strike anyone else.

Thomas leapt forward... but neither Williams nor Lina

was in any condition to seek another weapon.

Parts of Lina's torso had been pulped by the blast, fragments of bone and steel rested in a bed of red and black; her intestines gleaming. Blood splattered up to her chin, and from where he stood, the angle of her head shadowed her eyes, adding to the image of a skull.

Williams, however was not dead... yet.

His torso, arms and face had taken a lot of the blast. Bloody streaks and wounds everywhere, it seemed. But the man lived, blood bubbling upon his lips as his ruined lungs laboured.

A faint expression of shock lingered and his limbs twitched.

He would not last much longer.

Thomas stared down at the wreckage of the last Dirt King and found only a bitter taste in his mouth.

He knelt over the tyrant.

Something lingered in Williams' eyes – a desperation, somehow he clung to life.

"No," Thomas said. He retrieved the revolver and jammed it into the man's chest with a grunt. "You don't get to stay."

Thomas pulled the trigger with a muted bang.

And the Dirt King was no more.

He sat back, a little numb.

History had literally exploded right before him. Change was surely afoot but what did that actually mean? This doesn't feel... it doesn't feel... I don't know. Whatever it is, it's not enough. There was some relief, to know his tormentor – a tormentor of so many – would be no more but there was no rush of exhalation either.

Thomas laughed but it was a soft, bitter sound.

The air was no sweeter but it should have been after such a victory.

Is it just exhaustion? "I thought this would be different," Thomas told the old man's corpse with a frown.

Then he rose, turning to find Mia nearby, holding Ethan's hand, her own relief clear at the faint smile she wore. Felicity was glaring at the bodies but said nothing. *Thinking about what to tell the Queen?*

At the least, Elisabeth no longer had a reason to attack the city... so long as she could be told about what happened.

Footsteps started to shuffle away.

"No," Thomas said as he looked up at the servants. "We have questions."

Both froze, one man swallowing and the other more defiant, though his body shook. His dark hair was a little unkempt but his overcoat was quite finely maintained. "We worked with Silas. We know nothing about the king."

"Even better," Thomas replied. "Where is the Alchemist?"

"Gone," the younger one said.

"Ricky, hush," said the second.

Ricky frowned up at his fellow, his eyes wide. "I don't think we should lie to them, Peter."

"What do you mean by that?" Thomas asked. "Has he left the palace? The city?"

Peter shook his head. "Maybe both, we don't know. He's been gone for weeks already. He did not mention whether he was returning – but he left this, his final creation: the Thinking Globe."

"What is it?" Ethan asked.

"A device that can think. It can store knowledge and memories too," Ricky said, some excitement creeping into his tone as he gestured, a little wildly. "It's probably the greatest invention in the history of the nation."

"How?" Mia asked.

"Well..." Ricky looked to Peter.

"You know who I am, right?" Thomas asked. "What I can do?"

Peter nodded. "Please, it is his legacy."

"Whose?" Ethan asked.

"Not the king," the man said, waving his hands, revealing yellow hourglasses on his wrists. "Master Silas is responsible for this work of art. King Williams wanted us to use it to create new weapons, new ways to stop the *Clara* and control the people and we were... well, lying to him. Trying to delay him until the Master returned."

"Gutsy," Ethan said.

"That man was no-one to give us orders," Ricky said, nostrils flaring.

"We aren't planning on hurting you but show us what it can do before we're interrupted," Mia said. "You said it can store memories."

"Yes."

She nodded. "And this is what Silas left behind, of himself, for after he fled, right?"

Peter gaped, then shook his head. "Forgive me for staring, but yes. If you are Thomas' sister, then I think I know how you are aware of those things."

"Access his memories about our parents."

Chapter 48.

Peter led Thomas to the 'stand' and up close, the column and top plate *was* similar to that found at the sky-port. *How? Does this mean that Silas had been up there? Or that something of that time survived down here, and that the Williams line stole and concealed it?* But differences were present; it was not a map but a circular panel of switches surrounding what seemed to be a cross-shaped keyhole.

It also featured a square panel of buttons painted with letters and numbers.

And when the man removed a heavy key from his pocket and inserted it, he smiled. "It is connected via a maze of written information beneath us; we can access its memories by asking specific questions here. You will see the answers on the sphere – let me show you."

The man turned the key and it clicked once to the left. Then, he flicked two switches. Rumbling from below followed and Thomas focused on it... large pieces of metal were moving, crossing a vast space that far exceeded the dimensions of the chamber they stood within.

And it, too, was a mix of regular metals, Orichalcum and the new mineral that seemed blue, like the sphere.

"That should be long enough," Peter said. "I've chosen Memories about History and I have to give the Thinking Globe one of three commands first."

"It has more than one category, you see," Ricky added. "But over the years we've been struggling to house all the knowledge."

"Please continue," Ethan said. He spoke with a smile but was obviously focused on the possibility of attack from remnants of Williams' forces as much as Thomas was, by his glances back to the passage.

Peter waved everyone closer, and Thomas leant over the panel. "First, I give the Direction 'Seek'." He struck each letter on the panel to spell the word. "That tells the machine to find the topic I choose next."

"It can also 'Store'," Ricky added from where he was bouncing on his heels, eyes alight.

Thomas raised an eyebrow – hard not to be impressed by the possibilities of what Silas had left behind. Yet as before, he still had one ear for the passage they'd used. Who knew when or whether anyone would come looking for the king, and set off an alarm?

"For now, we'll just show you this side of things," Peter said. "Next, I describe the topic." This time, he struck the letters faster, spelling out Cataclysm. More rumbling from below, faint but unmistakable, and once it ceased Peter continued. "Now that it has located the knowledge-block, I give the next Direction: Retrieve."

Once he did so, the sphere began to revolve.

Twin screens slid across at the same time, revealing a flat, smooth surface that did once again seem to be a mixture of metals, though it was closer to black than blue this time.

But a whirring and clicking followed – then a regular clacking from behind the dark surface began. It seemed to run across the sphere and then down, the sound of each invisible impact faintly musical. *It's almost like each strike is made by something of a different size or shape?*

"Nothing is happening," Felicity said.

"Just a moment," Peter replied.

Shapes of light appeared – blazing letters following the sound of the strikes, and each one offering a word, and then a sentence until the Globe stopped. And while the brightness of the letters was fierce at first, they soon dimmed enough to be clearly legible.

Peter raised his voice a little. "It says the following, 'Seven Centuries ago the Two Decade Cataclysm was born from the folly of our ancestors, a heinous mix of greed and fear that created a regression which levelled cities and mountain ranges alike. Species disappeared, never to be seen again and humanity survived by eking out a barren existence at the furthest corners of the globe. Today, we await a unity free from the tethers of such a dark past. So it is written by Henri during the Cloud Era'."

Silence followed his words.

"What of our parents?" Thomas eventually asked.

"Spell out the Direction 'Seek' and once the machine is ready, the words 'Revolutionary Paths'. Again, give the Globe a moment before typing your name or your sister's."

Thomas did so, the buttons firm beneath his touch, and it took him longer than when Peter used the panel. But he eventually spelled out 'Mia' and waited. The letters for the cataclysm were already fading while the machine rumbled. The name of the 'knowledge-bank' was somehow optimistic but whatever the purpose, being someone else's tool, being experimented on, was not erased due to a possible noble purpose.

The whirring and clacking returned, letters being struck into light.

He read aloud. "With regard to Thomas and Mia, I have more extensive notes: Seek Experiment Two Hundred and Forty One. You may consider this entry as an initial overview."

Thomas paused. *Two-hundred and forty experiments before us?*

"Thomas, is that all?" Mia asked as she stepped closer.

"Sorry, there's more. 'It is not clear whether their conception or early lives exposed to the *Nautilus* had an impact on the swift development of their respective gifts. Perhaps their father's abandonment of Siobhan conceals more truths? We have done what we can for her, like the others, but I cannot convince her to stay; her fear is too great'."

Thomas swallowed a lump in his throat – his mother had a name! Yet what had she feared? *Why did she leave us here with Silas? And why did Father abandon her? Us?* A flash of anger tensed his every muscle.

But instead of lashing out, he took a breath and set the questions aside for the moment. He turned to Mia and took her hand, giving it a squeeze. She squeezed back as the words continued to appear on the sphere's surface. "What else does it say?" she asked softly.

"It's about me first, I think. 'In any event, Thomas responds well to the serum, both via injection and mixed in with his milk. Unlike the others, he has not fallen ill with fever, nor had his liquids drain from the various orifices. He is the one we have fought all these years for – from him will come a new world, if we can protect him long enough'."

Now Thomas' stomach flipped at the words he spoke. *How many children? How many years?*

"Now it's changing to you, Mia. 'Mia possesses a gift to rival her mother's – I suspect. It is difficult to design experiments to test this, while she is so young. When she can speak, I believe we will see swift improvements and, I hope, manifestation of ancient magics left from her father's side. Even above Thomas, she must be protected at all costs'."

Mia exhaled, almost a hiss.

The words did not cease. "'Together, they must restore the legacy of Gatehouse and those who survived before. Without them, change will only come at the cost of such bloodshed that I would not envy the survivors – even the Federation would struggle in such a chaotic time'."

Ethan placed a hand on his shoulder. "That you have done, both of you."

Thomas nodded. "Maybe."

"Is there more?" Mia asked, but the clacking had already started.

The pale fire of new letters soon appeared. "One more line only," Thomas said. "'So recorded by Silas of Birnhale in the Fifth Year of the Birnhale Standard Calendar'." *Twenty-six years ago.*

Mia turned toward Peter and Ricky, facing them for the most part, voice taut with anger. "What other entries relate to us?"

"Ah, several detailed accounts of... your time here when very young, but there is one you might wish to hear first – it's a message from Silas, actually," Peter replied, his voice faltering. To Thomas he said, "Seek 'Messages', then your names."

Thomas followed the instruction and soon the huge machine was working, letters appearing upon the strange metal-surface of the sphere. "I leave this message for you both, should you wish to learn more about what you have heard today – follow me to the New States. Silas."

Chapter 49.

"That is exactly what we will do," Mia told the machine after Thomas finished reading, and his own urge was exactly the same.

"We don't know how Silas escaped, but with the airship you can, at least, follow him," Ricky said with a rather nervous-looking smile. Maybe it was the way Mia stood, fists clenched, probably glaring at the sphere beneath her blindfold, that made him uneasy.

"Let's find out a little more, first," Ethan said.

"And it might be time to call on everyone else," Felicity added.

"Everyone else? Do you mean you're planning to liberate the city?" Peter asked. "I know Williams is dead now, but his generals and the other nobles will merely see this as an opportunity of their own, once they find out."

"Queen Marianne will have something to say about that," she replied.

"Then I wish her a swift victory," Peter replied.

As if on cue, from above, the sound of booted feet, still

distant, filtered down. Thomas spun to the passage, but no-one approached. *Who knows what's going on above us? Wilkins might have stormed the capital... but that isn't too likely, surely?*

"We might be running out of time, Thomas – get it to search for the Nautilus," Mia said.

"Are you sure?" Ethan asked.

"I am."

"Right." Thomas tapped the letters and waited. "It's not a long entry. 'The Nautilus is a trans-continental submarine thought to predate the Cataclysm, but the whereabouts of its sunken wreck are unknown. Its original crew was said to have hailed from lands unrecorded'."

"Our parents were once crew members aboard that underwater-ship," Mia said.

"You feel it?" Thomas asked.

"I do."

More noise from above. Ethan was glancing up to the ceiling. "I think we need to know what's going on up there before we research more here."

The growing rumble of footfalls neared – coming from the passage now.

"We need another exit," Thomas said. "Where did Lina enter from?"

A voice echoed from within the passage. "Ethan? Are you still there?"

"It's Genevieve," Ethan said.

His seconds soon appeared, Genevieve and Carlo leading the rebels – some two dozen men and women, many familiar faces though not names. Most were similarly bruised, their motley of clothing and armour just as battered.

But they were all armed, all smiling.

"Where to, boss?" one of the younger men asked. Distant booming still reached them, faint though it was.

"The walls – I want to know what's happening in the city, first."

"Let me take rear guard," Thomas said, and let Mia and the others pass. He paused, glancing once more to Williams' corpse and then Peter and Ricky. "To be safe, you might want to move that somewhere else."

"Ah, right," Ricky said and Peter only nodded.

Then Thomas was charging after the fading light, his pulse skipping a few beats. *I hope all that noise from above isn't Elisabeth destroying parts of the city – I have to tell her what happened here.*

Everything moved quickly then, first rushing through the passages and then the brighter halls as a fairly formidable group. Only once did they have to skirmish with Fortress soldiers, coming across what seemed to be an urgent meeting of five troops and their commander, but the rebels felled them almost as a reflex.

Despite the roar of gunfire, it attracted no more attention as they climbed stairwells.

"This is making me nervous," Thomas shouted ahead. "We should be facing a lot more trouble here."

"Let's not ruin our luck by questioning it," Ethan called back. "But I know what you mean."

When they reached one of the walls and its vantage point, Thomas finally understood why. It wasn't the men guarding the wreckage of the Ogre-cannon, nor the line of troops streaming toward the trail of smoke at the arena, its underside lit by fire, and it wasn't even the men and women in black trying to create a makeshift platform for a smaller cannon to fire on the shadowy *Clara* above, but the harbour.

Faint shouts rose from the ships, along with more glowing fire and smoke, as soldiers flowed toward the docks.

But it was the *Iron Whale* that housed the flame, its cannons silent as the *Albion* fired from a position in the bay. Other ships were already sinking beneath the waterline, tops of masts or stacks still visible.

"We need to take advantage of this," Ethan said, eyes narrowed as he stared down.

"Here?" Thomas asked.

"If we storm the armoury, we might be able to clear out a lot of rats, if the Palace really is as undermanned as it seems."

"Send them on but you're not leaving my side," Mia said. "The danger hasn't passed, just because Lina is dead."

He hesitated. "I think we could change things faster if we succeed."

"Let's leave that up to the Queen, for now," she said. "I want to ask you to help Thomas and I search for Silas."

Carlo grinned. "Leave it to us – you've saved my life three times already; we can handle this part."

"I–"

Now Genevieve gave him a slap on the shoulder. "He's right. Let us do this. Just make sure that you convince the Queen that she needs to listen to us."

He smiled. "I will."

"Then we're going to follow Silas right away?" Thomas asked.

"We might have to convince Elisabeth and the others to drop us off, but I think we should."

I want to do exactly the same thing... but is it fair? "Will we even be welcome in the New States?"

"We have to find out – let's head back to the *Clara*."

"What about Birnhale and the other cities and towns?" he asked, but what he wanted to ask was whether Queen Marianne could be trusted, but it seemed Mia understood what he would not say in front of Felicity.

"I hope we've done enough."

Chapter 50.

"Do you think the Queen's plan will actually be effective?" Thomas asked Elisabeth where they stood in the ruins of the Ogre-Cannon, its twisted surfaces catching the dawn light well-enough despite the mess.

Even the flagstones and earth were torn in places and a hole still stood in the wall. Beyond, flickers of light and shadow came from the city but not enough to see clearly. Even the scattered bodies were still vague lumps upon the ground, waiting for the day.

From the Fortress itself, gunfire had died away; Genevieve and Carlo and their force – now assisted by Felicity, the Queen and even Captain Donovan – were probably firmly in control of the palace itself.

Not the city, of course, but with the sunken ships in the harbour and mines still under threat from the Sand-Hog, the lack of leadership, the shock, the fear generated by the *Clara*, it was probably going to be enough to take full control in time... hopefully.

"Her plan? You mean the nobles' bloodbath?" Elisabeth shrugged, dark smudges beneath her eyes. Though she stood with one hand upon her hip, she seemed more resigned than relieved. "If she fools enough of them with her offer, and half the merchant population too, why not?"

"You don't seem all that confident."

Elisabeth glanced at him, a small smile. "Oh? Maybe I'm not so interested, in the end."

"Meaning?"

She moved closer. "Meaning, I'm feeling a little empty – how you probably felt down there with his body."

"Williams."

"Who else? I stood over his filthy corpse for long enough and it wasn't as good as I'd hoped." She paused. "And you know what? I was going to tell you before, that I wanted to be the one to kill him. That I *should* have been the one. I gave that up to keep an eye on things on the airship for you… but now I'm not so sure it would have made a difference, so I'm not going to bother saying any of that."

She's right. Vengeance hadn't been as satisfying as famous stories always made it out to be – but maybe it didn't matter. Williams was dead and the last of the line of Dirt Kings would die in a prison somewhere. The dynasty was finished and both goals that Jean and Gatehouse fought for had been achieved too. People would recover from the poison they did not even realise they had been forced to live with, and Marianne would put an end to slavery, in Birnhale at first and then hopefully elsewhere in the Kingdom. "Then what now?"

Elisabeth's gloved hand caressed his cheek but she did not answer right away. Her eyes were hard to read; she was holding something back. "Asking me to come with you?"

"I might be," he replied, and they weren't quite the words he'd expected to say.

"Surprised, Thomas?"

He sighed. "Maybe I am. Even after you threatened the entire city; I want your help."

She grinned back at him – and still, her expression masked something far less carnal than her response seemed to suggest. "That all you want?"

"Come along and find out."

"Well said, Thomas."

***

Mia let the hum of the *Clara* in flight, calm her, the breeze too – if she looked back on the struggle and desperation of the past weeks, memories of sitting or standing at rails and letting the air flow across her would be one of the strongest.

She shifted her legs where she sat. *Why is that? A sense of freedom? Of movement?*

Hope was connected to that sense, to the trip they were now making with their expanded crew, though Hawkins at least would probably leave before too long. The distance to the New States was unclear, using the airship would make everything faster but what dangers would they face upon arrival?

Williams was finally dead, the Kingdom being restored by Marianne and a bright new alliance with the Federation but a sliver of guilt lingered within Mia. *I've certainly set that aside quickly enough, left others to rebuild.*

The urge to survive, and then *escape* had been such long

parts of her life – and even when her focus changed to saving the lands and then seeking Silas to learn the truth, but now... *Our mother could be alive. We might have a family and a past, some heritage.* And while Nyath may or may not have blocked her from chasing Silas and those answers via the *chromata*, the Thinking Globe had offered more.

And not just about the *Nautilus.*

"And what about you, Father?" she asked softly.

No matter how many times she and Thomas had discussed it, they could not hope to guess at what happened. The bitter relief and cautious joy at learning about their mother – even her name – had been tempered with familiar fears being confirmed.

Maybe.

Father *had* abandoned us, and it might not have been connected to Silas at all. *Just one more man to hunt down.* And as much as Williams' death was its own victory, was the true villain Silas? Father? *Is that why I still don't feel much satisfaction?*

"There you are." Ethan.

"I am," she said with a smile.

His silhouette neared as he lowered himself beside her. She took his hand, the strength of his grip welcome.

"Thinking about your parents?"

Mia chuckled. "No prizes for that guess. But I can't seem to stop – I thought I'd closed off that part of me, the part that cannot help but I want to know. Everything's changed."

"Could be a good thing."

"I hope so." She leant against him. "Any guesses on how close we are?"

"We can go and ask Hawkins and Copper, if you like?"

"No, it's fine for now," she said. "Let's just stay like this for a little longer."

He kissed the top of her head. "Okay."

A NOTE FROM ASHLEY

Hi! I hope you enjoyed *A Crimson Wolf* and thanks for joining Thomas and Mia for their third adventure.

I'd like to ask if you could help me out by leaving an honest review of the story at your place of purchase? Long or short, bad or good, it all helps!

AND if you'd like to sign up to my newsletter (www. ashleycapes.com) you'll be the first to know when an eventual fourth *Slaves of the New World* book is released. You'll also have first access to preview chapters and pre-release editions of the story, in addition to being automatically added into the draw for giveaways.

ACKNOWLEDGMENTS

Thanks again to the large cast of folks who helped me with this book.

I must of course thank my wife Brooke for her endless support but also my writing group, the Alchemists, along with my editor Amanda and also Nick Deligaris for yet another stunning cover image! Thanks also to Vivid for the superb typeset too and also to those of you who spent your time with my characters!

Ashley

City of Masks - Sample
Book 1 of the Bone Mask Trilogy

Chapter 1

The chill of prison bars against his temple did little to ease Notch's headache. Decades of dank didn't help either, nor snoring from another cell, where someone was impersonating a bear. Or dying. In the poor light it was hard to tell.

Notch squinted. Noon sun barely crept through the small, grated windows on his side of the building. Even cells across the way were shadowed. Sunlight, in addition to a piece of bread and some water, were high points, while the straw 'bed' and stale body odour of criminals were typically unpleasant. Worse places than Anaskar City prison existed. At least he hadn't been beaten yet – a twinge in his shoulder reminded him how much some guards enjoyed their work.

His cellmate raised his voice and Notch turned. The man had probably been speaking for some time; his drawn face was expectant. Years of imprisonment had washed out his Anaskari tan.

Notch leaned against the bars. "What is it, Bren?"

"Did you kill her, truly?"

"No."

Bren nodded. "Innocent then." He knelt in the corner, his fine coat of blue long since gone to grime, his face pressed against the stone wall. "Listen to this one." He scratched at an armpit with some vigour. "It's hard to see but I think it says 'death to the Shields of Anaskar' and it's got a signature, but I can't make it out."

Notch grunted. Nothing special for a convicted man to write; since waking on a pile of old blankets that morning and meeting his cellmate, he'd heard a dozen similar sentiments. Through Bren's meandering introduction, Notch had winced, probing his body. Both arms and chest were heavily bruised and his head so fragile he wouldn't be surprised to learn a wagon rolled over it last night. Possibly twice. He wasn't drunk, though the smell of ale was on his breath. One damn drink, that was all.

And there was blood.

His leathers and tunic were splattered a dark red. Not his own blood, the City Vigil told him as much when they hauled him off the street, as if he couldn't figure that much out. But whose? His own memory was unreliable, which made no sense. He hadn't been drunk, truly drunk, since right after the war. When he bore another name. A name he left on some tavern floor, after making a convincing go of drinking the memories away. A good bath did for the sand on his body, but the blood-soaked sand in his mind? No amount of ale had washed that away.

And now the Vigil were telling him he'd been so intoxicated he had to be dragged to the prison?

Unlikely.

"The Shields probably caught him doing something bad, that's why he wrote this," Bren continued, tapping on the wall. His too-bright eyes looked up at Notch.

"I'd say so."

"Like us, Notch. We've done bad things, we have."

"So you keep saying."

Bren laughed, its shrillness cutting through Notch's skull. If it hadn't been unsettling, Notch would have thumped him, but there was something wrong with Bren. Any fool could see that.

"The guards say you've got a few days. That they can't hang you sooner, because there's too many in the queue. Waiting to hang."

"Thanks, Bren."

A moment of quiet fell between them. Distant voices drifted from beyond the prison walls. Notch clenched his jaw. He should have been out there. On his way to another job. The Blue Lady, a fat merchant ship, would have sailed with most of his possessions on board.

His father's sword.

No chance of seeing it again. He wrapped his hands around cold bars and squeezed.

"The guards say it too, the guards say you killed her," Bren said, unperturbed.

"I know."

He crept forward. "So?"

"So I don't remember." He frowned. "But I wouldn't harm a child."

Bren grinned, as if he thought it all a joke, and went back to the wall. A scraping sound followed. "This one says 'down with the Shields' and has no name. I wonder how many people have been here before us, eh Notch?"

"Maybe just you, Bren," he muttered, rubbing at his temples.

Bren prattled on. "I could deal with the Mascare too, you know. They aren't so powerful. It's just their precious bone masks. And their robes. All that crimson. They scare people, the faces. And the eyes too. Did you ever meet any, Notch, before you murdered that girl?"

He ignored the last bit. "I've seen the Mascare plenty of times."

"And were they protecting 'the city, the people and its history' as they love to claim?"

"Each time?"

Bren laughed. "Ever ask them why they won't show their faces?"

"They aren't very talkative, Bren."

Bren stopped scratching and moved to a spot beneath the window, running a set of cracked fingernails over the stone. "This is my favourite. I think it's the oldest one."

The clank of a key in a lock did not deter Bren from his examination, but Notch took hold of the bars again, letting the man's voice recede into the background. At the far end of their row, the guard, a scruffy man who'd made some effort to straighten his blue and silver uniform, led three figures toward the cell.

"Quiet now, Bren," he said as the group approached, their footfalls echoing. A slender woman – a Lady no doubt – stopped before Notch's cell. She was accompanied by a girl and a stony-faced man with broad shoulders, the orange tunic and gleaming breastplate of a Palace Shield in stark contrast with the prison keeper's appearance. The woman's hair was pulled back from her face, fanning down around her shoulders and covering the collar of an impeccably clean white dress. Bone earrings swung when she turned her head. A sneer that must have been permanent marred her otherwise smooth face.

Notch adjusted his grip on the bars. To come to Anaskar Prison in such clothing – she was either mighty vain or mighty important. Most likely both. Which meant trouble.

The girl stood in similar attire and shared the sneer but had trouble meeting his gaze.

"Here's the mercenary, my lady." The prison guard pointed with his key, making a low bow before scurrying off.

The woman took a single step forward, glaring at him. Her footfall clapped. "Your name?"

He blinked. Her distaste was like a battering ram. "Notch."

The palace guard bristled and she waved a clean hand at him. "Bring the torch, Holindo."

"Yes, my lady." His voice was a rasp.

Behind him, Bren shrunk back into the corner. He did not resume his scraping.

The woman levelled a finger at Notch. "You will address me as 'Lady Cera,' or not at all. Now, do not move."

"Can I ask why, Lady Cera?"

"Because if you do not I will have the Captain here gut you."

Notch did as he was told. The impulse to wipe her face clean of its expression was strong enough that he had to school his features. Palace folk. Even before he'd taken to the life of a hired sword, they'd looked down their noses at him. 'Mountain Family', they'd say to each other and snigger.

When Captain Holindo returned, the soldier thrust the torch forward, catching Notch's shoulder with his free hand. He narrowed his eyes but said nothing, only adding a crease to his brow. Did Holindo recognise him? Notch couldn't place the man.

"Be still now," the solider said.

The flames singed a little of Notch's hair and he started to sweat. No-one moved or spoke, though the girl he took for Lady Cera's daughter stared wide-eyed at the blood on his clothing.

"Well?" The Lady snapped. "Look. Is it him? Is that the man?"

"I… I think so, mother," said the girl.

Lady Cera and her captain shared a glance before she addressed her daughter again, her tones becoming honeyed. "Dear, are you sure? This is the man they caught by her body, in the street on our way from the harbour –"

"It's hard to tell. I didn't see him that well." She met his gaze. "I suppose it could be this man."

Captain Holindo withdrew the torch. "We have other witnesses, my lady. You've done far more than enough by coming here; it will satisfy the Justice. Furthermore, your own daughter identified the prisoner, that's enough for any man of law." Such a long string of words strained the man's voice, and for the first time Notch noticed a long, faded scar crossing his throat.

She gave a short nod. "Truly. I've had more than enough of this stench in any event. Take my daughter back to the palace."

"Of course, Lady Cera."

He ushered the girl toward the exit. Lady Cera did not follow. "I don't know the whole truth of what happened. But you are a criminal, of that I have no doubt."

"Mercenary, Lady Cera."

"Do you think there's a difference?"

"There can be."

"Well, Notch the Mercenary, I will ensure you hang for this. The girl might have only been a pale-skinned, half-blood brat, but I can ill-afford to replace her."

Notch sneered. "That all she was to you? Something to be replaced?"

She raised her arm but he stepped back.

"Fool." Lady Cera spun and stormed off.

Notch spat. He was already going to hang, what did it matter if some bone-headed noblewoman wanted him dead? Bren shuffled forward and placed a hand on his shoulder. Notch had forgotten him. "She knows what you are. What we are."

"You might be right," Notch said, sitting on the floor and scratching at a new, disturbingly persistent itch in his hair. "But I didn't kill that girl."